THE GALILEO GAMBIT

VATICAN SECRET ARCHIVE THRILLERS
BOOK SIX

GARY MCAVOY

RONALD L. MOORE

LITERATI
EDITIONS.

Hardcover ISBN: 978-1-954123-32-8
Paperback ISBN: 978-1-954123-33-5
eBook ISBN: 978-1-954123-34-2

Library of Congress Control Number: 2023908070

Published by:
Literati Editions
PO Box 5987
Bremerton WA 98312-5987
Email: info@LiteratiEditions.com
Visit the author's website: www.GaryMcAvoy.com
R0723

BOOKS BY GARY MCAVOY

FICTION

The Galileo Gambit *

The Jerusalem Scrolls

The Avignon Affair *

The Petrus Prophecy *

The Opus Dictum

The Vivaldi Cipher

The Magdalene Veil

The Magdalene Reliquary

The Magdalene Deception

NONFICTION

And Every Word Is True

* co-authored with Ronald L. Moore

PROLOGUE

J ust off the coach from Rome—where he had endured a trial for heresy against the Catholic Church for contradicting Holy Scripture—Galileo Galilei strode into the opulent parlor of the Episcopal Palace, home of the archbishop of Siena, the Most Reverend Ascanio Piccolomini.

Though Siena wasn't Galileo's beloved Arcetri—his home in the hills west of Florence—it was a lot closer to Rome, and he was grateful for the opportunity to stay here. And while he was here he was hopeful for a brief respite to visit his two daughters in the San Matteo Convent.

The room was a dizzying feast for the eyes, with riches draped everywhere: wondrous rugs and gilded furniture, walls adorned with heavenly treasures, including a haunting representation of Christ's martyrdom. As he sat there waiting, Galileo could hardly draw his gaze away nor ignore the painful parallels between his own suffering and that of Christ's.

Glancing around, however, it was difficult to consider this as suffering in any form. Galileo had taken up residence in the home of the Florentine Ambassador to Rome while the trial had taken place and for the ensuing ten days awaiting the verdict. Now, he braced himself while the court determined where he would serve his imprisonment.

The uneven pulse of approaching footsteps—two people, he surmised, both men by their long strides—snapped him out of his reverie. Just as he stood up, the archbishop's herald swept into the room and announced, "His Excellency, the Archbishop Piccolomini."

Piccolomini entered the room, clad in his purple cassock, a white rochet overlaying it, a hooded mozzetta covering his shoulders, and a purple zucchetto atop his balding head, with a gold pectoral cross on a chain around his neck and secured over his right breast.

"Forgive me, dear Galileo, for keeping you waiting. I was celebrating Mass this morning."

As the archbishop approached his guest he extended his right hand. Galileo instinctively knelt and kissed the archbishop's ring, a sign of loyalty and obedience to the Church.

"Your Excellency, thank you for seeing me and allowing me to reside here in your magnificent palace during my imprisonment. I promise not to bring you trouble," he said, rising from his kneeling position.

"Have you been so thoroughly humbled, my friend? That is not the Galileo I have come to know. Here, do sit down." Piccolomini gestured toward a pair of luxurious chairs set off to the side of the room near the fireplace, the wooden logs within crackling fiercely as orange and yellow sparks leapt from the flames.

"Come, tell me all that has transpired, for it has been some time since we spoke, and while I have heard fragmentary accounts, I would prefer to hear the whole tale from you yourself."

"As you wish, Excellency. As to the beginning of it all, we have spoken of it before, so I will be brief. But for the sake of the memory, I will go back to where I think it all began.

"You might recall that in 1609, or perhaps the following year, I became aware that a Dutchman had created a device consisting of a tube with glass lenses at either end, which was capable of magnifying vision such that far away objects appeared closer. A 'telescope,' he called it. I was able to divine its operating principles such that I was able to build one myself and improve upon its capabilities.

"It was simply a matter of the shape of the lenses and the length of the tube. Those who were using the device in other places were using it merely to observe ships and troops at a distance, which has obvious tactical advantages and for which the device is eminently useful. I believe I was most probably the first to point a telescope at the heavens. Truly, the experience was illuminating. You have, of course, had this experience yourself, Your Excellency?"

"Yes, Galileo, I have. One of your disciples, if one may call him that, passed this way and made his device available to us. Some among my advisors cautioned against looking through it, claiming that it produced visions by way of witchcraft...that God had not meant for man to view the heavens in any other way than with the eyes God gave him, for fear of being confused and deceived by its false images. Yet, against such counsel I chose to look through the device. And indeed, I saw the moon and the satellites of Jupiter, just as you had described them! It was this experience that compelled me to begin our correspondence and now our close acquaintance."

"Very good, Your Excellency. Very good, indeed. You

can see, then, why I became so very excited and enthusiastic about using this device to observe the heavens—for I was making discoveries that nobody else in the world had seen and for which few men had the appreciation. It became clear to me, having read the work of Copernicus, that these discoveries supported his interpretation of the heavens: that the Sun, and not the Earth, stands at the center of the universe. And that the Earth and the movable stars—the planets such as Jupiter, Saturn, Mars and Venus —all revolve around the Sun, too, and that the Earth itself turns on its axis, fixed at the North and South, rotating toward the East, and that the moon revolves around the Earth.

"And furthermore, I observed that Venus, in a similar fashion to the Moon, exhibits phases, waxing and waning, showing that it indeed revolves around the Sun, and that the moons of Jupiter revolve around it, as our moon revolves around the Earth. I observed that Saturn is not one body, but three which move together, and that the outer two fade and return over time. I observed stars in the Milky Way galaxy that cannot be seen by eyes alone and craters and mountains on the Moon. And all this, taken also with the evidence from the tides—which are caused, I believe, by the movement of the water as the Earth revolves—convince me that Copernicus was right. I have spoken to many people, learned men and Churchmen and those among the nobility, and many have been convinced by this evidence. Many, but not all."

"Yes," the archbishop concurred, "and some of those who do not agree with you see themselves as ardent Defenders of the Faith whose mission is to resist heresy wherever they find it. You have made more than a few enemies, Galileo. Some very powerful."

"Indeed, though I did not fully appreciate the extent of

my peril. And it seems now, in retrospect, that was not so much due to my scientific observations as to how I attempted to reconcile the apparent conflict between the Holy Scriptures and those observations. I wish now that I had never written that letter to Grand Duchess Christina."

"Then why did you, my friend?"

"Benedetto Castelli, a Benedictine, if you recall, was one of my students and I discussed my discovery with him. Very bright and more than a little ambitious."

"Ambitious, you say?" the archbishop chuckled. "Go on."

"Yes, well, it is said one notices his own faults most in others. In any case, Benedetto had occasion to break fast with Grand Duke Cosimo de Medici, Ferdinando's son and his wife, the Grand Duchess Christina, and Cosimo Boscaglia, who is teaching at the University of Pisa, like Benedetto, and who does not like me even a little bit.

"Boscaglia apparently took great exception to Benedetto's representation of my work and propounded a great many Scriptural oppositions to it. Benedetto did his best to refute them, but after the meal, Benedetto was called into audience with the Grand Duchess to make further answer on the theological points. When Benedetto informed me of this occurrence, I subsequently decided that it might be best if I addressed the Grand Duchess's concerns myself. I did not anticipate the extent to which copies of that letter would circulate. Certainly not all the way to Rome! I sent that letter to her in 1615, and by early the next year it had become clear to me that I was going to have to go to Rome and defend my opinions and reputation before I was summoned by the Inquisition."

"So you went to Rome voluntarily?" the archbishop inquired. "You were not summoned?"

"Yes, I went voluntarily. I did not know that I had

already been referred to the Inquisition. But I did not meet with them formally, and there was no trial or even questioning."

"Hmm, I heard many rumors to the contrary. So, what did happen?"

"Well, earlier in 1616, Monsignor Ingoli instigated a discussion about the matter, and I defended my observations and their interpretation, including my opinions about reconciling Scripture with the clear implications of scientific observations. Once I got to Rome, I attempted to obtain an audience with His Holiness, hoping for a decision from the highest authority. But before I could do so, Cardinal Bellarmine requested my presence and informed me that the works of Copernicus and several others of the same bent were to be placed on the Index and that I could not hold the opinion of Copernicus nor teach or defend it. I understand now that after the Inquisition made their findings and presented them to the pope, he directed Bellarmine to give me that warning.

"A short while later, I had the opportunity to speak with His Holiness, who reinforced the Church's position, so I began preparations to return home. But already, rumors circulated that I had been summoned to appear before the Inquisition, had been tried, found guilty, and punished!

"None of these rumors being true, I asked Cardinal Bellarmine for a letter explaining what had transpired, which he graciously provided. Little did I know at the time how important that letter would become. I returned home and let the matter rest for the most part, as I had teaching responsibilities and my children to attend to. Vincenzo was only ten years old then, and the girls fifteen and sixteen."

"And had you left it there, you would have been safe," Piccolomini observed. "So what possessed you to write that book?"

"Ah, well, the root of that must be in my dispute with Jesuit Father Orazio Grassi over the comets. The man is a blithering idiot. His arguments on the comets weren't even his, they were Danish astronomer Tycho Brahe's, and he presented them poorly. I responded with my *Discourse on Comets*, in which I dissected his stupidity. Of course, Grassi responded, not even man enough to put his name on the reply. He used the name of one of his students.

"Obviously, I could not let that lie, so I wrote *Il Saggiatore, The Asssayer*, perhaps my greatest written work. Since he could not dispute the science any further without looking foolish, he resorted to theology in his last response. And from what I understand, a similarly worded complaint was filed a couple years later with the Inquisition.

"But I would not have written *The Assayer* at all if Cardinal Barberini had not been elected pope that same year, 1623. I went to Rome after his election and spoke with him some half-dozen times. When I left, I was sure I had permission from His Holiness to discuss heliocentrism, as long as I did it in a purely hypothetical manner, not defending or extolling the view but merely explaining how my scientific observations seemed to support the conclusion.

"His Holiness felt that since God had the power to make the universe as described in Scripture, and yet have it appear as the observations supported, we could never know the truth of the matter from observations alone.

"So I returned home to write the book, careful not to defend the Copernican model, but only to show how the observations supported the model so as to explain the appearances. I felt myself very clever to have hit upon the idea of structuring the book as a dialogue, much like that of Plato's work.

"But that is where the seeds of my destruction were

planted, watered by my ego and illuminated by my arrogance, only to reap a crop of woe. Well, you have read it. I put the pope's argument in the mouth of the simpleton. He took it worse than I imagined. In my defense, I had obtained imprimatur from the censor in Rome where it was originally intended to be published. But then bubonic plague hit, and I could not return to Rome, so I obtained the second approval from Florence."

"So, when the Holy Father heard of the book, he had the Inquisition call you to Rome?" Piccolomini asked.

"I admit, as I did when I was questioned by the Inquisition, that my biggest fault was an over-exuberance in my own cleverness in trying to show how the scientific evidence might be so convincing if it were not for the contrary light of Scripture.

"The thing of it all, however, seemed to come down to whether I had received a formal injunction not to hold, teach or defend the Copernican model all those years ago, at the meeting with Cardinal Bellarmine. The Inquisition had minutes from the meeting that confirmed I had been so enjoined. I don't think they were aware that I had the later letter from Cardinal Bellarmine that stated the opposite, that I was only given an informal warning. The Inquisition was stymied when I revealed that, and the prosecutor came to me after the questioning and suggested that if I were to confess to my over-enthusiasm in emphasizing the support given by science to the Copernican model over the Scriptural truth, that I might be convicted only of Slight Suspicion of Heresy and released with a light punishment.

"But, having agreed to this, when I returned to give my confession, I was informed that the bargain had been revoked, I believe by His Holiness, and that on pain of torture I was to renounce to their formula and be convicted of Vehement Suspicion of Heresy and punished with a lifetime of imprisonment, as well as being forbidden to do any further work in this area. And thus, now, I find myself at your mercy and in your debt for however you managed to have me remanded to your custody."

"Well, for all your irascible ways, Galileo, you still have friends in this world, and I number myself among them. I think you are right—though I cannot say that publicly, of course. So I must limit my support to hosting you here and making sure your imprisonment is not too onerous to bear.

"But I must go now. I have duties to attend to. Wait here and enjoy the warmth of the fire. When your things have been placed in your apartment, someone will come and take you there. We will speak again soon. And as you contemplate the fire in the hearth, be grateful that you are not staked to a burning pile of rushes."

"Indeed, Your Excellency. Indeed."

CHAPTER
ONE

PRESENT DAY

D
r. Alice Hastings, Dean of Loyola Law School, paused at the door to the conference room and checked herself. Law school administration, especially at Catholic institutions, was still largely a man's world, and she had to be perfect just to be considered adequate. The law school had only had one female dean before, and Hastings was not going to let them down.

The legal conference and trial exhibition coming up this weekend would be the first of what she intended to be a series of events to raise the public profile of the law school, part of her focus as the new dean. She had taken over from someone who had served in that role for over twenty-five years, and for the last several of those, at least, had become more of a caretaker and figurehead than an active leader. This had left the school pulled in many directions by some faculty asserting their own interests over those of the school. None of those directions appeared to have a chance at strengthening the overall program, only pet projects, let alone increasing profitability to the university. The need to bolster the coffers from what was now her department now rested on her shoulders. Alice Hastings was going to right the ship and get everyone pulling in the same direction. This trial exhibition, the crowning event of the Historical Trials Conference, would begin to accomplish that. It was common for law schools to do this type of historical re-enactments periodically to revisit old cases to see if the same result would be reached using modern legal methods. But she needed more. She needed this conference to help put the school back on the map and on people's minds.

Satisfied that she at least looked the part of a competent academic administrator—outfitted in a dark gray pin-striped suit and a cream-colored silk blouse with a pleated jabot—she took a deep breath to settle her nerves and entered the room. The three men already there stopped talking and rose in unison.

"Gentlemen, please be seated. Thank you for taking the time from your busy schedules to join me both today and in this moot trial for the conference. Let me make the introductions."

The three men glanced at each other as she began. She gestured to the first man on her right.

"Professor Thomas Anderson has been helping me get acclimated as dean and has assisted me in outlining a schedule of events that will revitalize the law school and increase our public impact. He's been at Loyola for about twenty years now, holds a PhD in Renaissance studies from Sapienza University in Rome and an LLM from Oxford focusing on medieval legal systems including canon law. He writes primarily on the impact of historical trials on modern jurisprudence. Tom will be acting as the conference chair, as well as taking the position of advocate for the defense in the trial."

Professor Anderson lifted the Styrofoam cup of coffee in front of him and raised it in salute, then took a sip and set it back on the table.

"Working opposite him as prosecutor, I'd like to introduce Bishop Vijay Sharma, Deputy Prefect of the Vatican Dicastery for the Doctrine of the Faith, known more colloquially as the Holy Office, or historically as the Inquisition. Before coming to the Vatican, Bishop Sharma was director of the Canon Law Society of India. He holds a doctorate of theology from Christ University in Bangalore, and a masters in canon law from St. Peter's Pontifical Seminary and Institute of Theology, also in Bangalore."

The bishop stoically bowed his head in acknowledgment but gave something of a hard look at Tom. Dean Hastings wondered what that was about, but she went on.

"And on my left is Professor Emeritus Luigi Bucatini. Luigi recently retired from teaching philosophy at the University of Padua. He holds a PhD from Harvard University in the philosophy of science, and over his distinguished career has written extensively on bioethics, environmentalism, and the intersection of science and religion. It is in this last area that he will lend us the most support, as the Galileo affair has been a pet project of his for decades. He will be portraying Galileo himself, though in my discussions with him—attempting to convince him to be a part of this project —I can tell you that he is much more agreeable than Galileo was. He assures me that, when the time comes, he will manifest a most historically accurate and irascible persona."

Professor Bucatini smiled, then shifted to a menacing scowl before breaking into affable laughter.

"Now, we have a couple of weeks before the conference

to plan out the trial. Members of the law school faculty, some of our prominent alumni, and a few local clergy will serve as members of the jury. The trial will start on Friday, the second day of the conference, with opening statements and the first witnesses for the prosecution. On Saturday the prosecution will finish and the defense will present their side, and on Sunday, after Mass, I expect closing statements. The jury will deliberate, and we will get their decision at the conclusion of the conference Sunday afternoon.

"Tom had the wonderful idea that it would be nice if we could get the original Galileo documents from the Vatican and have them available for display at the conference and trial, properly preserved from potential damage, of course. The Fielding Museum here in Chicago is going to have a Galileo exhibit at the same time as the conference and would love to display the documents for as long as possible before the trial starts and before they are moved here."

Bishop Sharma raised his hand and addressed the group. "The Dicastery for the Doctrine of the Faith has its own archives, and our records from the actual trial of Galileo are stored there. I have arranged to have as many of those documents as possible brought over with me when I return for the conference, so I can make arrangements to be here for a couple of days before the event to allow them to be displayed at the Fielding Museum. Some of these documents have never before been viewed outside the Vatican.

"Of course, I will need to arrange for security to keep an eye on them. The dicastery has a special contingent of Swiss Guards assigned to us. Perhaps I can arrange for some of them to come along to keep watch over the documents. However, I suspect the Vatican Secret Archive may have additional documents related to the Galileo affair that are not in the possession of the dicastery. We operate within our own little spheres and are not involved with other departments in the Vatican."

"Well, then we are in luck," Professor Bucatini said with a knowing smile, "for I know just who to call at the Secret Archive."

CHAPTER
TWO

As he sat at the old, red oak desk in his office overlooking the Vatican gardens, Father Michael Dominic, Prefect of the Secret Archive, studied an inventory of digital documents from a small cathedral in Prague.

In response to the devastating Notre-Dame blaze of 2019, Pope Ignatius had initiated a preservation process that sent Vatican archivists all over Europe—and eventually, the world—to help digitize each cathedral's records. Too much precious information had been lost in the Paris fire, and with the advances in digital imaging technology, it would be possible—indeed preferable—to prevent such further losses.

This project melded perfectly with the already daunting mission of digitizing the Vatican's vast archives and Church records, a task that could never be finished. With millions of documents on more than eighty kilometers of steel shelves situated in the underground archive, it was already a challenge to keep track of what was there, let alone know what was yet undiscovered. Nevertheless, Michael and his crew had to do it, despite their already thin ranks being stretched even further by this new task.

Fortunately, his team was only responsible for training each cathedral's people in such matters as the Vatican's archival requirements and the correct equipment to make digital images of the records and such. Local staff would take it from there, mostly interns recruited from nearby universities and seminaries. Pope Ignatius had decided that one of his legacies would be to safeguard the history of the Church. It had not gone unnoticed by some, however, that the project also expanded the purview of the Prefect of the Vatican Archive—who, as it happened, was also the pope's son.

Father Dominic's illegitimate parentage had been revealed in Malta on live television by the late Cardinal Fabrizio Dante during what was purported to be "The Last Mass." This was an apocalyptic fraud perpetrated by the now-defunct Knights of the Apocalypse. Since then both Michael and Pope Ignatius had been forced to deal with that unfortunate disclosure, which until then had been a closely guarded secret. Michael had been the product of a clandestine love affair between then-parish priest Enrico Petrini (now Pope Ignatius) and his housekeeper, Grace Dominic.

Once the child had been conceived, Enrico and Grace ended their intimacy, but Grace stayed on at the rectory where she was allowed to raise their son Michael, with Enrico assuming the role of a loving, supportive mentor. Michael had followed "Uncle Rico" into the priesthood, obtaining a degree from Fordham University, though also spending a couple of summers at Loyola University in Chicago, before taking his Jesuit formation at the Pontifical

Institute at the University of Toronto. Topping off his training with a masters degree in medieval studies with an emphasis on paleography and codicology made him a natural for work in the Vatican archives. His facility with languages and computers also helped a great deal. Michael himself had only recently learned the truth after Petrini had been elevated to cardinal and later Vatican secretary of state and had brought Michael to the Vatican as a *scrittore*, or archivist.

Over the past few months, Michael had known that the pressure on Pope Ignatius to resign had been growing, instigated by far-right conservatives in the Curia. Some hard-liners could not stomach the fact that the pope, being human, was imperfect. The Holy Father reminded them that Jesus himself had called on some of the worst sinners he could find to follow him and be his disciples and founding fathers of the Church. Surely, if the cardinals believed that the Holy Spirit guided the selection of popes, from whom nothing was hidden, then this pope's election had been determined and approved by God himself.

Still, there were those who felt very strongly that it was inappropriate, even shocking, for the Catholic Church to be led by a priest with a bastard son, especially in light of other crises the Church was facing. The pope's offspring was continually brought up in those discreet discussions among detractors of the Church's leadership. It made defending the institution that much more difficult.

But the pope was less concerned with defending the Church than he was about ferreting out bad priests and healing the damage caused by their abhorrent conduct in various scandals. His Holiness had, for the most part, shielded Michael from this criticism and the pressure being put on him. Working in the archives was a world unto itself, and while the pope was certain that Michael heard the gossip in the cafeteria and in the halls, still he did not face the brunt of what was directed at the Holy Father himself.

THE PHONE on Michael's desk rang. Looking up, he noticed the U.S. country code and the Chicago area code on the caller ID display. He wondered if this had anything to do with the death of Father Jonah Barlow, whose nearly completed manuscript on the Third Secret of Fatima had set the Knights of the Apocalypse off on their twisted path the year before. Tragically, one of the Chicago police detectives investigating Barlow's death had herself been killed at the end of that misadventure.

Curious, Michael answered the phone. "*Pronto*, Father Dominic speaking."

"Hello, Father Dominic. My name is Alice Hastings. I am dean of Loyola Law School in Chicago."

"Of course, Dean Hastings, hello. How can I help you?"

"Well, the law school is going to be conducting a conference on historical trials, and the featured presentation this year will be a three-day retrial of Galileo. Bishop Sharma of the Dicastery for the Doctrine of the Faith will be bringing a number of original documents from the actual trial to Chicago for the conference, and they will be on display for a couple of days at the Fielding Museum's Galileo exhibit.

"It was suggested that I contact you to see if the Apostolic Archive had any other documents that would be relevant to the retrial that might be brought to Chicago for display at the museum and the conference. Having some of the original documents would be quite a draw for the conference exhibition. We would be willing to fund your attendance at the conference and cover expenses for as many of your staff as you think necessary to care for the documents while they are here. We have secured funding from a few prominent alumni who would like to see this conference be as special as possible."

"An interesting proposal," Michael said. "I do know we have a number of Galileo documents, although I don't know specifically which ones. To be frank, I didn't know that the DDF had its own historical archives, although it makes sense that they would. Also, I believe the Vatican Museum has the original telescope Galileo gave to Pope Urban the Eighth when he came to Rome in 1623, just after the pope's election. Perhaps I can also arrange to bring that along."

"Oh, my! That would be marvelous! Does that mean you'll accept my offer?"

"Well, I do need to make sure I'm not otherwise committed during that time, and that we have something of substance to offer, but yes, I agree in principle. When is the conference?"

"It starts in three weeks, on a Thursday and ending that Sunday. It would be wonderful if you could arrive on Monday or Tuesday that week so the documents and telescope could be on exhibit at the museum for a couple days beforehand. I know it's rather short notice, but we hadn't actually thought of having the original documents on hand until our organizational meeting of the principal participants yesterday."

As Dr. Hastings was speaking, Michael checked his calendar. "That should be fine. It looks like I am free that week. Let me see what documents we have available and I'll call you back tomorrow. Is this a good number to reach you?"

"Yes, this is my direct line. I'm very excited that you might be coming, Father Dominic. It will really boost the profile of the conference. Thank you so much."

"It's my pleasure. I'll give you a call tomorrow, then. Goodbye for now, Dean Hastings."

Michael wandered down the hall and peeked into his assistant's office, but Ian wasn't there. Walking out the entrance doors of the Archive, he stopped to greet the Swiss Guard stationed there, Sergeant Dieter Koehl.

"Hey, Dieter. Have you seen Ian, by chance?"

After a smart salute to the priest, Dieter assumed the more casual Guard's position, his hands folded in front of him. "Well, Father Michael, you didn't hear it from me, but I'd check the Restoration Lab." He smiled knowingly, nodding his head down the main hallway toward the lab. "Ian has been sneaking off down there quite a bit lately. I think it has something to do with that cute young Roma girl you have working there."

"Oh, has he now? Good to know. Thanks, Dieter."

Just then, Ian emerged from the Restoration Lab and turned up the hallway toward the two men. He stopped when he saw Michael and Dieter looking at him, realizing he'd been caught. Head down, he resumed walking toward them, slowly now, trying to come up with a good reason to have been in the lab.

"Uh, hey, Boss," Ian quipped, with a sheepish look on his face. "I was just—"

"Never mind, I don't want to know. You're allowed to have a life. Just make sure it doesn't interfere with the work. And be discreet. You may not be of the clergy but still you know how rumors fly around here."

"Thanks, Michael!" Ian beamed. "Was there something you needed?"

"Yes. Feel like a field trip to Chicago? I just got a call from the dean of Loyola Law School. They're putting on a conference and a retrial of Galileo's heresy tribunal. I need you to determine what our Galileo holdings are and where they might be located. I've got to go have a chat with the curator of the Vatican Museum and see if I can borrow a certain telescope."

~

LATER THAT AFTERNOON, Michael had returned to his desk when his phone rang again. This number he recognized immediately: the Rome bureau for *Le Monde*, the French newspaper where his friend Hana Sinclair worked as a reporter.

"Hana!" he answered brightly. "What a lovely surprise. What are you up to?"

"I was about to ask you the same thing! I just saw a press release come into the newsroom from Loyola Law School stating the Vatican was sending some of the original Galileo documents for a conference and moot retrial in Chicago. My editor said it sounds like a good story for me, especially with some investigation into the Galileo affair itself. It's the 400th anniversary of one of his major publications, *The Assayer*. So, are you going to the Windy City for the event?"

"I am, indeed. The conference is paying for me and a few of my staff to attend the conference and safeguard the documents. Were you thinking of going as well?"

"Well, actually, I'd love for all of us to go together if you don't think I'd be a distraction. I'm sure we could get Grand-père's jet. Save the conference some money on airfare and increase the level of security for the trip. Sound like a deal?"

"That would be terrific! It's always great spending time with you, and we haven't yet been to the U.S. together."

"Okay, then, it's set. Send me your conference details and my assistant will make the arrangements. I'm so looking forward to getting away for a bit. The Rome office is nice, but since we're a French publication, the space is a lot smaller than working at the main office in Paris, and we are literally tripping over each other here. Besides, I've always wanted to spend some time in Chicago. Big American cities are so different from Europe's. Didn't you go to school there for some time?"

"I did, yes. A couple of summer programs at Loyola while I was getting my degree at Fordham. But that was a while ago now. From what I've read, the city has grown substantially since then and is not necessarily the safer for it. I'm bringing Karl and Lukas for security—both for the documents and for me." He laughed. The two Swiss Guards had become friends with the priest while serving as his protectors over the years. Though Michael never felt he needed protection, there had been certain threatening times when he was more than happy they'd been with him.

"Well, I'd love to see some of the sights, if there's time," Hana added. "I'll also check on available rooms at the conference hotel, or someplace nice nearby. This is an academic conference at a Catholic law school. I imagine they don't have a lot of extracurricular activities planned. You're not participating in the trial, are you?"

"No, I'm just an observer and custodian of the documents and perhaps another exhibit. I'm working on getting the telescope Galileo gave to Pope Urban. I've almost convinced the curator of the Vatican Museum to let me have it for the conference. He's reluctant to lend it out, but they do it all the time for reciprocal institutions, so it shouldn't be that big a deal. I'm sure the pope could put in a good word, too, if it came to that."

"Oh, you wicked boy... Well, it all sounds like fun anyway. I can't wait. I'll give you a call back when I've got all the arrangements made. I'd love some background on which documents you'll be taking, for the piece I'll be working on."

"We're still making that assessment, seeing what documents we have and which ones are amenable to travel. I'll know more in a few days, and we can talk again then."

CHAPTER

THREE

VATICAN CITY, TWO WEEKS LATER

In an office somewhere in the Vatican' Apostolic Palace, the phone on a desk rang. The person sitting there noted caller ID and picked it up.

"Hello, Your Eminence, I'm very busy right now. What is it?" Bishop Sharma asked.

The caller's response was curt, nervous. "You leave for Chicago tomorrow. Is it done?"

"No," Sharma answered. "As I understand it, there are processes involved that cannot be sped up. It will be a few more days."

"What are you going to do? This is becoming a problem. I thought it would be done by now."

"No, it is not a problem. I had planned on that. I'll call Father Dominic. Ask him to transport our documents with his. I'll tell him we could not spare the personnel to provide adequate security. I'm sure he will be accommodating. In fact, he is perhaps too accommodating; it's in his nature. And actually, I'm counting on that."

"Good. But what about the girl? She is going to Chicago, too."

"Yes, that is also part of the plan," the bishop confirmed. "Had Father Dominic not thought of bringing her, I would have insisted that she be part of the team to make sure the exhibits were properly preserved on display."

"So, you have left nothing to chance?"

"No, not so far as I am able. I'll make the call to Dominic. Once he is committed to taking the documents to America, I will make sure to have what I need, when I need it. Fear not. I have taken steps to anticipate contingencies that might unfold. You just do your part. I will worry about the rest. You will have what you are looking for, and I intend to win this trial as well, one way or another. No sacrifice is too great."

"And no detail too small," the familiar voice replied. *"Veritas vos liberabit."*

The truth will set you free.

IAN DUFFY POKED his head in Michael's office as he was heading back to his own desk.

"Well, Boss, I've done as thorough a search as I can, and it turns out that we don't have as many Galileo documents as you might think. I guess the Office of the Inquisition must have the bulk of them," Ian surmised.

"Be careful calling them that," Michael cautioned. "They can be a little sensitive about their image, and you really don't want to make enemies over there. They hold a great deal of power within the Curia. Their capacity to investigate misdeeds and violations at will gives them influence over a lot of people they've caught in various indiscretions. They have been known to withhold prosecutions in order to sway people to their positions on issues. It's practically blackmail, but it is within their purview to use discretion in enforcement. They just aren't supposed to use it for their own ends. It's supposed to be pastoral, not persuasive."

"Right, okay. So what *do* I call them?" Ian asked.

"Well, their new formal name is the Dicastery for the Doctrine of the Faith. We used to call them the Holy Office, but I think we should use their formal title when they are around. In here, we can just refer to them as the DDF."

"DDF it is, then. Anyway, we have some records from 1616 and 1623, from Galileo's trips to Rome, including a copy of the letter Cardinal Bellarmine wrote for Galileo describing the warning he was given at Bellarmine's palace. We also have a copy of the summons that brought him to Rome in 1633, and others related to his imprisonment after his conviction. There are also a few of Galileo's letters to various Church officials and the approvals for him to publish his 1632 treatise *Dialogue Concerning the Two Chief World Systems*. Plus, we have a copy of *Dialogue* itself."

"Well, that will have to be enough," Michael said. "I hope the DDF is bringing some good stuff for the exhibit. I'd like to see Loyola have a nice event, and for the Fielding Museum to have a compelling exhibit, since our name is going to be on it as supplying the records and the telescope —which, by the way, we just got approval for bringing with us."

"Awesome! Okay, so I've pulled all the records for your review to see which ones you think we should take. They are all down in the Restoration Lab so they can be prepped for transport. Say, why didn't you tell me Kat was coming?"

"Oh, so it's 'Kat' now, is it?" the priest asked, grinning. "Well, I was saving that as a surprise, but I guess 'Kat' beat me to it. I need someone with experience in archival preservation methods to assist with the display of the records.

And you are going as a reward for your help on my last couple projects. I want you to know I appreciate it." Michael reached out to squeeze Ian's shoulder in a moment of solidarity. "Besides, I might need a gofer while we're there..." Ian rolled his eyes but grinned happily.

The phone on Michael's desk rang. He glanced at the number on the display.

"Well, speak of the devil. It's someone calling from the DDF." He picked up the phone and answered, *"Pronto,* Father Dominic."

"This is Bishop Sharma at the Dicastery for the Doctrine of the Faith. I understand from the conference organizers at Loyola that you are going to be taking some documents to the Galileo conference and the Fielding Museum beforehand. Is that right?"

"Yes, Excellency. We are taking a number of documents, and a telescope from the Vatican Museum, the one Galileo gave to Pope Urban the Eighth."

"Very good. I need you to transport our documents, Father. I have to leave for Chicago early to prepare for the trial exhibition, but our archivists have not been able to complete the preparation of our own documents for travel yet. I expect you will be able to take our documents with you when you go over later in the week," he said in his typically curt manner.

"Of course. I don't see a problem with that. Did you need us to come pick them up or will you have them delivered here?"

"We will have them delivered to you there, and naturally you will need to sign for them to establish chain of custody. There will be a complete inventory. I expect you to check it thoroughly to ensure everything is there and properly accounted for. Then they will be locked and sealed in an archival transport case. You simply need to take them to the museum. I will come to the museum and oversee their unpacking and installation at the exhibition. I appreciate your assistance in this matter."

"I am happy to be of help, Bishop Sharma."

"Very good, then. I will have our archivist call you when the documents are ready. Goodbye, Father. I will see you in Chicago."

"Ciao, Excellency." Michael hung up, then turned to his assistant.

"Well, Ian. I guess the DDF is going to be sending their documents with us. We'll get to see what they're taking when we inspect the inventory before locking up the transport case. Can you make sure Ekaterina has a similar case available?"

"Yes, sir! I'd be happy to run down to the Restoration Lab for you."

"Yeah, I didn't think you'd have a problem with that."

FOUR

T he morning of the day before he was due to leave for Chicago, Michael called up to the pope's office to arrange to say goodbye. Father Nick Bannon, the pope's longtime personal assistant and gatekeeper whom Michael had known for many years, answered the phone.

"*Pronto*, Office of the Holy Father."

"Hi, Nick, it's Michael."

"Hey, Michael! I hear you're heading across the pond soon. Did you want to meet with His Holiness today?"

"I do, yes. I'm leaving tomorrow for the Galileo conference and wanted to see him before I go. How is he doing?" Michael appreciated that Nick had always been honest with him about the pope's health, even if the pope himself had asked Nick not to tell anyone about his growing infirmities. Nick had known about the relationship between Michael and the Holy Father longer than almost anyone except the previous pope, so he felt that Michael, more than anyone, had a right to know.

"I was thinking of calling you later today, anyway. Your

father has been pretty run down the last few days and we are restricting his schedule to give him some time to rest. Would you like to have lunch with him?"

"Yes, lunch would be perfect. What time should I be there?"

"Come up at eleven forty-five. And don't be shocked at how he looks. He's lost a bit of weight because he hasn't been sticking to his normal diet. Hopefully having lunch with you will stimulate his appetite. I'll let him know you're coming."

"Nick, level with me. Should I be concerned? I don't have to make this trip. I could just send the staff. I was just looking forward to seeing Chicago again. My last trip there, for Detective Lancaster's funeral, was rather short."

"Well, his doctors don't think it's anything serious. He just keeps a busy calendar that would tire a man half his age. There is so much he wants to accomplish, and he knows his time is limited, no matter how long that is. And he's been under stress since the revelations in Malta. There are factions within the Church that would use that against him, and the vultures are always circling. He has been shielding you from most of that, you know. But you would do well to watch your back, even more than you normally might."

"I understand, Nick. It's shameful that power is so important to some people, but what can you do? Anyway, I'll see you just before noon. And thanks."

"You're welcome, Michael. See you then."

Michael had just hung up the phone when it rang. The screen displayed "Diamond Ark Cathedral, Dallas, Texas, USA."

Michael groaned. *Oh, great. This can't possibly be good.* He decided to answer in Italian.

"Pronto, Archivio Pontificio, parla Padre Dominico."

"Michael, Michael, Michael..." a voice greeted him chidingly. A man with a strong Texas twang continued. "This is Pastor Gabriel Darwin of the Church of Supreme Divinity, calling from the Diamond Ark Cathedral in Dallas, Texas, in the good ol' U. S. of A."

Michael reluctantly switched to English. "Hello, Pastor Darwin. I'm curious, how did you get my direct line?"

"Well, Michael, I think you'll find I'm a very resourceful person. And I take it as a sign of God's favor that when I want something, God and I usually find a way to make it happen. Why, just look at the hundreds of Jewel Ark Chapels we've opened around the world to spread the good news of the prosperity guaranteed to us by the Lord in the Good Book. And I am a livin' example of that prosperity. In fact, I think you might have had the opportunity to visit one of those chapels in the Holy Land recently. I know some of your people were there..." Darwin let that hang in the air a moment, but when Michael did not comment, he went on.

"Well, all that aside, I'm callin' 'cuz I've had a new vision from the Lord, and I've been directed to make an addition to the Biblical Hall Museum that'll feature the original writings of some of Christianity's greatest heroes of the faith. People like Martin Luther, Calvin, Tyndale, Wesley, Wycliffe—why, even Oral Roberts! Speaking of whom, maybe I should look into starting my own university and a seminary... Hmm, I'll have to pray on that.

"Anyway, back to the addition. I hear you are going to be bringin' some of the original Galileo documents to Chicago soon. And I intend to buy one of them. I want the original letter from Galileo to Grand Duchess Christina as the centerpiece of the openin' of our museum's new addition. I think it's destined to be in my collection so that everyone who visits the Biblical Hall Museum can read it for themselves and rejoice in the presence of such history. I assume you're familiar with the letter? It's the one where Galileo explains why the Catholic Church is wrong to have taken a strict literal interpretation of the Bible in conformity with its tradition rather than in accord with proven science."

Michael was feeling testy with this tiresome man. "Pastor Darwin, I'm afraid the Vatican is not in the business of selling off its historical manuscripts. Plus, the text and digital image of Galileo's Letter to Grand Duchess Christina is readily available in a number of books and websites for people to read, whether they visit your 'museum' or not." The priest reflexively allowed an audible sneer color his pronunciation of "museum."

"Now, Michael. Let's not be too hasty. I could make a sizable donation to the Church. Think of all the good works that could be done with it. There could even be somethin' in it for you. I'm sure the Archive could use the additional resources, right? So don't say no just yet. Think it over. I've made arrangements to preach at the Jewel Ark Chapel in Chicago while you're there for the conference. Maybe we can talk again. My people will be in touch. Just make sure you bring the original Letter to Grand Duchess Christina with you. Adios, Michael." The connection broke off.

"Great. Just great..." Michael muttered to himself in the otherwise empty office. He logged into the Archive's inventory and searched for the Letter to Grand Duchess Christina. Michael knew that the original manuscript had been copied several times in its day and circulated around the Florentine court as well as among the powerful clergy in Tuscany and Rome, including those of the Inquisition. Michael found that the Vatican had an early manuscript copy, as well as the Italian and Latin side-by-side versions published in Strasbourg in 1636, since Galileo had been prohibited from publishing after the trial in 1633. A brief search of the internet failed to reveal where the original was. Perhaps in the private holdings of the remaining Medici family, or even lost to the ravages of time.

But he didn't have any further time to deal with that. The interruption and subsequent research had eaten up his morning and it was nearly time for his lunch meeting.

When he arrived at the Apostolic Palace, Father Bannon buzzed him in through the main doors.

"He's in a meeting with a few members of the Curia, but they are just leaving," Father Bannon warned him.

As Michael went in, he was received by one of the Gentlemen of His Holiness, personal lay assistants and stewards who see to the organization of the papal household, the conduct of guests to and from the papal apartments, and other duties under the pope's direction. One Gentleman brought Michael to the door of the pope's office and knocked briefly, while another Gentleman opened it from the inside.

"Your Holiness, I present Father Michael Dominic, Prefect of your Apostolic Archive," the Gentleman called out.

A cluster of bishops and cardinals in their various attire was still gathered around the pope's desk. The pope was dressed in a simple white cassock and zucchetto. In his declining health, such allowances for informality were made for his comfort, and none of them dared say anything about it. They began to file out as Michael was announced.

Michael recognized the Vatican Secretary of State, Cardinal Giovanni Greco, as well as the heads of the Dicastery for the Doctrine of the Faith, the Dicastery for Bishops, the Dicastery for the Clergy, the Dicastery for Institutes of Consecrated Life and for Societies for Apostolic Life, and the Dicastery for the Laity, Family and Life, as well as a number of their immediate assistants and the heads of subordinate institutions within the dicasteries.

As they left, many of them turned to regard Michael as he entered. Some of the looks Michael received were friendly, or at least neutral, but a few ranged somewhere between hostility and disgust. Cardinal Caputo, Prefect of the Dicastery for the Doctrine of the Faith—formerly the Holy Office of the Inquisition—gave Michael an especially antagonistic glare. Caputo was one of the most conservative members of the Curia, and had a particular dislike of the current, more liberal pope and his son. He considered Michael's existence so severe an affront to the sanctity of the pope's office that he felt the pope should have abdicated in disgrace after the news of his paternity hit. The previous pope had absolved then-Cardinal Petrini before Petrini became Pope Ignatius, but Caputo still headed a faction within the Curia that looked forward to a more conservative replacement, and the sooner the better. The Holy Father tried to remain above the criticism. What was done was done, and he tried to serve the Church as best he could, just as his son Michael did.

As the last of the group left the spacious room, Michael could finally see the pope seated at his desk—not in his normal chair, but in a wheelchair. Michael rushed to his side.

"Papa, are you okay?"

"Yes, Michael, I am. Just feeling a little run down, and the wheelchair allows me to conserve my energy for the important work. You young men do not appreciate how big the Vatican is and how much effort is required to get around in it. Come, take me over to the table and they will bring our lunch."

As if on cue, one of the pope's Gentlemen appeared through a side door with a wheeled cart holding two domed platters. The glinting silver cloches were pulled away with a flourish to reveal china plates with the gold and silver papal insignia on the china positioned at the top. The pope received a steaming bowl of pasta *fagioli*, a hearty soup containing sausage, beans, pasta and vegetables. This was accompanied by a small loaf of crusty bread, a small antipasti salad, and a glass of red wine. Michael received a steaming bowl of mushroom risotto with bits of crimini and portobello mushrooms peeking out from around the creamy arborio rice. This was topped with slices of morels, white truffle, and a dusting of Pecorino Romano cheese.

"This smells heavenly," Michael remarked as he leaned over his bowl to inhale the heady aromas.

"Yes, well, it's not like your mother used to make. She was such a good cook, our Grace. We always ate so well in the old days. Not that I'm complaining, mind you. But when your mother cooked, it must have been her love imbued in the food that made everything taste that much better."

Michael looked at his father questioningly. "You miss her, too, don't you?"

"Every day. After you were conceived, we were remorseful of our sin, and we repented, never again engaging in intimate relations. But you had to be raised, and you deserved as close to a father figure as could be provided under the circumstances. Your mother sacrificed much in those days, Michael. She bore the shame of having a baby out of wedlock and the sorrow of never being able to claim a father for him, or a husband for herself. I think in a way it was her idea of penance. But she took such good care of us both. I miss her terribly. Maybe more now than when she died. I find myself thinking often of what might have been, had things been different."

"How do you mean?"

"What would life have been like for all of us if I had left the priesthood, married your mother, and raised you in a respectable family? Or better yet, if the Church had allowed clergy to marry?"

Michael shrugged. "I didn't know any different. I think it worked out all right, though. But I know what you mean. Have you ever given thought to starting an initiative for the Church to allow priests to marry?"

The pope chuckled softly. "Oh, Michael. If there were even a remote possibility of it, I would issue a proclamation today. But the practices of priestly celibacy and self-denial are so deeply rooted in the ascetic impulses of Catholic culture, combined with the human quest for a closer relationship with Christ, that it would likely never gain traction with the conservative wing of the Church. But, I do have a possible plan—so for now, hold that thought.

"Speaking of self-denial...how are things with Hana?" he asked warmly.

Smiling, Michael looked at his father with great love. He was such an understanding and compassionate man.

"We are still very good friends, Papa, and we've agreed that must be enough for both of us unless something changes. Right now, I think I mentioned that my friend from Loyola, Aaron Pearce, is now here teaching classical studies at the John Felice Center across town. He and Hana have been spending a fair bit of time together recently. But she is coming to Chicago with us for the Galileo conference."

"Ah, the Galileo conference. I'm sure you will enjoy being back in the States for something less serious. Your last trip wasn't all that enjoyable. That whole mess with Father Barlow." He shook his head, sorrowful about the loss of a good priest. Plus, Michael had been in peril during that event, and the pope had worried for his safe return.

"I could stay, Papa. It worries me that you are slowing down so much."

"No, Michael. I'm fine. Go. I'll be working on my latest encyclical. It involves redefining the different roles in the life and structure of the Church. That is why certain members of the Curia were here when you came in, to give their input. So go. But keep an eye over your shoulder. You are not the only one to have noticed that I am getting older. They are like birds of prey now. Factions are forming. I would not be surprised if someone tried to use you to get to me. Make sure you take security with you to the U.S."

"Yes, Papa. Karl and Lukas are going, too. I will be careful. I would never let anyone use me to get to you."

As they finished their lunch, Father Bannon entered the office.

"I'm sorry, Michael, but the Holy Father's afternoon calendar beckons. I'm afraid we'll have to cut this visit short."

"That's okay, Nick, I was just about to leave." Michael leaned over his father's wheelchair and gave him a hug and a kiss on the forehead. "Goodbye, Papa. I'll send word from Chicago."

CHAPTER

FIVE

E arly the next morning Michael woke up, threw on a pair of dark navy sweat pants, laced up his Saucony trainers, and headed out St. Anne's Gate for his usual run through the Suburra neighborhood of Rome.

He hadn't gotten far—just north of the Vatican walls—when his pace slowed as he approached *Edicola Sacra,* the news kiosk on the Piazza del Risorgimento. He noticed a young woman sitting behind the cramped counter, framed by colorful magazine covers and blaring headlines across the world's newspapers displayed in racks surrounding her. She appeared to be around twenty, dressed in woolen trousers with suspenders, a flannel shirt, and a newsboy cap tilted on her head.

"Buongiorno, signorina," he greeted her, speaking in her native Italian. "I'm Father Michael Dominic, a friend of Signor Bucatini, the owner of this stand. I usually see him here every day; is he all right?"

"Oh, *sì, padre,* my uncle—well, great-uncle—he is fine," she answered with a generous smile. "And yes, he has told me about you. He just had to take a trip for a few days so he asked me to work the stand. I thought I should look the part." She gestured at her attire, touching the brim of her cap as she nodded her head. "My name is Carla, Carla Bucatini. Can I get you anything?"

Michael stood there, a thin sheen of sweat from his run just forming on his arms and face. "No, *grazie*. I'm in no position to read a paper just now," he grinned. "But you know, that is how I met your uncle, dripping sweat on his newspapers one day. Anyway, if you do speak with Luigi, please tell him hello for me."

"I will, *sì*...unless you see him first," she replied with a look of mystery on her smiling face. Michael glanced at her, his head cocked to one side as if there were some joke he wasn't in on. With a slight wave, he turned and ran off.

HAVING RETURNED to his apartment after an hour-long run, Michael showered and dressed, then packed a suitcase for the trip and took it with him to his office.

He headed down to the Restoration Lab to check on preparations for their flight to Chicago and found Ian and Ekaterina working at the lab's main table.

"Hey, you two...how's it coming?" Michael asked, gesturing to the materials on the table. Each page of the historical documents they were taking had been placed between two sheets of acid-free archival paper, and then sandwiched between two sheets of thin, clear, UV-resistant Mylar and fastened with clear plastic clips. Kat was just finishing placing the pages of the last documents between the plates and clipping them closed.

"Just about done, Father Michael," she murmured, her voice not as robust as usual. Finished with the latest pages, she placed them into a wheeled, metal travel case on the floor next to her. "I've color-coded the edge of the plates for each of the documents we are taking for easy reference. As you directed, we are taking Galileo's Summons to appear before the Inquisition, the letter Cardinal Bellarmine wrote to Galileo in 1616, the two Imprimaturs—the permissions to publish in Rome and Florence—and the pope's copy of Galileo's *Dialogue*."

"Excellent, good work," Michael said. Kat didn't look up, apparently focused on the task at hand.

"I've also prepared an inventory and shipping manifest as if we were sending these to the Fielding Museum by courier—but of course, *we* will be the couriers in this case. Father Michael, I just need you to check the page counts and validate we have all the documents. Then we can seal up the case."

Michael came over and peered into the metal case. He counted the pages of each color, then verified that each of the described documents was present and accounted for. Satisfied, he took the clipboard Kat had handed him, flipped the inventory over to the signature page at the back and signed it.

"Father, could you bring me that little pot of sealing wax on top of the burner over there? Be careful to hold it by the wooden handle; it's hot. Ian, please get a silicone pad from the drawer over there to set it on. I'll lock the case and then we can seal it. Did you bring your embossing seal, Father?"

"Yes, it's here in my pocket."

As Michael turned away and walked over to the side of the lab where the ceramic wax pot was warming on a Bunsen burner, Kat made sure neither was looking, then surreptitiously slipped another single-page document in similar packaging into the case, quickly closing it and twisting the keys in the two locks. Michael turned back and took the wax pot over to her, at which point she poured a quarter-sized disc of hot red wax onto the sealing port of the case, then set the pot on the pad.

"Okay, now press your seal into the wax. Quickly, before it hardens."

Michael sighed to himself; he'd used his seal enough times to know how it worked. He withdrew the brass seal engraved with the official insignia of the Apostolic Archive, then pressed it into the wax. He lifted it away to reveal the impression, which was rapidly hardening as the wax cooled.

"Thank you, Father," she said coolly, still avoiding meeting Michael's eyes.

There was a knock at the lab door.

"Enter," Kat said loudly. A young Jesuit novitiate pushed the door open, pulling a similar wheeled travel case through the door behind him.

"Ah, Viggo," she said. "Right on time. This is Father Dominic, Prefect of the Apostolic Archive, and of course you know Ian. Father Dominic, this is Viggo Pisano, a *scrittore* from the DDF."

Michael extended his hand. "Good to meet you, Viggo."

"Wow. Sir, it is such an honor to meet you. Ekaterina, I mean, Signorina Lakatos, has told me so much about you."

"Well, it's an honor to meet you as well, young brother, and good to see you're on our Jesuit team. I only recently learned that the DDF has its own archives. So, let's see what have you brought us."

Viggo took two keys from his pocket, used one in each of the two locks, then lifted the hinged lid of the case and removed the inventory packets and passed them to the priest.

"Let's see here... There are copies of the trial transcripts, one for each session. There is a copy of the notes from the meeting with Cardinal Bellarmine, a copy of Galileo's confession which he signed, a copy of the verdict signed by members of the tribunal, and lastly, a copy of the Sentence of Imprisonment. This is an excellent addition to what we're taking and will make for a marvelous exhibition."

Viggo looked like he wanted to say something but hesitated, then responded absently, "Uh...yes, Father."

Michael verified that all inventoried documents were in the case. Satisfied, he had Viggo lock the case, then took the keys. Kat poured another disc of red sealing wax into the inset area on the base, and Michael pressed his insignia into the wax. Now any tampering with the cases—and potential access to the precious documents inside—would be immediately detectable.

Another knock at the door interrupted them.

"Enter," Kat again shouted.

Karl and Lukas came into the room, both smiling and wearing dark suits instead of their usual Swiss Guard uniforms.

"Good morning, everyone. Are we on time?" Karl asked.

"Yes, perfect timing," Michael said. "We've just locked and sealed the two transport cases." He took one of the two keys to each case and gave them to Karl. "You take one key to each case, and I'll take the other set. Now, if you guys can take the cases out to your car, I'll grab my suitcase from the office and meet everyone in the parking lot. Viggo, again, nice meeting you."

Viggo glanced at the cases, then said, "It was a pleasure meeting you as well."

With that, he ducked out the door to return to the DDF. As Michael watched him go, it seemed to him the younger man was bothered by something.

As Viggo left the Archive building, he took a deep

nervous breath and let it out. There was something wrong with the document count. He knew exactly which documents were intended to be sent to America, for Bishop Sharma had been very specific on that point.

But it was the documents that were *not* in the case that concerned him.

So, where were they?

CHAPTER

SIX

Arriving at Ciampino Airport on the southeast outskirts of Rome in Karl's Jeep Wrangler, he, Lukas, Michael, Ian and Kat made their way to the FBO terminal for private aircraft and were directed to the hangar where Baron Armand de Saint-Clair's Dassault Falcon was parked. As the Jeep pulled up, the pilots were going through their preflight safety checks.

While Karl and Lukas were loading the document cases into the cargo area at the back of the plane, a courier van pulled up with the telescope from the Vatican Museum. Michael signed for the sturdy wooden crate, nearly two meters long by thirty centimeters square, and helped load it into the plane. He was a little concerned that Hana had not yet arrived. Stepping away from the tail of the plane, he was about to call her when he saw a little blue Fiat Cinquecento convertible rapidly approaching, Hana's hair tossing in the wind as she hung on in the passenger seat while the tall, handsome man at the wheel, Aaron Pearce, maneuvered around the parked jets.

When they came to a stop, Hana got out, pulled a hairbrush from her handbag, and tried to tame her windblown hair while Aaron unhooked the straps fastening her suitcase to the rack on the rear of the Fiat. He handed her the suitcase as she gave him a quick kiss on the cheek.

"Thanks for the ride, Aaron. I'll see you when I get back," she said, turning toward the plane.

Aaron waved to Michael and called out, "Have a great trip, buddy. I can't stay to see you off; got a class to teach. Call me when you get back." Making the sign of holding an imaginary telephone to his ear, he hopped back in the Fiat and sped off.

Michael turned to Hana. "Well, you two are getting along nicely."

Hana looked at him curiously. "He's just a good friend now. We went out a couple of times, but he's probably not right for me long term."

Michael just smiled. "I was getting worried…like maybe we'd have to take off without you." They both laughed as Hana playfully punched his shoulder.

"All right, everyone, climb aboard," the pilot called from the main cabin door. "We have a twelve o'clock departure slot we don't want to miss."

Michael and Hana took the airstairs up to the cabin door and entered the luxurious passenger lounge. Ian and Kat had already taken seats near the aft section, and Karl and Lukas were seated together near the front. Hana and Michael claimed a pair of mid-cabin seats.

"Hello, Ms. Sinclair. So nice to see you again," Frederic, the baron's flight attendant, said as she was seated. He then addressed the six passengers. "Ladies and gentlemen, it is a nine-hour flight to Chicago, but with the time zone change we will arrive at about two in the afternoon local time. Since it is such a long flight, I will be serving both lunch and dinner.

I shall start the lunch service just as soon as we reach cruising altitude, and then dinner at what would be six o'clock here in Rome. May I get anyone a refreshment before we depart?"

"Just a bottle of water for me, Frederic, thank you," Hana replied. Frederic made the rounds of the other passengers, then retreated to the galley to prepare the beverages.

"So," Hana asked Michael, "how is this Galileo retrial supposed to work? Are they going to be using the actual documents during the tribunal? I wouldn't think you would allow that."

"No, not during the trial. The documents we are bringing will be on exhibit in the Fielding Museum, which is just south of downtown. It's right next to Soldier Field, where the Chicago Bears play, and the Shedd Aquarium and the Adler Planetarium are also nearby. I'll have to check to see if there's a Bears game we might take in. But there will still be plenty of things to do besides the conference. Chicago is one of the most engaging cities in America. There is just so much to do. And the food! I know you have a taste for fine cuisine, but we're going to have to stretch your consumption boundaries, because Chicago has some of the best ethnic food enclaves in America, with small authentic restaurants everywhere. Then there's Chicago pizza and Chicago hot dogs. Greektown. Oh, we are going to eat so well…"

"Seriously, Michael? A *hot dog?*"

"You bet! And no need to be stuffy about it. Hot dogs are a cultural delicacy in Chicago. But I'll take you to a good place, not just a street cart. There's a Kim and Carlo's right by the museum, or we could go to Portillo's or the Dog House."

"Hmm. Well, we'll see. If you're that excited about it, it

must have some merit." She smiled in a coy but challenging way. Michael just grinned.

"Anyway, the exhibits will stay on display at the museum until the trial, when we'll move them to the Loyola Law School campus for display during the confer-ence. But during the trial, they'll be using copies of the trial documents. Having the originals there is just an audience draw because some people will be interested in seeing the genuine documents they actually used in the trial.

"As far as the tribunal itself goes, as I understand it, Bishop Sharma will be the prosecutor, presenting the orig-inal evidence to the people sitting in as jurors, and Professor Anderson will be working to counter Sharma's position, using modern legal rules, so it should be just a kind of demonstration of modern procedure versus historical meth-ods. I'm curious what the jury will decide, given nearly four hundred years of intervening history in which Galileo was shown to be right—not only about the science, but with the fact that the Church has largely moved away from a strictly literal interpretation of Scripture in those places where literal meaning conflicts with proven facts. Now the passages are given a more poetic or spiritual interpretation. I expect Galileo to be exonerated, frankly. But it's kind of old news anyway since in October 1992, a commission at the Pontifical Academy of Sciences—after thirteen years of study and debate—found that Galileo's conviction should be overturned. It just wasn't the right time for Galileo to have been so vocal about his discoveries and so confronta-tional toward the Church. And as you know, the Church makes changes very slowly. It wasn't until 1835 that Galileo's *Dialogue* was taken off the *Index of Prohibited Books*."

"That's a lot to digest," Hana said. "When I get to writing the piece for *Le Monde*, I'm definitely coming to you for more background. But if the commission already found Galileo not guilty, why this moot trial, even though it's just an exercise?"

"I really don't know for sure, but I can think of a couple possible reasons. The Galileo affair has been used as a symbol of the Church's opposition to scientific progress and to support the argument of the superiority of faith over science. There is an undercurrent of that same sentiment flowing in the world again now, especially in America, though it seems to be, ironically, mostly among certain Protestant denominations. In his day, the Protestants championed Galileo's resistance to the Church's position. Now they seem to be taking the Church's old position against modern science. Perhaps the pope encouraged Bishop Sharma to participate in order to emphasize that it is no longer the Church's position.

"On the other hand, while I don't know him, from what I've heard, he has a reputation as a very tough and skilled prosecutor. Maybe he thinks he can win."

"Well," Hana said, "maybe this isn't going to be as routine as I was expecting. This should be more than just interesting and potentially a good story."

IN THE FRONT SEATS, Lukas had leaned over and rested his head on Karl's shoulder, exhausted from working the overnight shift. They kept their relationship a private matter while at work, but could be open now, in the presence of their friends. After lunch, Lukas was looking forward to a few hours of sleep to catch up. As he napped, Karl held his hand while looking out over the vast ocean below them.

In the back, Kat also sat and watched the great blue

expanse out the window, but she was clearly unsettled—a departure from her usual demeanor.

"You okay?" Ian asked with some concern.

"Yeah, I guess so," she replied without looking at him. "I'm, uh…not much of a flyer. Feeling kinda queasy."

She kept looking out the window, fearful of letting Ian know it wasn't the flying that made her nervous.

CHAPTER
SEVEN

After eight hours in the air, the pilot's voice came on over the cabin speakers. "Well, folks, we just got word from O'Hare that the planes landing in front of us have been experiencing a fair bit of turbulence on descent. So, I'm going to ask you to take your seats, lock them in position and fasten your seatbelts for the duration of the ride. I'll do my best to smooth it out, but it's likely to get pretty bumpy on the way in. We'll be on the ground in about forty-five minutes."

Kat turned to Ian and grimaced. He reached over and took her hand.

Hana turned to Michael. "Think your boss can do anything about the wind?"

"I think the pope is probably already in bed." Hana glanced at him with a glint of humor, then pointed up. "Oh, that Boss. I don't think it works that way, but it doesn't hurt to ask." Michael closed his eyes for a few moments. "There. The rest is up to the pilots."

"Thank you. Now I know we're in good hands." While there were a few uncomfortable dips in air pockets, the approach was not as bad as the pilots had been led to believe by Aviation Weather Services.

As they came in across Lake Michigan, Hana marveled at the Chicago skyline. "So many tall buildings all crammed together. And look at all the cranes; they're constructing even more."

"Yes, it never stops. The skyline is constantly evolving. I just read that there are currently twenty tower cranes operating in Chicago right now. Back in 2017 there were actually fifty-three. It's just a funny little thing I used to keep track of when I was here for school. I thought it was fascinating to see how the buildings go up in an already overbuilt area. I looked it up again before we came over."

"You never cease to amaze me," Hana said. Then she looked up and ran her hand across the short stubble on his head. "Your hair's growing back, finally. Soon it'll be just as long and silky as before."

"Well, I don't know about silky," Michael muttered, a shadow crossing his face at the memory of his recent imprisonment in Egypt. He shuddered thinking about it.

Once they were on the tarmac, it took over thirty minutes of taxiing to finally reach the private air terminal. At the Chicago FBO, the van they had arranged was waiting for them. They loaded up the exhibits and made the eighteen-mile drive to the Fielding Museum in only an hour, a spectacular feat given typical Chicago traffic.

AT THE MUSEUM, the team was met at the loading area by Stacy Grzelewski, the Director of Special Exhibitions. They were led into the museum and directly to the Founders' Room, an event space with an elegant chandelier and inviting fireplace that served as one of the several spaces available for rent by museum guests or used for temporary exhibitions, like for the Galileo documents.

"Oh, Father Dominic, I'm so glad you've arrived," Director Grzelewski greeted him pleasantly. "Here's my card with my cell number on it. Note that my name is pronounced 'JHUH-LEV-SKEE,' in true Polish fashion.

"Oh, and Bishop Sharma has been here for an hour, pacing rather impatiently, I must say, waiting for you to get here." She did her best to offer a weak smile, clearly happy to have the priest and his crew here to serve as a buffer for Sharma.

"I'm sorry, it took us a little while for our jet to get from the runway to the hangar and then to drive downtown. You know Chicago air traffic... Anyway, allow me to introduce my colleagues. This is Hana Sinclair, a journalist from *Le Monde* who's doing a piece on the trial. Then there's Ian Duffy, my right-hand man at the Apostolic Archive, and Ekaterina Lakatos from the Vatican's Document Restoration and Preservation Lab. And these are Sergeants Karl Dengler and Lukas Bischoff, both Pontifical Swiss Guards, who are taking charge of security for the Vatican's materials."

"Well, very nice to meet you all. Let's get those document cases inside and arrange the exhibits, shall we? We're somewhat short on time as it is. I'm not sure you were made aware, but the conference organizers and museum administration have arranged a champagne reception for museum donors and law school alumni to give them an early opportunity to view the exhibits. We are hoping all of you will be able to attend as well. It starts in just a few hours, at seven-thirty, so I'm afraid there isn't much time to get the displays set up and allow for you to go to your hotel to freshen up."

· · ·

Two rows of document display cases had been installed in the center of the room, with a special display case against one wall for the telescope. The fabricators had made the display cases approximately standard waist height, with interior pedestals for rare documents that would position them at an angle to avoid glare and give visitors the best view through the glass covering. Each case was two meters long by one meter deep to accommodate a series of documents spread out on interior glass shelves, and constructed such that the laminated, safety glass was permeated with wires connected to the museum's alarm system.

Bishop Vijay Sharma had been waiting in the room with his two security agents—Akachukwu Ibrahim, who went by Bram, and Somchai Nguyen—when Michael and his team wheeled in the mobile exhibit cases, with Karl and Lukas carrying the telescope in its wooden case.

"Well, it's about time you got here," the bishop cried in the loud and annoying, high-pitched monotone he was known for. "I've been waiting forever, it seems. I thought your flight was supposed to land at two!" Sharma nearly accused Michael of staging his tardiness simply to upset him. The bishop brusquely set down his briefcase next to the exhibit cases.

"Good afternoon, Excellency. Yes, it was about two when we got to O'Hare, but then it took some time to get the plane to its hangar, load the van, and make it here through Chicago traffic. Surely you haven't been inconvenienced…"

"This whole conference is an inconvenience. But I do what I'm told. Let's get these cases set up and check the inventory. I need to speak with you while your people get the documents into the displays." Sharma gestured toward the cloakroom, where they could have an uninterrupted conversation.

First, Michael and Karl took out their keys, and under Sharma's careful watch, the cases were unlocked and the seals broken. Kat removed the inventory sheets and tucked them under her arm.

Turning to Michael, she said, "If you'd like, Ian and I can get everything organized and ready for you while you have your conversation with the bishop."

"Yes, that's a good idea," the bishop said, grabbing Michael's arm and leading him away. Unaccustomed to being hustled like that, Michael gently shrugged his arm and broke away from the bishop's grasp, who didn't seem to notice.

Kat took over management of the document cases. "Ian, can you get the manuscripts out of the DDF's case and line them up on the display case on the left side, and I'll do the same with ours on the right. Karl and Lukas, can you stand by the doors and keep an eye on the room?"

Taking their positions on either side of the main entrance to the room, Karl and Lukas—looking dapper in their suits but bearing a commanding air of surveillance— were equipped with curly earbuds plugged into their ears and linked to museum security.

Hana wandered over to speak with the director. "Stacy? Can you give me a bit more background on who will be attending tonight's reception, in case there were any digni- taries coming who I might interview for the piece?" Grzelewski gave Hana a short list of the more prominent people invited, names she immediately recognized as being heavy hitters in both global politics and philanthropy— even a former U.S. president.

Once everyone was distracted, Kat discreetly opened the case with the Archive's exhibits and removed the single page she had inserted back at the Restoration Lab, then furtively placed it inside Sharma's briefcase, the one he'd held when they arrived. She took the remaining exhibits and arranged them inside the display cases, ready to be removed from their protective sleeves and placed on exhibit.

Michael and Sharma came back into the room, and Kat met them with the inventories on a clipboard. She held the clipboard closely, read off each manuscript—except the one she'd secreted to the Bishop's briefcase—from the inventory, including the number of pages. Michael checked each one, and she flipped the inventory over and had him once again sign the acceptance page, affirming that each page had been delivered to the museum.

They followed the same procedure on the inventory for the DDF exhibits. Then each set of documents was placed into the exhibit cases and securely locked. The transport cases were stowed in the cloakroom with all protective sleeves inside.

"If you don't mind, Michael," Lukas began as the priest approached him, "we will stay here while you all go back to the hotel and get spruced up, then we'll head back to the hotel. I think Karl and I will skip the reception tonight. We're both pretty tired. But there will be museum security here for the reception and I assume the documents will be secure in this room once they lock up for the night."

"Sure, Lukas, that's a good idea. We'll take the van back to the hotel, come back and relieve you, and then you can go back to the hotel, maybe have a late bite, and turn in. We'll meet up for breakfast at the hotel in the morning."

IT WAS after dark when Michael, Hana, Ian and Kat returned to the museum, now freshened up and formally decked out for the evening's event. Michael was dressed in his Pian Jesuit attire, a black wool cassock trimmed in black silk, with a black silk skullcap. Hana looked stunning in a simple black cocktail dress. Ian, not having planned for a formal reception, had run out and picked up a blue herringbone sport coat with a red tie that complimented his tan Dockers, pale-blue, button-down shirt and burgundy sweater vest, looking every bit the part of a visiting professor. Kat also had to scout for a dress downtown, finding a black number with silver vertical stripes and high heels, all of which complimented her youthful figure.

The group mingled among the patrons and alumni. Michael spoke briefly to Dean Alice Hastings. She introduced him to Loyola Professor Thomas Anderson, who would act as defense for Galileo in the retrial. Michael was just about to ask Anderson what he expected from the trial when he heard a booming voice calling out his name from across the room and coming closer.

"*Michael, Michael, Michael,*" he heard the Texas twang repeat.

Michael froze, closed his eyes and took a deep breath. The voice he had dreaded hearing, the man he hoped had not been informed about the night's reception.

But he had been warned. Pastor Gabriel Darwin was indeed a resourceful man.

And now, here he was.

CHAPTER

EIGHT

Michael did not want to turn around and greet the man, but it would have been odd not to since his name had been hailed so loudly from across the room.

Turning slowly, he watched as Darwin approached him.

"Pastor Darwin... Imagine seeing you here."

"Well, you shouldn't be surprised, my boy. I *told* you I was gonna be in town while you were here. We spoke about my acquiring Galileo's letter to Duchess Christina, remember? But I was lookin' over the rare exhibits, and I didn't see it here. Did you bring it and just not put it on display?"

"Actually, Pastor, I did make it pretty clear when we spoke that the Vatican does not sell its historical holdings. Besides, we don't—"

"Now, never you mind that," Darwin interrupted him. "I'm sure the Vatican could make an exception here. I find that most rules are only convenient suggestions. With enough motivation, a different rule could be established. The way things are is not set in stone—except for the Ten Commandments, o' course. Instead, man's rules are just accepted because we decide that's how it should be. If we changed our minds, then the rule would change, too. Am I right? Or am I right?"

Just then, Darwin's cell phone rang. He removed it from his pocket and looked at the small display.

"'scuse me a moment, son, hold that thought. I need to take this."

The preacher walked a few feet away from the others, covering his mouth with his hand so nobody could see or hear what he was saying.

"Where are you?" he whispered to the caller, then listened for a few moments. "Never mind. Get over to the Fielding Museum. We're in the Founders' Room. I'll forward you a copy of the invitation to get you in. Take a look around at the exhibits. I might have a job for you later." He ended the call, then turned back to Michael.

"Now, just to prove my point, remember that silver scroll in Israel? The one everybody was chasin' all over the Holy Land? Well, God has seen fit to deliver it into my hands. At this very moment, it is being set up for display in the Biblical Hall Museum in Dallas. And I take it as God's blessings of abundance upon me that He will similarly deliver Galileo's letter."

"But, Pastor Darwin, you're missing the point. We simply do not have—"

"Don't bother me with buts, son," Darwin insisted, interrupting Michael again. "I'm not interested in Why-Nots. I'm only interested in How-Tos. But I do need to leave now for some pressin' business. So, *you* think about how we're gonna make this happen, and I'll write the check when you're ready. Arrivaderchee, Michael. Talk soon."

Before the priest could say another word, Darwin was trundling off, his large frame pushing through the crowd.

· · ·

LATER, as the reception was winding down, Michael rounded up Hana, Ian and Kat.

"I had a run-in with Pastor Darwin this evening. I'm not sure what he's up to, but I don't trust him. He desperately wants a particular letter from Galileo for his museum in Dallas." Michael made air quotes when he said *museum*. "He won't listen to me tell him that we don't even have the letter he's looking for. Anyway, I have a gut feeling he's going to try to get one of the exhibits. Maybe not him personally, but in Israel, he had a rather clever but hapless agent working for him who stole the silver scroll and several other valuable parchments. He told me tonight that he's finally acquired the silver scroll—presumably from Sarah Geffen, that former Mossad agent, who had it last— which shows that he is determined to get what he wants, and the fact that he acquired it is an act he interprets as a favor from God. That makes him very dangerous.

"I've arranged with the museum to leave two of us here overnight to keep an eye on the exhibits, given their value and any potential threats. Karl and Lukas are back at the hotel and probably already asleep. I'd like them to be fresh for tomorrow. So, I'm proposing that we divide into three teams, each taking an eight-hour shift watching the exhibits until they are moved to the university. Kat and Ian, do you want to be Team One?"

"Sure," Ian said a little sheepishly, looking over at Kat. "If that's okay with her."

"Yeah, that's fine by me," she replied, smiling at Ian.

"Good," Michael continued. "Now, do you want to take the first shift or come back in sixteen hours? The other team will get word to Karl and Lukas to return and relieve them in eight hours."

"I'd just as soon get it over with and then get some sleep. Is that all right, Kat?"

"Sure, we can go first."

"Great. Hana and I will go back to the hotel, then. Now, the director of the museum tells me that the entire facility will be locked down at night and the usual sensors and alarms will be set. There will be one guard on duty, but he primarily stays in the security office and monitors the video feeds. The cameras will be on in here, but they will shut off the motion detectors to accommodate our presence here. Your comms earbuds are linked directly with the security office. One of you should stay in the room here at all times, even if the other uses the restroom, which is right through that door, so you won't really be leaving the event space."

Ian nodded. "Right, we got it. And Karl and Lukas will relieve us in the morning. Have a good night, you two," he said to Michael and Hana as they left the room.

After everyone had departed, the security guard locked Ian and Kat in the exhibit suite, then returned to the security office. Half of the museum lights had been turned off, leaving the room they were in dimly lit. They sat next to each other on one of the small couches in the Founders' Room.

"I wish we could go looking around the museum," Kat whispered to Ian. "I bet this place is really creepy and fun in the dark. All those dinosaurs and big cats staring at you. And the African masks. Gives me the willies just thinking about it."

Ian pulled her in closer. "You just stay with me. Nothing is going to get to you in here—well, besides me, anyway." He gave her a playful kiss, which she returned.

"Come on," Kat said, "I don't want some guard watching, or worse, recording us. Let's go into the cloakroom. There are no cameras in there."

They pulled one of the small couches into the small chamber, sat down and snuggled in closer again. They made out softly, gently for a while, but the comfortable couch and the dark room—as well as the jet lag and the long day—combined to put them both to sleep in short order.

IN THE MEN'S restroom nearest to the security office, a ceiling panel was lifted and pushed aside ever so quietly. A man dressed all in black and wearing a ski mask slowly emerged from his hiding place in the overhead crawl space and silently lowered himself into the room. Turning off the restroom light, he waited in a stall, the door closed but unlocked.

About an hour later, the three cups of coffee the night guard had consumed got the better of him, and he left the security office for the restroom, having disabled the motion detectors in the hall so he did not set them off himself. As he entered the darkened restroom, he was caught off guard by a powerful arm encircling his neck, rendering him airless and, some thirty seconds later, unconscious.

The man in black used the guard's handcuffs to bind his wrists, then withdrew a six-inch piece of duct tape from a shred of rolled wax paper in his pocket and affixed it over the guard's mouth. Taking out two zip ties, he bound the handcuffs to the toilet fixture and left him in the stall.

The intruder went into the security office and disabled all the silent alarms and motion detectors and turned off the cameras. He then went to the back door, opened it, and let in an accomplice waiting there. Together, they made their way up to the outer door of the Founders' Room. One of the two men took out a set of lock picks and began working on the lock, careful not to make any noise that might alert the two people whom they knew to be inside.

· · ·

UNAWARE THAT ANYONE besides a guard might be in the building, a man named Remi Shapiro—an unscrupulous antiquities agent working for Pastor Darwin—had been surveilling the museum from his car parked at the rear of the building, trying to figure out a way to break in.

While he was watching, he was surprised to see a rear door open, a man in black silhouetted by the inside light holding the door open, then another man dressed in black emerge from the shadows of the parking lot to join his comrade inside. The door closed.

What fresh hell is this?! Remi thought. *This is my heist!*

Emboldened that someone else had the same thought, Remi waited a short while, tucked his Beretta APX inside the back of his belt, then got out of the car, ran through the shadows, and when he reached it, gently tried the door handle.

They left it unlocked!

Carefully, he pulled open the door, peered inside and, seeing no one, made his way quietly toward the foyer of the Founders' Room. As he came upon it, he saw the two figures in black huddled at the door, apparently using picks to open the lock.

Remi could not believe his luck! On the one hand, he didn't have to figure out how to break into the building, which would have been a dumb move anyway given the obvious tight security of the Fielding—though he had often found ways around such obstacles in past exploits. But these two boneheads had done it for him.

Since they were breaking into the same room he had targeted, it was likely they were after the same exhibit materials he was—the Galileo manuscripts. He was loath to allow another fiasco like the mess in Jerusalem a couple of months earlier on another task for Pastor Darwin. As soon as these two got the door open, he would take care of them with his trusty Beretta and some zip ties. He turned back around the corner and withdrew the pistol from behind him, but in doing so, his elbow slammed into the wall. Cursing himself silently, he held still, hoping no one had heard him.

A minute later, he rounded the corner and made his way in the shadows to the Founders' Room door.

Only one man stood outside that door now, and by the looks of it, he'd managed to pick the lock open just fine. Watching as the man peered inside the room, Remi made his move. He slowly approached the guy from behind.

Suddenly, an arm closed around his neck and grabbed for his gun, pulling him back and down onto the cold tile floor, choking off his air, until Remi was out cold.

THE NEXT MORNING at six o'clock, Karl and Lukas arrived at the museum by taxi. They telephoned the security office to be let in, but there was no answer. They walked around the building, checking doors and windows, peering inside for signs of life or trouble.

Finding the back door unlocked, they entered the museum tactically, weapons drawn. Slowly clearing the hallways, the two Swiss Guards headed for the security office, only to find it empty and all cameras off, monitors dark. Heading back out into the hall, they cautiously opened every unlocked door to check each room. When they explored both restrooms across the hall, Lukas found the security guard handcuffed to the toilet, his mouth taped shut. He bent down next to him and carefully removed the duct tape.

"Finally," the guard gasped. "Thanks. Someone was

hiding in here when I came in a few hours ago, and he took me by total surprise, choking me out before I could react."

"Well, they're gone now. Where are your handcuff keys?" Karl asked.

"They should be on my belt, right side."

Lukas took out his knife and slit through the zip ties, then unlocked the handcuffs, at last freeing the guard. "Now, where is the Founders' Room?"

"It's on the right side of the south entrance. It has one door on the west side, and several on the north side."

"Okay, wait here in the hall. We'll be back shortly," Karl said.

Karl and Lukas made a quick but careful approach to the Founders' Room. With weapons drawn, they entered, finding neither Ian nor Kat. They swept the suite, eventually entering the cloakroom and finding the two lying next to each other, asleep on a small couch. The sudden exposure to bright light woke them up.

"*What the hell are you two doing?*" Karl exclaimed. "You're supposed to be awake and on duty!"

"Karl," Lukas said sternly, having examined the room. "You'd better come out here."

Karl, Ian and Kat all emerged from the cloakroom and looked beyond Lukas.

"*Oh, shit…*" Ian muttered, his face paling.

The cases were empty. All the exhibits were gone.

CHAPTER
NINE

Earlier the prior evening, Michael and Hana had taken a cab to the Ritz-Carlton, the conference hotel just a block from Loyola Law School. During the drive they spoke about the reception.

"Darwin had some nerve showing up at the museum after the thieving shenanigans he pulled in Jerusalem," Hana said, her arms folded in anger.

"Yes, but he's a pretty determined character, and for some reason he's decided he desperately needs a letter from Galileo for his museum."

"Why would he want that?"

"Something about expanding the museum to include writings from famous and mostly Protestant theologians, or people who had issues with the Church, like Galileo and Martin Luther."

"So, now Darwin wants to purchase documents from the Vatican Archive? On the face of it, that's absurd."

"Yes, he made that pretty clear. But we don't even have the original letter he's asked for, not that he'd let me speak long enough to tell him that. In any event, of course, I would never give it to him if we did.

"Hey, I'm famished. I didn't eat anything at the reception. Do you want to grab a bite near the hotel? There's a great pizza place, Giordano's, just a couple of blocks away. They have a stuffed deep-dish you won't believe."

"I'm not sure I could eat another bite! I *did* take advantage of the goodies, and those hors d'oeuvres at the reception were incredible. You missed out on braised mushrooms stuffed with pork sausage and breadcrumbs... Greek olives stuffed with goat cheese and bruschetta with buffalo mozzarella and fresh basil... and steamed and fried gyoza. Oh, and chicken teriyaki meatballs served in a miso broth. Those were incredible. So, no room for pizza, even Chicago's famous pie. But I'll join you just to see the place. I wouldn't want you to have to eat alone."

They diverted the cab driver to drop them off at Giordano's. Michael ordered a slice of deep-dish pepperoni and sausage and a 312 Urban Wheat Ale. Food and drink in hand, he chose a table against the front window, with Hana sitting next to him, so they could see Chicago's nightlife for a block along the Magnificent Mile.

"Drinking tonight, are we?" Hana asked.

"Yeah, just a beer to help me relax. Darwin irritates me, and I'm nervous about what he's up to. I also have a feeling we should have left Karl and Lukas instead of Kat and Ian to watch over the exhibits. I'd feel better with our Swiss Guards watching the room our first night."

"I'm sure they'll be fine," Hana said as she teetered toward Michael, then reached up to grasp his shoulder as she steadied her balance. "Whoa, sorry. I had three glasses of champagne at the reception. They just kept refilling my glass. I guess the way to a donor's wallet is through a champagne bottle. I'm still feeling a bit lightheaded."

"Your honor is safe with me, my lady," Michael said gallantly with an endearing smile, and then covered any further show of emotion by diving into the pizza.

"I know that," she replied, and in her slightly tipsy state, "She leaned over to whisper in his ear. "Actually, I think it might have been four." In his peripheral vision, the priest saw her lean toward him and simply turned to face her. They nearly accidentally kissed, pulling away quickly when they realized how close their faces had come, but not before a bright flash of light appeared from outside the window—likely from a passing car, Michael thought.

"Oops," she uttered giddily. "That was supposed to be a whisper in your ear. *Awkward...*"

"Oh, don't give it a second thought," Michael said, blushing. "Okay, I'm pizza'd out now; that deep-dish did me in. Let's get back to the hotel. Tomorrow is going to be one busy day."

BRAM LOOKED at the photo he'd taken with his cell phone from across the street. The newest cameras were getting quite good, even at this distance. It looked like they were kissing from this angle. Bishop Sharma said just to keep an eye on them and make sure they didn't come back to the museum before morning, but this was even better. He might even get a bonus.

He texted the photo to Sharma.

AT SIX THIRTY the next morning, Karl stood with Ian and Kat outside the police tape at the Fielding Museum. Lukas was speaking with the museum's chief of security and Chicago

PD officers who responded first on the scene. They were waiting for the CSI team and detectives to arrive.

Ian was devastated at the consequences of his irresponsibility, and Karl knew it. "Well, do you want to call him? Or should I?" Karl asked.

"You do it," Ian said glumly, his heart in his throat. "I don't think I can speak to him yet. He's for sure gonna fire me and send me home."

"You think he's gonna fire *you?*" Kat lamented. "I'm more likely to get the axe. My father will never forgive me for betraying Michael's trust like that."

"Okay, I'll call him," Karl acceded. "But you owe me, Ian." He tapped the speed dial button for Michael's cell phone. It rang five times before being picked up. His sleepy voice answered.

"Hey, Karl, what time is it? Did I sleep through breakfast?"

"Uh, sorry to wake you, Michael. But I've got some terrible news. The museum was robbed last night. All our exhibits are gone. Kat and Ian are okay. They, uh, fell asleep in the cloakroom and missed all the activity."

Michael quickly sat up in bed as his heart sank. Those exhibits were his responsibility. Clearing his mind, he tried to think.

"All right. I'll fill Hana in and be there as soon as I can. Have you called Bishop Sharma yet?"

"No, the museum director did, though. She was going to call you, too, but I told her we would take care of notifying you."

"Okay, I'm on my way."

On hearing the news from Michael, Hana would not be left behind. She met him in the lobby carrying two to-go cups of coffee and a Danish for each of them from the hotel coffee shop.

"Hey, eat up," she urged. "You're going to need something in your stomach and it's likely we'll both lose our appetite once we get caught up in everything."

They arrived just as Bishop Sharma emerged from a black Lincoln Navigator, dressed in his usual attire—a black cassock with a fuchsia sash around his waist and matching zucchetto—along with two intimidating men in dark suits, each wearing a black beret adorned with a small red flash on the front. Michael also noticed bulges under their left arms, and wondered why a mere bishop would need an armed security detail. He sighed and mentally shook his head on seeing the all-too-frequent waste of Church resources that certain self-entitled bishops and cardinals often flaunted. Then again, in the face of last night's robbery and the lack of security his own team provided... well, Michael couldn't fault the bishop for being overprotective.

"Father Dominic," he sputtered, launching into a nonstop tirade. "I am extremely disappointed in you. If you had suspicions that the exhibits were in jeopardy, I should have been informed immediately. As you can see, I have my own security here that could have been of assistance. I would have expected you to leave your own security personnel there last night rather than entrust such treasures to a computer technician and some gypsy girl.

"Well? What do you have to say for yourself? I have already informed Cardinal Caputo. I don't know if he is going to speak of this to the Holy Father, but you have really stepped in it this time, Dominic. And there *will* be consequences."

Michael restrained himself from getting angry. Cardinal

Boris Caputo was Prefect of the DDF, Sharma's boss and a most unpleasant man of some importance.

Responding tersely, Michael said, "Excellency, I am truly sorry. I did not think to alert you because I also didn't think the exhibits were at any risk of being stolen. Leaving people in the museum with the exhibits was just a precaution. This is, after all, the esteemed Fielding."

"I can hardly believe you. If the documents were not in danger, museum security would have been sufficient. You, however, saw fit to leave additional personnel with the exhibits. There must have been some suspicion on your part. I should launch an investigation into your security practices. What aren't you telling me?" Bishop Sharma demanded, his high-pitched monotone exacerbating Michael's already dark mood and trying his patience.

"Okay, I probably did have *some* underlying concerns. There was one man—Pastor Gabriel Darwin, a televangelist in Dallas—who was at the reception. I had an encounter with him in Jerusalem earlier this year. I suspect he was ultimately behind the theft of some first-century artifacts that were recently found in an Israeli cave. He contacted me in Rome before we came over here, looking to acquire an original Galileo letter for his own museum. When he showed up here, I admit I was slightly concerned he might try to acquire one of the exhibits or have it stolen on his behalf."

"Well, now, *that's* an interesting story," said a voice from behind Michael. Turning, he saw a man approaching from a few feet away. He looked vaguely familiar.

"And you are Father Dominic, right? I remember you from Rebecca's funeral. I'm Detective Mancini from Chicago PD's Special Investigations Unit." He extended his hand. "Call me Joe."

Shaking it, Michael now remembered meeting him at

the funeral of the cop's partner, Detective Rebecca Lancaster, who had been investigating the suspicious death of a Catholic priest in Chicago a year earlier. That adventure had taken them to Scotland and ultimately Malta, where Lancaster had been brutally poisoned by Cardinal Fabrizio Dante in a bizarre scenario.

"Of course, Detective Mancini...Joe. Good to see you again, although I'm sorry to be meeting this way. You remember Hana Sinclair? She was with me at the funeral, as were Sergeants Dengler and Bischoff.

"And this," Michael said, realizing his faux pas too late, "is His Excellency Bishop Vijay Sharma of the Dicastery for the Doctrine of the Faith, and his security detail. About half the exhibits were from his department's collection, the rest from my own, the Vatican Apostolic Archive."

"Well, I'm gonna need statements from everybody about where they were last night. Who they talked to. Anything suspicious they saw. All that. So don't leave, okay? I'm gonna go talk to the CSI people real quick. Be right back."

As Mancini turned away, his cell phone rang. Answering it as he walked, he stopped where he was. After a brief exchange, he ended the call, then returned to the group.

"Any of you know some guy named Remi Shapiro?"

CHAPTER
TEN

As if Gabriel Darwin's presence weren't sufficiently vexing, Michael groaned at the thought of now having to deal with Remi Shapiro too—Darwin's antiquities agent from Israel.

"I know of him, yes," he grumbled to Mancini, who heard his name being called by someone else at the same time.

Turning, he saw a tall female officer in a navy-blue CSI jumpsuit standing on the steps of the museum, gesturing to get Mancini's attention.

"Hold that thought, and don't nobody go nowhere." He walked over and had a short conversation with the officer before making his way back to the group.

"Okay, who's this Remi guy?" he asked.

Michael answered, "He's an agent for Pastor Gabriel Darwin, the Texas megachurch televangelist—you know, the Diamond Ark Cathedral and the Jewel Ark Chapels around the world? There's even one of his chapels here in Chicago. And as it happens, Pastor Darwin was at the reception last night. Remi tried to steal a couple of very rare and extremely valuable scrolls that were discovered in Israel recently, under Darwin's direction. Darwin came here looking to acquire a letter from Galileo for his museum, actually wanting to buy it from the Vatican. I told him—or at least I tried to tell him—that the Vatican doesn't even have the letter he wants, and obviously we wouldn't sell it to him if we did."

"Interesting," Mancini muttered indifferently. "Well, he was found this morning duct-taped to a chair that was tied to a piling at a dock on Bubbly Creek. Up to his neck in polluted water, he was. He kept jabbering about the tide coming in and drowning him before the sharks got him. He wasn't hurt, but he was pretty shook up mentally. Somebody addled him pretty good. He wasn't talking other than that."

Michael laughed. "You did tell him there are neither tides nor sharks in the Chicago River, right?"

"Ya know, come to think of it, I forgot to mention that," Mancini smiled wryly, "though I *might* have said something if he'd been more forthcoming. Anyway, CSI has finished their processing of the scene. There were literally thousands of prints on the display cases and a lot of glove smears. I suppose we could run all prints through the database. We have the guest list, the fabricators and museum staff, and the roster of food servers working last night, so we could get exemplars from all of them, which would be a ton of work. And time. There were no prints on the inside of the cases, though.

"The museum security office has the interior surveillance camera footage already rolled back to the end of the reception. Father, I'd like you and Bishop Sharma to go there with me now to view the recording and see if you recognize anyone or anything that might be helpful. CSI will be out to take exemplar prints from the rest of your team."

Before leaving, Michael looked over to Hana, Karl and Lukas to make sure they heard Mancini. Then he glowered at Ian and Kat. "I'll speak with you two when I get back."

Both of them hung their heads, expecting the worst.

As the three men headed to the security office, Michael turned to Mancini. "So, Joe, I didn't expect to see you at a burglary. You handle homicides, don't you?"

"Yeah, well, after Rebecca died, I just didn't have it in me anymore. When I first got partnered with her, I was coming out of a divorce, and there just wasn't much making me want to get up in the morning. I was hitting the bottle pretty hard, too, on a nosedive to nowhere.

"But as we got to know each other, she made it worthwhile. Becca still had the passion for the work and thought she could make a difference. And that energy was what pulled me out of my downward spiral. She was a great partner. And then she was gone. It's ironic. The last thing I said to her was '*Have fun in Italy. Don't get killed.*' I didn't even get to say goodbye." His voice cracked a little, and he swallowed. "Anyways, I only got a couple of years till retirement. Don't want any lingering cases. So I asked for a transfer, and here I am."

"I'm so sorry, Joe," Michael said, empathizing with him. "I still feel responsible for that whole thing, myself. Dante was really after me. And Rebecca was incredibly brave, trying to save someone else. She died a true hero."

Mancini was silent but reached up and gruffly wiped his eyes as they entered the security office.

With Michael, Mancini and Sharma now clustered around a large computer monitor, the security supervisor replayed the footage from the night before. The display was segregated into six windows, each showing a different view of the event space. The supervisor tapped a few keys and the footage streamed at twice the normal speed, showing people zipping around unnaturally. After a minute, Michael said, "Wait! Stop it there! Now, back it up just a bit..." The supervisor did as instructed.

"See there?" the priest asked. "In the view of the lobby, that's Pastor Darwin, and he's talking to Remi Shapiro. I never saw Remi in the exhibit space last night! Is there any audio available?"

"No, just the video," the supervisor said.

They watched as Darwin and Remi spoke, then Darwin exited the room, and Remi went to the doorway and looked into the exhibit hall but did not go in. He was apparently making mental notes of the layout of the interior, glancing up at the cameras in the ceiling, noting their positions. Then he turned and left.

They continued watching the playback as the reception wound down and the people left, once again sped up to double time. At the end, they saw Ian and Kat sit down on the couch and start making out. Michael reddened, both angry over and embarrassed by his employees' behavior. He watched as they dragged the couch into the cloakroom out of view. Then nothing happened until the screens went dark. Michael heard Bishop Sharma make a disapproving grunt behind him.

The security supervisor tapped a few more keys and the monitor now showed six different views of the museum interior. They saw the security guard leave the security office and walk down the hall to the restroom. A short time later, a different man exited the restroom, this one wearing black clothing and a ski mask. He retraced the guard's steps to the security office and then the displays again went black.

"Roll that back to the closest view of the perpetrator,"

Mancini directed. "There," he said, pointing to the screen. "Gloves, mask, and no shoes. He's wearing socks or something, and his pant legs are tucked into them. Very quiet. No shoe prints. No fingerprints. This guy's a pro. Hey, roll it back farther and let's see if we can find him going into the restroom."

The operator rolled the security footage backwards, this time at triple speed. People backed into the restroom as they left, and then backed out, when they'd entered. As they watched, near the end of the reception, a man in a waiter's uniform—like one of the servers from the reception —carried a backpack while he backed out of the restroom. But they hadn't seen him back in. Which means he never left. The supervisor paused the playback. The person, apparently a male, was wearing a hair net and beard net, like the ones cooks wear to keep facial hair from falling into the food—which, in this case, also conveniently obscured his features. And they saw he was wearing glasses: thick, horn-rimmed spectacles that veiled his eyes from brows to cheeks.

"Like I said, this guy's a pro. Can't get an ID off that, but I'd love to know where he got one of the server uniforms. Do you have any outside cameras?" he asked the supervisor.

"No, but the city does. They have systems in place on all the parking lots and pathways around the museum, the planetarium, and the stadium. It's all online, too. I do have access credentials and can log in from here if you'd like."

"Well, then, Cliff, what are you waiting for?" Mancini asked with a grin.

A bit more tapping on the keyboard and the screen filled with a login prompt for the city's camera system. Cliff logged in and entered the camera ID numbers for the three devices closest to the museum: one facing the loading dock, one over the parking lot, and one at the front entrance. They watched as cars came into and out of the parking lot. At one point, a cargo van pulled into the back lot near the loading dock and parked, but no one got out. Whoever was inside was just waiting.

"That's not suspicious at all," Mancini noted sarcastically.

Then, after some time, two men exited the van, both wearing black clothing, with hoodies pulled close over their heads. Each was carrying a large backpack. They faced away from the camera and walked behind the dumpster, where they disappeared from view.

"When they were sitting in the van they must have been scouting for security cameras. They didn't get out until they knew where the only one was, and then avoided facing it."

Sometime later, one of the food servers came out and went behind the dumpster.

"What's he doing back there?" Mancini asked no one in particular. "Maybe they had a guy on the inside."

Then they saw a flare of light, a faint glow, and a puff of smoke appear over the top of the dumpster.

"Ah, maybe not. Just sneaking a smoke. So why would —*Whoa!* Holy shit!" They watched closely as the server was suddenly hoisted over the side and into the dumpster, wearing only his underwear, with his hands and legs bound by duct tape. "Obviously, that's how they got a server's uniform. Clever bastards. Have they picked up the trash today, Cliff?"

"No, not till tomorrow, Detective."

Mancini pulled out a two-way police radio from under his coat, switched it on, and pressed the transmit button.

"Hey, Johnson, this is Mancini. You copy?"

"Copy, Joe. Go for Johnson."

"Hey, check the dumpsters out behind the museum. There might be a body in one of them."

"Stand by. I'll grab a couple of uniforms and get back to you."

They resumed watching the video, and observed one of the two men, now wearing the server's uniform, enter the museum through the loading dock. Cliff speeded up the video as they watched the staff and servers leave, then the loading dock went dark. A short time later, the loading dock door opened, and the second man emerged from behind the dumpster and went in like his colleague. Then, not long after that, a third man, also dressed in black but not wearing a mask or gloves, went to the loading dock door and, finding it unlocked, went inside.

"That's Remi Shapiro!" Michael said.

The video kept playing. Soon they saw the two men emerge, each now carrying backpacks, and one was also carrying a long tube, all of which they loaded into the van in the parking lot.

Then they both went back into the museum, and when they emerged again, they were carrying the third man, who was now taped—arms, legs and chest—to a chair, and blindfolded. They loaded him into the van, got in themselves, and drove off.

"Well," Mancini said, "that tells me this Remi character might have *wanted* to be the thief, but someone beat him to it. Think your Pastor Darwin might have hired a backup set of superior thieves, Father? Or is there more than one perp who might have wanted those exhibits?" Michael just shrugged, mystified by what he'd seen.

Mancini then led both priests back outside to the rest of the group.

"Father Dominic," Sharma said, "I need to make a report to Cardinal Caputo. I suggest you inform the Holy

Father before he does. It might be better if he hears this from you first." The bishop secretly enjoyed the thought of Michael having to inform the pope that the exhibits had been stolen and Michael's own personnel had been to blame for not stopping it.

"Yes, I suppose you're right."

As Sharma and his security detail trudged off toward their SUV, Michael turned to Ian and Kat.

"I watched the video from the cameras in the exhibit space. You said you fell asleep. You didn't say you fell asleep after moving a couch into the cloakroom so you could make out in private. I must say, I'm very disappointed in both of you."

Ian was the first to apologize. "I'm so sorry, Michael. I don't know what to say."

"I am, too, Father Michael," Kat murmured, her eyes cast to the floor. "I know I let you down. But, if there is an upside here, I think I know who the thieves are."

CHAPTER
ELEVEN

Aghast, Michael responded swiftly, his voice low. "You have got to be kidding! How could you possibly know who did this since you were asleep? Or were you?"

The group gathered around Kat—Michael, Hana, Karl, Lukas and Ian. They all leaned in to hear her explanation, careful to keep the conversation from being overheard.

"Okay, let's hear it," Michael demanded. "Who do you believe the thieves were?"

Kat was clearly torn, her face a mask of frustration. "I... I'm afraid I can't tell you."

Michael was beside himself. "What do you mean you can't tell me?"

"I mean, I just *can't*. I would have to violate another trust if I told you. But I think I might be able to get the stuff back. Please, Father, don't be mad and send me back to Les Pèlerins. Give me a chance to fix this. Just a couple of days. If I can't get the exhibits back before the trial, then you can send me home."

Michael considered the options. If he did send her back, and she did know the thieves, he would have lost his chance to get the exhibits back. But at this point, it was difficult to trust her.

"*Si kado jekh ši Roma?*" he asked her in Romani. *Is this a Roma thing?*

"*Va,*" she replied with a nod and no hesitation.

Michael paused a moment, fuming. "All right. I'm going to give you this one chance. You pursue your angle. Meantime, we'll go with the other possibility, that Darwin is somehow responsible for this. Ian, go back to the hotel. I'll stay here for now with the others and think about our next steps. But now I have to call the pope and break the news to him—a conversation I am not looking forward to having."

After Kat and Ian left, Michael excused himself and walked away from the museum toward the Shedd Aquarium and Lake Michigan. He dialed the pope's office. As usual, Father Bannon answered.

"Hello, Michael. We've been expecting your call," Nick said glumly.

"Hey, Nick. What, did Cardinal Caputo already call him?"

"No, but let me just put you through to him." There was a pause and a couple of clicks on the line before Pope Ignatius came on the phone.

"Hello, Michael."

"Good morning, Your Holiness. I've got a bit of a mess on my hands."

"Yes, it would appear so. How could you let yourself get caught like that?"

"Well, while I knew Pastor Darwin was here, I really didn't expect that he or anyone else would really try to get into the museum and steal the exhibits, and I did leave two people in the museum to watch over them, as well as museum security."

"That's bad enough, but it's not what I'm talking about, Michael. Haven't you seen the news?"

"News? No, I've been here at the museum taking care of this mess. What news?"

"Turn on a TV. Any news channel should do. It's one of the top stories. Then call me back." The line went dead abruptly. Michael was stunned. *What could possibly have caused the pope to react that way?*

He opened a web browser on his phone and searched for the Associated Press portal. Clicking on the AP link, he opened the Breaking News tab, and there it was, the headline: *"Vatican Priest Kissing Girlfriend While Exhibits Stolen."* And right beneath it, a picture, a little fuzzy from the distance and angle, showing what appeared to be a kiss between Hana and him at Giordano's the night before.

Michael suddenly got dizzy, then angry. He recalled seeing a flash of light in his peripheral vision at that moment, like from a quickly passing car, but he had been so distracted he hadn't thought anything of it. Now he realized it must have been a camera's flash. Which means somebody had been following him with the intention of taking pictures of him. The photographer had gotten lucky and caught the innocent but embarrassing moment. Probably just what they wanted. The Holy Father and Nick had both warned him that people might try to use him against the pope. And he had just given them the opportunity on a silver platter. He read the rest of the article.

A priceless collection of Galileo documents and the irreplaceable telescope Galileo gave to Pope Urban VIII were stolen overnight from the Fielding Museum in Chicago. Sources indicate that the people guarding the exhibits were otherwise engaged in a closet, then fell asleep together while the crime was being committed. The Prefect of the Vatican Apostolic Archive, Father Michael Dominic, was seen at a local pizza restaurant with his longtime female colleague, Hana Sinclair, engaged in similar activities instead of watching over the collection.

Police have not released any information about the suspected thieves but are asking the public to report anything suspicious they saw in or around the museum last night. Father Dominic was reportedly revealed to be the pope's illegitimate son last year during an incident in Malta involving a former cardinal. The Vatican did not deny the accusation, nor have they responded to the accusations of nepotism in giving such a young priest such an important role in the Vatican's administration. The Holy See was contacted but had not commented by press time.

Great, Michael thought. *That would play right into the hands of the people opposing the pope and looking to replace him. How could I have been so stupid?*

But it was an accident! They hadn't even kissed. And how could he have known they were being followed? He closed the browser and redialed the pope's office.

"Hi, Nick. So, obviously, you've seen the news, then?" Michael asked.

"Yes, I did. I'm afraid it's spread through the Vatican like Curial gossip on a freight train. You know how the rumor mill is here. Phone's been ringing off the hook. Everybody wants an official comment. We're holding off on saying anything for now. Unfortunately, all this stress isn't helping your father's condition, Michael."

Michael was crushed. Everything had gotten out of hand. "If I could make it all go away, Nick, I would. But thanks for letting me know. Now, could you put me through to the Holy Father again?"

AT THE HOTEL, Ian followed Kat up to her room. She took out her phone, but just stared at it for a few moments. This would not be an easy conversation. Maybe not as bad as the one Michael was having to make, but still in the running.

"Do you want me to leave?" Ian asked.

"No, I think I'm going to need the support."

"Can you tell me why you think you know the thieves?"

"Well…you're going to hear it on the phone call anyway, but you have to swear to me that you won't tell anyone. Nobody. And especially not Father Michael."

"Sure, I promise."

Kat reached into her pocket and removed a small piece of thin red silk. Holding it in her palm, she held it out to show Ian.

"This is a silk rose petal. I found it next to one of the display cases in the museum after the thefts. I've told you a little about my family, and about the Roma in general. But I have two cousins. Both boys, or really, young men now. They are thieves, burglars. And they are very good at their work.

"But they also have a code: they only steal from those who have much, and give back the proceeds of what they took to the poor among the Roma.

"Anyway, one of them, when he was first getting started, stole a very valuable painting, and next to the painting was a vase filled with artificial roses having silk petals. He took one of the roses, too, but left one petal at the scene. Since then, on all his big jobs, he leaves one red petal from this rose. It is his signature. A calling card. It's him bragging, 'Yes, it's me again, and you still haven't caught me.' He has said when the rose runs out of petals, it will be time to retire."

"But, how do you know this?"

"Because when I was younger, I used to help them. I wouldn't actually steal anything myself, but I would be a decoy or a lookout, or, when I was old enough, I was their driver.

"But that wasn't my primary role within the Roma. I have always had a talent for calligraphy. And hand in hand with that, you might say I could study a person's cursive, then reproduce writing just like theirs."

"You mean, as in forgery?" Ian asked, grinning mischievously.

"Well, now you put it that way..." Kat said, blushing. "At one point, I got into trouble with the police and the Italian Art Squad. They thought I'd forged some documents, but I didn't, really. Well, not the ones they thought I had, anyway. But still, the thought of going to jail scared me, so when Father Michael intervened at the request of my uncle, I decided to clean up my act and live right. And I was doing pretty well, I thought."

"But, Kat, taking something from a crime scene...that's evidence tampering. You could go to jail for that alone. The authorities could even make you out to be an accessory or part of a conspiracy, if it really was your cousins doing the deed."

"I realize that. But you have to understand: among the Roma, family comes first. Family is everything. And the closer they are, or the higher up they are in the family, the stronger the bond. My uncle is the clan chieftain, the *voivode*. If he asked me to do anything, I would do it without question. It's about honor, duty, and obligation. They are the old ways, yes, but they are our ways. So when

I saw the petal, I had to take it. I had to protect them. I didn't really have a choice."

"So, what are you going to do?"

"I have to call Uncle Gunari. I need to tell him a few things."

TWELVE

After his second phone call with the pope—who was now angry at whomever had sent the photographer, especially after Michael's explanation that they had not actually kissed—Michael returned to the group to take Hana aside.

She watched as he approached, his face showing dismay. "You look pretty downcast. Didn't your call with the pope go well?"

Deflecting an answer for the moment, he asked, "Have you seen the news?"

"No, I don't follow U.S. news much. Besides, I've been here with you. Why?"

"It isn't in just the U.S. news." Michael handed her his phone, opened to the browser page he had just read.

As she took it and absorbed what she was reading—not to mention her shock at seeing the photo of her "kissing" the priest—Michael watched as a medley of emotions played across her face: embarrassment, anger, fear.

"Oh, *Michael!* I am...*so* sorry. That was completely misconstrued! And what kind of person follows a priest around Chicago? I can only imagine how this must be going over in Rome." After a moment's pause, she added, "For that matter, I should check to see how they're taking it in Paris, too. So, what's going to happen to you, or to the pope?"

"Nothing for right now, I imagine. He thought about recalling me to Rome. That's what Cardinal Caputo is pushing for. But the Holy Father is hesitant to give Caputo anything he wants, so that argues for keeping me here, thankfully."

"That's good to hear, anyway." Reaching for her own phone, she checked for new messages and email. Clearly this had become newsworthy enough to warrant a couple of wisecrack texts from friends, along with an email from her editor.

"Well, apart from snide remarks from a couple of girl-friends, nothing serious on the Paris front. My editor wants to talk later, but she doesn't seem upset. We've had journalists caught doing worse things. But we aren't held to the same standards as a priest."

"Hana, I should tell you the pope suggested we might not want to be seen together for a while. Reflexively, I pushed back. I don't appreciate being unfairly treated for committing no crime at all. But he does have a point, politically, so I need a favor from you."

"Anything, Michael, name it. I feel like this is all my fault. I never would have wanted this to happen. I feel so bad about it."

"Don't. That was a sincere moment of caring on your part, taken advantage of by some rapacious paparazzo. We'll just have to deal with it. But my 'favor' involves you going to Dallas to interview Pastor Darwin, with a focus on the Biblical Hall Museum. We need to know if he was behind the thefts. And I'd feel better if you took Karl with you. Maybe have him act as your photographer or something.

"Besides, this is a good opportunity for you to flesh out your piece on Galileo for *Le Monde*. Your journalistic sleuthing skills will obviously be of great value. Get a tour of his museum and see what you can find, maybe even a private 'behind the scenes' tour. His ego would surely respond to a beautiful young woman professionally 'fawning' for his attention if my intuition is right. He's obviously seen the news by now, so ask him about the thefts here and if that might disrupt his plans for the new exhibit. I trust your instincts, Hana, and want to know if *you* believe he might have been responsible. I'll stay and manage things here and see where Kat's lead takes us. We really need those exhibits back, and soon. There are too many things at stake now."

"You bet, Michael. I'm on it." She started to lean in to give him a hug, but instantly pulled back, thinking better of it. Their eyes met, knowing that's how it would be for a while. Then they just smiled shyly, each with a hint of melancholy in their gazes.

Turning, Hana walked off to find Karl and discuss their trip.

BACK IN HIS HOTEL ROOM, Ian sat on the bed watching Kat pace back and forth, waiting for the call from her uncle, Gunari Lakatos, chief of her Roma tribe, who hadn't answered when she called a few minutes earlier. She left a message, including a code word that indicated she had an emergency. Finally, the phone rang. She rushed for it.

"Hello?" she answered in Romani.

Gunari responded in kind. "Hello, Ekaterina. And are

you well?"

"As well as can be expected, *Voivode*."

He paused. "What's going on? How are things with that new job in Rome?"

"I am not in Rome at the moment, Uncle, and I've got a bit of a mess on my hands. Can you tell me: where are the boys?"

"My boys? Milosh and Shandor? They are not here in Les Pèlerins. Why do you ask?"

"Right now, I am in America, in Chicago, with Father Michael for a conference. And I strongly suspect my cousins were involved in stealing the Vatican Archive exhibits that were displayed here in the Fielding Museum. We brought an important selection of Galileo manuscripts and a telescope with us, but they were stolen last night by two very accomplished operators."

Gunari's voice was now tinged with anger and defensiveness. "But *why* do you think my boys were involved? Do the American police also think this?!"

She well understood his prickly reaction, for historically, Roma were always the first to be blamed for such transgressions, especially in Western European communities.

"No, the police do not see them as the culprits yet. But where are Milosh and Shandor now?"

"They are...away, on a mission for the American branch of our family. I cannot say more. So why do you think *they* were involved? I need to know more if they are in trouble."

"Milosh leaves a signature on all his jobs, Uncle. I recognized it."

"What do you mean, a signature?"

"Hmm. Well...if you do not know, perhaps I should not have said anything. Please, let me have Milosh's phone number. I must speak with him."

"*Ekaterina Maria Lakatos!* You tell me what you know

right now, or there will be consequences!"

Kat sighed. "All right. Milosh leaves a red silk rose petal behind when he takes something of value on a job. He considers what he does to be not really stealing, but more of a trade. Something of his for something of theirs.

"I found one of the petals at the museum after the theft was discovered, right there at the scene of the crime. I took it before anyone else saw it. I *knew* it was Milosh's work then, but I didn't want him to get caught. So as you can see, I need to speak with him. I must get those exhibits back, Uncle. If I don't, it will be very bad for Father Michael, which will be very bad for me."

"But how do you know this was *his* rose petal? Maybe it was just a piece of trash. It could be a coincidence." Kat reasoned that Gunari was stretching for any reason other than letting blame fall on his people. Again.

"Uncle, I have seen these petals before. Yes, it could be a coincidence, except that, as you yourself just said, the boys are here, in America. And this was a job only someone of their skills could pull off. That simply cannot be coincidental. It was them, I'm sure of it. And even though I kept that evidence, if I can figure it out, the police may be able to as well. I need to talk to Milosh."

"That stupid idiot! Does he want to get caught? Okay, I will give you his number. Find them. But I must tell you, this is something much bigger than you are aware of, Ekaterina. It needs to be handled delicately—"

"Uncle! You knew about this?! Is there something you're not telling me?"

Gunari paused a moment. Then he sighed, relenting to his niece. "There are some things that I know and some things that I do not know," he said cryptically. "I will tell you more when I see you. You find them for me. I am coming to Chicago."

THIRTEEN

A young archivist, Viggo Pisano, was making his way down the long, marbled hallway of the DDF's executive wing on his way to the archives downstairs when he heard a cell phone ring.

He was quite surprised since Cardinal Caputo, prefect of the dicastery, had forbidden the audible ringing of cell phones within his domain. As a Benedictine, the cardinal was accustomed to silence and considered cell phones an affront to God.

It rang only twice, then was quickly answered by the person on the other side of a door that was slightly ajar as Viggo was passing it.

"I told you not to call during work hours, especially on this number. This had better be important."

Curious, Viggo slowed his steps. This was Bishop Sharma's office, but Viggo knew he was currently in the U.S. for the Galileo trial. Should someone else be in the bishop's office? He tried to make out the voice, but it was muffled.

There was silence while the person at the other end of the call was obviously speaking. Then...

"Yes, of course I know about the theft of the exhibits. Nothing goes on over there without my knowledge. You didn't lose the letter, did you?"

There was another pause as Viggo lingered outside the door, certainly more intrigued now but trying not to be conspicuous should anyone discover him eavesdropping.

"Good, start the trial without the exhibits. You have the digital copies of both their manuscripts and ours. You just do your job and let me worry about the rest. You got lucky having Father Dominic followed, by the way. That photo of him kissing the woman was priceless. He'll turn out just like his father, an embarrassment to us all. I can't wait to be rid of them both. They are a stain on the holy garments of Our Lord.

"The girl has done even better than I had hoped, even falling asleep while guarding the exhibits! Those two were not even supposed to be there, but that could have been dealt with... No, do not worry. Everything is under control. You do not need to know the rest. Better for you not to know, actually, at least for now. You worry too much, anyway. Veritas vos liberabit. Ciao."

Viggo quickly and silently picked up his pace as the call apparently ended. No one else was in the hallway, so he hadn't been seen. Reaching the staircase, he double-timed it down to his office two floors below. Sitting at his desk now, he began to tremble.

What he had overheard was shocking. Scandalous! *Someone* was trying to get rid of the Holy Father and the Prefect of the Apostolic Archive! Of course he had read about the thefts, and he had seen the picture of Father Michael. Everyone had. It was all over the Vatican.

But to think someone in the DDF had a hand in it was vexing.

So, what should I do? What can I do? I am here in Rome, and Father Michael is in Chicago. And I am but a clerk. This is way above my pay grade. And going up against Sharma or Caputo or God knows who could very easily make the rest of my life here miserable.

For now, at least, he would just wait and see what happened next.

Personal interview requests for Pastor Gabriel Darwin were typically routed through his megachurch's media relations staff in Dallas. But when a request had come in from an investigative reporter at Paris's *Le Monde* newspaper, it caught the attention of Miss Lyla Buckley, the media relations director herself.

Having seen the name of the reporter, Lyla made the surprising connection and realized that Hana Sinclair was the very same woman who had been caught in that embarrassing photograph with the Vatican priest in Chicago.

Poor darlin', she clucked to herself. *Violatin' the Seventh Commandment like that…*

She immediately called Pastor Darwin aboard his jet as he was returning from Chicago and informed him of the request.

"I'll handle this my own self, Lyla. Thank you for letting me know. Yes, I'll call her now."

Spread out on the tan leather sofa in the Gulfstream's main cabin, Darwin pondered how he would handle Hana

Sinclair. After a time, he sat up and dialed her number. She answered.

"Hey there, Hana! It's *me*, your old friend Pastor Gabriel Darwin. How you be?"

"Why, Pastor Darwin. I'm fine, thank you. Are you responding *personally* to my request for an interview? If so, I'm impressed."

"We aim to please, Hana. And I would be delighted to be interviewed by you, even honored. I assume you'll be comin' to Dallas?"

"Yes, and I was hoping we could get a tour of your museum, if that's possible. My assistant, Karl, will be with me, which I hope won't be an inconvenience."

"Not at all, not at all. The more, the merrier. We'll put on the dog for both of you, with a VIP tour and everything. I'll even put you up in the Sapphire Suite at our Divine Favor Retreat Center adjacent to the cathedral campus.

"But I gotta tell ya, Hana, my schedule is tight, and we need to do this tomorrow. Can you be here by tonight so we're ready to go first thing in the morning?"

Hana was surprised at the seeming urgency in Darwin's voice, but since she and Karl were already prepared to act quickly, she acceded.

"Of course, Pastor. We can fly out tonight. It's only two hours or so from Chicago."

"Good. Call my assistant when you book your flight. We'll have someone waiting to pick you up at the airport. See y'all then, Hana. Buh bye now." He ended the call.

Well now, this is an interesting situation, thought Darwin, as he plopped back down on the sofa and grabbed a handful of shelled peanuts from a crystal bowl on the table. He'd wanted to know how important this interview would be to Hana, so given his push for meeting the very next day

—and his insisting they travel tonight—well, she'd shown her hand.

Too, he figured she was important to Father Dominic, and having her here in Dallas rather than in Chicago with Michael could very well play into his own blessed hands. He did find it coincidental that right after the Galileo exhibits had been stolen, she was being delivered to him. But, he took that as a sign of God's multitudinous favor, and would not reject the convenience of this particular gift.

Having resolved the weighty matters of the day, he called out to the flight attendant, "Rosie, darlin', bring me a root beer, will ya?"

Having arrived at Dallas–Fort Worth International Airport later that evening, Hana and Karl were met at the private aviation terminal by the driver of a Lincoln Navigator limousine with the Diamond Ark Cathedral's logo indiscreetly emblazoned on the sides.

Already suspicious of Darwin's motives in any situation, Hana sat quietly in the back as she looked out over scores of softly lit nodding donkey heads on the oil well fields dotting the otherwise dark landscape and pondered her opening moves in the game that was about to begin. If the good pastor was up to something—and especially if he were behind the stolen exhibits—she aimed to find out.

Michael spent most of the day with Lukas at the crime scene in the Fielding Museum, silently lamenting the loss of historically important Galileo materials and the predicaments that resulted for him and the pope.

He'd checked with Kat and Ian twice, but they had very little to report. Kat told him that she had spoken with her uncle and that while he did not have the information she needed, he had given her a next step to take, and they were pursuing that lead.

Michael believed if this was a family matter, he knew which family members it involved: her cousins, Milosh and Shandor.

Michael knew both boys well, having met under morally ambiguous circumstances a year or two earlier. He had gotten them out of trouble more than once, had further engaged their special talents on particular occasions, and in doing so had earned the respect of Kat's uncle, the Roma clan leader Gunari Lakatos—which was how Kat had come to be in Michael's employ in the first place. He was tempted to call Gunari himself, but intuition guided him to wait and give Kat a chance to redeem herself.

For her part, Kat spent most of the day pacing her hotel room. She had repeatedly called the number her uncle gave her for Milosh, but each time the call had gone to voicemail on the first ring as if the phone had been turned off. Finally, she turned to Ian.

"Isn't there anything *you* can do?"

"Me? I don't know anything about this! Why are you asking me?"

"I have to find my cousins, and Milosh isn't answering his phone. Uncle Gunari is on his way to Chicago, and I'm supposed to find them before he gets here. But I have no other clue how to reach the boys. Isn't there some kind of computer thing you can do to find a phone?"

"Kat, I don't do that kind of thing anymore. It's illegal to hack into the cellular system."

"But you know how, yes?"

"Well, yeah, I do know how. But aren't we in enough trouble?"

"Ian, my cousins could be in even more trouble. I *must* find them. And we *are* doing this to get the exhibits back for Father Michael, you know. The ones that were stolen while *we* were supposed to be guarding them instead of sleeping. It's our fault they're gone!"

"I don't know...if we get caught it could mean years in prison."

"And if we don't do anything, it could mean Father Michael's job, and mine, and yours, and maybe even the pope's!"

"Kat... I don't—"

"Ian, come on. If you loved me, you would do this for me. If you understood the Roma—how important family is and how hard it is for me to ask for help—you would do this for me without my asking. If we succeed, you will have the gratitude of our entire family. Not to mention Father Michael's."

"Well...when you put it that way. But we should go somewhere else. Not our hotel room. The internet cafes are monitored and firewalled against what I need to do. I need someplace with super-fast internet access but low security, or maybe even an outlet store for the carrier."

"How do we find out who the carrier is?"

"I can get that much from the phone number itself. The carriers have to register every block of numbers they use. But then we'd have to find one of their local stores and use one of their computers. You'd have to create a diversion while I opened a back door and hacked location services to find Milosh's phone. Give me the number and hang on a second." Kat handed him the number on a piece of paper.

Ian used his phone to run a check on it through a special public database.

"All right. That number is registered to SixG Cellular."

Kat checked the map on her phone. "Found it! There's a SixG retail store less than a mile away down by the river."

"I'm regretting this already," Ian lamented.

CHAPTER

FOURTEEN

K at and Ian walked a few blocks down to a retail mall on the edge of the Chicago River at the end of the Magnificent Mile. On the way, Ian stopped in a competing cellular shop and—thinking their appearance might come in handy for his mission—picked up some brochures explaining their company's cellular plans.

On arrival at their destination, they had only just opened the door when the lone and clearly ambitious sales-clerk greeted them.

"Welcome to SixG Cellular, the future of cellular technology! How can I help you?" *Good*, Ian thought. *Ambitious is good*.

"My girlfriend wants to upgrade her phone, but I have a couple of questions first." Ian laid out the competitor's brochures on the counter to establish his quest as legitimate. And while he was engaging the salesman, Kat occupied herself looking at a rack of phone cases.

"As you can see, we've been shopping around, but we haven't found the deal we're looking for yet. I think SixG might be the right fit—*if* we can work out a good deal."

Ian asked several questions that the clerk was able to answer without having to do any research, but finally, he hit on a topic that the clerk couldn't answer off the top of his head.

"Let me look that up for you," he said as he walked over to a computer on a demo table. As Ian followed him, he activated his phone camera, then stood looking away but aiming his phone on the keyboard, where he could see the clerk typing in his employee login and password.

As the clerk was busy with the computer, they both heard a noise from the front of the store. Kat had started to climb up the rack of phone cases to get to one near the top. The rack creaked under her weight and started to tip.

"*Oh, no! Please* don't climb up there. If you want something from the top, let me get a stepladder and I'll get it for you."

Too late. Kat started to step down but leaned back, reaching with her foot for the floor and putting most of her weight as far back as possible. The rack broke free of the wall and started to fall towards her. She hit the floor and crashed down as the phone cases cascaded all over her and across the floor. She shook her hands in front of her, making cases fly even farther while she made a whining cry. The clerk hurriedly ran over to her and moved the rack aside.

"Oh, my goodness! Are you okay?"

In his haste to get to Kat, he had not bothered signing out. Ian stepped up to the computer, glanced at the interface and, using the mouse, navigated to the service module. He typed in the phone number of Milosh's phone and got its service history. Then he queried the system to list the last cell towers the phone had pinged, and the signal strength. He snapped photos of a series of numbers and backed out of the service tab. The whole exercise had taken well under a minute.

Meanwhile, Kat was trying to pick up the phone cases, shakily handing them to the clerk and dropping them so he was having a hard time grabbing them. She appeared flustered, distraught. Done with his work, Ian joined them.

"I'm so sorry," he said. "She has anxiety issues. This probably isn't the best day to do this. We'll come back when she's doing better. Thank you so much for your help." He helped Kat to her feet, put his arm around her shoulders as if to soothe her and they left the store, the clerk looking after them, a little miffed that he might have lost a sale, but more so that he had to put the rack back up and sort all the phone cases in their original order.

Ian and Kat walked part way back and found a coffee shop where they could use Wi-Fi. Finding a quiet booth, Ian took out his laptop and connected to the cafe's network. He brought up a mapping program and entered the cell tower identification numbers he'd acquired. The mapping program dropped pins that triangulated the location of the three towers.

"What are you doing now?" Kat asked.

"Every cell tower has an identification number. The phone needs to know which towers it's communicating with. The phone tries to connect to the closest one, but in order to not drop calls if that one gets busy, the phone also keeps track of the next-closest ones in case it has to switch. It's called dynamic rerouting. The cellular system is completely transparent to the end user, but the phones and towers are constantly communicating to manage the traffic load and make sure calls aren't dropped to avoid customer dissatisfaction. So the system places a high priority on keeping calls connected.

"What I'm doing is looking at the location of the last three towers Milosh's phone connected to. Not that he placed a call, but the phone was making sure it knew which towers were available if he did, a process called handshaking. The telephone system stores the tower ID and the signal strength. I looked up the tower locations from their ID numbers, information that's easily available online. Then I plotted the locations on a map. Now I'm trying to plot the signal strength to try to get an idea of the distance the phone was from each tower. Each one will give me an approximate circle in which the phone *could* be—but it *should* be in the area where the circles intersect. I can't give you the house, but I can get within a short block or two."

Kat came around the booth and sat next to Ian. She put an arm around him and leaned her head against his shoulder, looking at the computer screen.

"Thank you," she said softly.

"Don't thank me yet. We haven't found them, but we still might."

The plotting program completed its calculations and drew the signal strength circles around the tower locations, revealing the intersecting areas.

"It looks like Lincoln Park. We should be able to get there if we keep walking west of Halsted and north of Armitage. That's about three miles from here."

"Sounds good. Let's go."

It took a little more than an hour, walking at a steady pace, for them to get to the Lincoln Park neighborhood. The residential streets were lined with trees now showing the effects of a Chicago winter. Shades of orange, red and brown graced the leaves, some still clinging to the trees but most of them having found their way to the ground below, swishing around and crunching beneath their feet.

"So, the phone was around here somewhere," Ian said. "Any ideas?"

As they passed one of the houses, Kat noticed a man looking out the third-story window, apparently sitting and watching the cars and pedestrians as they passed. Another man was sitting on the front steps, reading a newspaper. He also glanced up periodically, observing the goings-on in the neighborhood.

"Just keep on walking," Kat suggested. "Don't turn around, and don't look to your left. Just keep talking to me about soccer or something and look straight ahead like you know where you're going."

"Sure, soccer is definitely an interesting sport. At least, that's what we call it here in the U.S. My favorite team is the LA Galaxy…" Ian continued chattering, making up facts about imaginary soccer players and pretend matches as they passed a few houses ahead, gesticulating for dramatic effect. Kat then grabbed his hand and abruptly took a sharp right turn into an alley between two houses. As soon as they were out of sight, she scurried around to the back of the houses, where all the garages and trashcans were located.

"Did you notice the person in the third-floor window back there?" Kat asked. "At the same house with the man on the steps?"

"No, because you told me not to look!"

"They are Roma. One gypsy can spot another."

"Do you think they noticed us?"

"I hope not. Let's go over to Halsted and hang out for a while. Maybe get something to eat. I want to look at the area on a map so I can get a feel for it. We'll come back tonight after dark."

THE MAN in the third-floor window picked up his cell phone and dialed a number. The man on the steps felt his phone vibrate in his pocket. He pulled it out and answered it.

"Yeah?"

"See those two who just walked by?"

"Yeah."

"That girl is Roma. I'd stake my life on it. Keep a sharp eye out for a while. I'm going to call the boss and get a couple of guys here for the night shift, and then I'm going to have a conversation with the boys in the basement."

CHAPTER
FIFTEEN

The Diamond Ark Cathedral was located in Lakewood, Texas, to the northeast of Dallas, on the eastern shore of White Rock Lake. The cathedral was oriented such that in the morning the rising sun illuminated the 18,000-seat auditorium through a brilliantly conceived arrangement of stained glass and skylights, so the full glory of the sun bathed the room in morning light without blinding the congregants.

To the north of the main, ark-shaped stadium was the four-story main office building. Darwin's office took up the entire north side of the top floor of the circular office building, where he could see both sunrise and sunset over the campus. The Ark was situated such that it appeared to be floating on the lake when viewed from the opposite shore.

To the south of the stadium stood the Biblical Hall Museum, and slightly further north the Divine Favor Retreat Center. The accommodations in the adjoining Sapphire Suites of the retreat center where Hana and Karl were housed were unusually luxurious. Each suite had two main rooms and a large bathroom with a dressing area. The bedroom featured a view across the lake towards the downtown area's city lights at night. The main room featured a salon with a corner office, kitchenette, dining area and sitting area with a large, flat-screen TV.

After a long, relaxing bath, Hana had finished toweling off and had just wrapped a plush robe around herself when she heard a quiet tapping on the door. Looking through the peephole she saw a young Latina woman in a black uniform with a maid's cart, obviously one of the hospitality staff. Hana opened the door.

"Good evening, Señorita. Is there anything you require before you sleep? I would be happy to turn over the bed," she stated in slightly broken English.

"Oh, you mean turn down the bed?"

"Yes, that is it. Turn down the bed. My English is not so good."

"Don't worry," Hana answered in Spanish, "my Spanish is pretty rusty, too."

They both shared a giggle. The maid came into the suite and headed toward the bedroom. She pulled the tightly-tucked blankets and top sheet down and folded them out on a diagonal so that Hana could easily slip under the covers and pull them up.

"If you feel cold, the controls are there on the wall, and there is another blanket in the closet."

"*Gracias...*" Hana paused, looking for a name tag. "Señorita..."

"Juanita, Ms. Sinclair. I am called Juanita."

"Thank you, Juanita. I'm very pleased to meet you. Do you live around here? This is my first time in Texas."

Juanita paused, suddenly uncomfortable. She cast he eyes downward and wouldn't meet Hana's gaze. Hana sensed the change in her demeanor.

"Yes, I live very close by," she said quietly, nearly whispering.

Hana had just been trying to make conversation, but the change in tone piqued her curiosity.

"Were you born here in the U.S., or maybe somewhere farther south?"

"I was born in Mexico City."

"Oh, very nice. So how long have you been here?"

"Only a week or so."

"So, what is it like working for Pastor Darwin?"

Juanita paused, a look of fear on her face. "I am sorry, Ms. Sinclair, I need to get back. But do call housekeeping if you need anything," she gestured toward the phone on the desk, "and one of us will be here right away."

And with that, she scurried from the room, leaving Hana...curious.

She was about to call Michael and let him know she had arrived at Darwin's campus when there was another knock on the door. Through the peephole she saw it was Karl. She opened the door and Karl greeted her with his finger to his lips. His backpack was slung over a shoulder and he was holding his phone, which he lifted up so she could read the screen. In an unsent text message space, he had written:

Don't speak. My room was bugged. Going to sweep your room now.

She nodded. Entering the room, Karl pulled an RF detector out of his backpack and scanned for radio frequencies coming from any wireless transmitters. After circling the room, he took out his cell phone and dialed a number that connected to a special constant tone. Walking around the suite again, he listened for disruptions to the tone.

Finally, he checked the suite for known types of hidden

cameras and microphones. He pulled a USB charging cube from the wall socket and inspected it. On the front of it, there was a small black circle above the USB port, similar to an LED indicating it was active. But on the back Karl found a micro-SD card—indicating the black spot on the front was not a light but a camera, and the device recorded what it saw to the micro-SD card. He took out the card and put the cube back in the socket. He also located a tiny hidden microphone in the heater vent in the ceiling, then pulled it out and snipped the wires with his pocketknife. He tapped out another message on his phone.

I think we are safe enough, but no sensitive phone calls unless you are outdoors and away from the buildings. I'm just down the hall if you need me. Speak guardedly.

Hana nodded again. She was unsettled at the thought that someone could have been listening to her talking to Juanita. Or singing to herself in the tub, for that matter. But it did explain why Juanita had gotten nervous after one question about Darwin.

She would have to do something to get Juanita alone, outside, and have a little chat with her. That would be a task for tomorrow.

SITTING in his office with the lights off, Pastor Darwin peered through binoculars down toward the retreat center buildings. He watched as the lights went out in Hana's suite. A few minutes earlier, thanks to the microphone planted in her room, he heard a tapping at her door, then someone walking around—but strangely, no talking. Then the audio stopped. It was probably her "assistant," an inference that gave Darwin pause.

This Karl Dengler person was awfully fit and seemingly too cautious to be just a journalist's assistant and photographer. Something about him felt military. Darwin was familiar with the type. He would have to be careful with that one. His interactions with Hana should involve only the two of them. He still wasn't sure how the negotiations were going to play out, but he already knew his chances would be better if the assistant weren't with them. Divide and conquer.

"Get some sleep, Ms. Sinclair," Darwin muttered to himself. "I'll deal with you and your escort in the morning."

CHAPTER

SIXTEEN

With nothing left for him to do at the crime scene, Michael returned to the hotel later that afternoon. He sat in the lounge with Lukas, sipping coffee and wondering how this trip could possibly get any worse. Lukas asked how his conversation with Detective Joe Mancini at Chicago PD had gone.

"He told me they released Remi Shapiro, who told them he'd just been walking around the grounds of the museum after meeting someone at the reception, whom he refused to identify but *we* know was Pastor Darwin. He said he saw the thieves enter the museum, and he followed them in to alert security but was subdued before he could take any action.

"He said the thieves asked him a lot of questions in some room—questions about who he was, who he worked for, and what he had been doing there. Then they took him to the river, taped him to a chair, and tied it to the piling before dawn, telling him that the tide would come in with the sunrise and he would surely drown—if the sharks didn't get him first—unless he confessed to them the rest of what he knew.

"But as he didn't, they left him there. The water was cold, but Remi wasn't really in any danger. Obviously, there are no tides or sharks in the Chicago River. Mancini mentioned something about Remi having a flight out in a day or two."

"They should have tied his chair a little lower in the river and done the world a favor."

Michael was shocked at Lukas's comment.

"What?! The guy is a thief and a liar," the young guardsman said defensively.

"Christ was crucified between two thieves," the priest reminded him. "One repented and was received into heaven. Even Remi Shapiro deserves that chance, Lukas. For that matter, I think Remi's chances are better than his boss's. Jesus had a lot to say about the self-righteous and false teachers."

"Hmph. Well, if you say so, Father Michael... Hey, have you heard from Hana?"

"No, and I'm a little worried. Have you heard from Karl?"

"Just a couple of text messages. They made it to the retreat center at Darwin's cathedral in Dallas. He's supposed to call me later."

"Well, if there was something up, I'm sure he'd let us know."

Thomas Anderson, the law professor presenting the defense for Galileo, was wandering through the hotel lounge carrying a stack of papers and file folders in his arms when he spied Michael and Lukas. They had met, though briefly, at the reception. And, by now, all participants were refiguring their efforts in light of the stolen documents. Joining them, he plopped down in a seat at the table and set the papers down.

"I've been making copies of the trial manuscripts at the business center since the originals won't be available now. I guess we weren't really supposed to be using them anyway. Bugger that they were stolen. Any news on that front?"

"No, not really," Michael said glumly. "A couple things are in the works, but I've no idea how they're going to pan out."

"Sorry to hear that, Father. Oh, I, uh…saw your picture in the paper, by the way. How did that happen?"

Michael sighed deeply, then cupped his chin in a hand, his elbow resting on the table. "Bad camera angle, not bad behavior. Hana was whispering something in my ear, Tom. But I accidentally turned to face her just as she was coming in. It was pure bad luck that some lurking photographer was prepared for at that moment."

"Do you know who took it?"

"No, I don't. But somebody must have been following us, hoping to catch something tabloid-worthy."

"Unless they were following you for some other reason and just got lucky…"

"I'd have to know *who* it was to have a guess as to *why* it was."

"Well, back to the matter at hand," Anderson continued, "I wanted to talk to you about how the trial will proceed tomorrow. I assume we'll talk about the original tribunal manuscripts. And the theft will surely come up in conversation. We might have to put you on the stand to authenticate the copies of the manuscripts since you are the only one who has seen the originals. Then we'll do opening statements and maybe have one witness, probably the stand-in for Galileo. But it's likely we'll only get to the direct examination, which means that Bishop Sharma will get to question him, and I'll have to wait until the following day before it's my turn. That's unfortunate since the jury has overnight to think about Sharma's questions and 'Galileo's' answers before I get a chance to clean things up."

Thinking back to how this trip could get any worse, Michael now had his answer. He was going to have to take the stand and authenticate the copies of the manuscripts that were stolen. He hadn't planned on taking such a visible role.

"So, will there be much media covering the trial?" he asked.

"Oh, sure. Probably a lot more now, thanks to news about the theft. Apart from the utter rottenness of the act itself, one couldn't have asked for better publicity. It's like it was written for a tabloid. You'd think Sharma himself had planned it. It's certainly going to bump up his visibility if he wins."

"Hmm. Yes, perhaps so," said Michael. "But there's not really any chance he could win this, is there? I mean, how could the jury find him guilty if the Vatican already cleared Galileo over thirty years ago. This is just a demonstration, right?"

"Well, yes, it is just a demonstration. But Sharma's a pretty bright guy, not to mention a very determined advocate. I don't think he would have agreed to do it at all if he didn't think he had a chance to win. I realize he's a priest, but I have to say, I don't trust the man at all."

Michael sought to veer the conversation away from Sharma, not wanting to admit to his own disagreeable feelings about the bishop. "Why are you holding this trial, anyway?"

"Well, for a number of reasons," Anderson replied. "First among them is that it's good for the school. The new dean is really trying to put us back on the map, back on the cutting edge, so to speak, after years of coasting under the previous administration.

"As for why I'm doing it, it's good to have the dean owe you a favor. Plus, this is right up my alley. My PhD is in Renaissance studies, and my LLM is in medieval legal systems, so the Galileo affair fits right in that intersection. It's also a chance for me to appear on the national stage, which would be a nice addition to my C.V. Plus, I've always had a fascination with how Galileo's case was handled."

"What do you mean? I know the basics of it, but I haven't really explored the whole trial background in depth."

"Well, based on my research, I'm convinced the pope at the time, Urban the Eighth, personally intervened in the case, which would have been unusual. The prosecutor knew he had a proof problem. Galileo was on trial not so much for his heretical beliefs as for violating a prior injunction from the Inquisition *not* to teach or write about them. But when it came time for the trial, the prosecution couldn't find the actual injunction, which—if there had really been one—Galileo himself would have signed.

"Faced with that, the prosecutor met with Galileo and worked out a deal. Galileo would confess to over-exuberance in expressing the argument for heliocentrism in his book, then the Inquisition would convict him of only Slight Suspicion of Heresy, for which he would have received a much lighter sentence."

Anderson shifted in his seat, leaned forward and continued. "Based on what I do know about men in those stations of power, I have a theory about what happened behind the scenes. You see, when Galileo discussed writing a book about heliocentrism during Pope Urban's reign, the pope argued that God could make the universe look one way but be another. So it might look heliocentric but still be geocentric in accordance with Scripture. When Galileo wrote his book, though, he put that argument in the mouth of Simplicio, a character who was a simpleton, a fool—which really upset the pope.

"So, with pride presumably as his motivation, Pope Urban directed a different outcome. Galileo was ordered to solidly renounce his beliefs on pain of torture, which he did, and was then convicted of being 'Vehemently Suspect of Heresy,' for which he was sentenced to life in prison, which a short time later was commuted to house arrest under the guardianship of Archbishop Ascanio Piccolomini."

Michael was fascinated with the professor's clear and reasoned explanation. "But I gather there is no evidence that directly implicates the pope in this?" he asked.

"Not that I've ever seen. And, like I said, no one has ever found the original signed injunction that was allegedly read to Galileo in 1616, which he would have signed."

"Well, I don't know what the DDF has, but I can tell you that I'm not aware of anything like that being in the Archive that I oversee. Not that that's a guarantee, mind you. If you knew the amount of uncatalogued material we have, and the amount of work it would take to get it all indexed, you'd be appalled. Some days it's downright overwhelming. Maybe soon we'll have the AI capability to catalogue and index all the holdings, but it still has to be manually scanned, and that alone is a monumental task. And after the fire at Notre-Dame, we are asking that all Catholic cathedrals scan their records for inclusion. As you can imagine, the digital storage requirements are enormous."

"Yes, I can imagine. I'd love to see your Archive sometime. I'm afraid as far as I've ever gotten is the reading room. I did my PhD at Sapienza, so I was over there fairly often, but before you were prefect. Dr. Ginzberg has helped me a lot, too."

"Yes, he's still there, and we've become good friends."

"Well, do tell him I said hello when you get back. Now, I've got to get upstairs and get ready for the morning. I'll see you in court," he said jokingly.

"Yeah, I guess so," Michael replied as he watched Anderson rise and leave. "Okay, Lukas. I'm going up to the room to change and take advantage of the gym here in the hotel. I like running around Chicago, but generally not at night. See you a bit later."

CHAPTER
SEVENTEEN

K at and Ian finished off their tapas at a restaurant on Halsted, a couple of blocks from the presumed place where Milosh's phone was, and hopefully, Milosh with it. He still wasn't answering, and that had her concerned. He always answered, or he called back promptly.

They hadn't realized how hungry they were, and the food had been excellent, with small plates of chorizo-wrapped dates, spicy roasted potato slices with aioli, and beef tenderloin sliders with blue cheese and chips. Ian felt a little guilty eating so well while who knew what was happening to Kat's cousins. On the other hand, he considered, they probably *were* the ones who stole the exhibit items, and he *had* hacked the SixG computer to get the location of the cell phone—so his hands were as dirty as anyone else's in this mess.

With Kat looking on, Ian pulled a small laptop from his backpack and set it on the table and pulled aerial views and street-level images of their location from Google Earth. He scrolled up and down the street where the suspected house was located including the alley behind the house. The views were limited, but they gleaned a general layout of the property between the trees and cars that lined the street and the fences and garage doors along the alley.

They decided that it would be better if they came in from the back, through the alley, and ended up along the space between the houses to see what could be seen in the window that opened into the basement.

"You're sure they're in there?" Ian asked.

"Sure? No. But it makes sense. The house is right in the middle of the cell phone map, and there were two Roma guys keeping watch on the street. How likely is that?"

"You're probably right. But what are we going to do if Milosh and Shandor *are* in there? These other men could have guns. What do *we* have?"

"The element of surprise?"

Now THAT IT WAS DARK, Ian and Kat walked back to the alley behind the house and crept toward their destination. There was an old, beat-up panel van parked against a garage a couple of houses away and a dumpster in an alcove on the fence line, its lid slightly raised due to trash bags stacked up on one side. The only streetlight was at the entrance to the alley, and the house they had been scoping out was at least six houses down from the cross street.

As they crept closer, Kat gestured toward the trash enclosure and whispered to Ian, "Stay here, behind the dumpster. I'll go check the window." She slipped between the houses, walking silently, staying in the shadows. She lay down and did a low crawl, her elbows propelling her along the wall until she got to the first window of the basement. She carefully shuffled forward, trying not to make a sound. Then she listened for any signs from within.

Nothing. Inching forward, Kat looked in the window. The room was dark, and she couldn't really see anything inside. She slowly moved forward to the next window, one that had blinds covering it, but there was a light on in that room. As she got closer, she could hear voices. She moved closer and listened as best she could.

"How many times do I gotta keep askin' you da same question?" a gruff voice asked, his accent indeterminate.

Then she heard her cousin Milosh's voice! "As many times as you want the same answer," she heard him say.

There was a slapping sound and a muffled grunt.

"You keep smartin' off and I'll cut that smart tongue right outta your smart mouth."

"Well, then, I definitely won't be able to give you the same answer."

Another smacking sound, and another grunt.

"I thought we were your guests! How come you tied us up like this?"

"Answer the question—who else knew about this job? Who did you tell?"

"I told you. We haven't told anyone. Not a soul, I swear!"

"Then how come there's some Roma girl casin' da joint now? How does *she* know you're here? We took your phones. I know they're turned off." Then the voice shouted, *"Who did you tell?!"*

Milosh was not talking.

While remaining silent, Kat was angry and frustrated. They'd seen her. She had compromised Milosh and Shandor's safety.

She had to get out of there. Getting to her feet, she started back toward the alley.

"Ian! Come here!" she stage-whispered.

She hurried the rest of the way to the alley and met up with Ian, both now standing next to the dumpster.

"We really should get out of here," Kat urged. "Those two men saw us earlier. They'll *expect* us to come back."

"And so you did," a deep, accented voice said, surprising them. Suddenly, a man emerged from behind the dumpster, aiming a gun at them.

Just then, the front door of the nearby panel van creaked open, and another man got out, also holding a gun aimed in their direction. He approached Kat, speaking to her in Romani.

"What family are you with, girl?"

"*Lakatos*," she replied fiercely, her chin jutting forward with pride.

"Ah, the French contingent. Well, aren't *you* a long way from home? Come for a family reunion?"

"Mind your manners, *bengalo*," she spat, risking calling him an idiot. "You don't know who you're talking to."

"Well, you are as feisty as your cousins. Turn around," he demanded. She reluctantly turned around, her back to him, her arms slightly raised.

Suddenly, his right hand came around and covered her nose and mouth with a damp cloth as his left arm held her in place. The fumes from the cloth were noxious, and she began struggling—but then the click of a cocked gun hammer against her temple made her still, and moments later her world went black.

EIGHTEEN

H ana was awakened by a doorbell chiming somewhere. Forcing her eyes open as she lay in bed, she remembered she was at Pastor Darwin's retreat center. But who would be at her door this early?

Getting out of the bed, she slipped into a white terry robe and made her way to the door as it chimed again. Then there was a gentle tapping, and before she could answer, she heard, "Señorita Sinclair, I have breakfast for you, please."

"Coming," she called as she walked toward the door. Looking through the peephole, Hana saw Juanita standing beside a cart with shiny silver domes covering various plates. She opened the door.

"Good morning, Juanita. I don't remember asking for a wake-up call *or* ordering breakfast."

"*Sì*, Señorita. Pastor Darwin, he is very busy today. He arranges for you to tour all the places here before he meets with you."

Juanita pushed the cart into the room and arranged the

breakfast dishes on the dining table, moving a vase of flowers from the cart and placing it on a corner of the placemat.

"You're here awfully early for having worked so late last night. What time do you start work?"

Juanita looked uncomfortable, but rather than reply to Hana's remark, said, "I do not know what you like for breakfast, so I bring many things. There is fruit, bacon, eggs, potatoes, oatmeal, bread, juice, coffee and milk."

"My goodness. There's enough for three people here. I'm really a light breakfast person. I'll just have fruit, a Danish and coffee. Will you join me, Juanita? I'd hate for the rest to go to waste."

"No, sorry. It is not allowed. But food will not go to waste."

Hana was nonplussed. Clearly something was going on with the staff that Juanita was not supposed to talk about. Then she recalled the listening devices Karl had removed last night. She decided to take a chance.

"Juanita," she said in a whisper, "I know about the listening devices. My assistant came in last night and disabled them. Made them not work. You can speak freely. Nobody is listening."

Juanita said nothing but pointed at the cart emphatically. Hana understood. Another listening device had been placed on the cart. The maid also pointed at the vase of flowers. *Another bug in the flowers, too?*

Hana sat down and began to eat breakfast while pondering how to disable the listening devices without arousing further suspicion. Whoever was listening probably knew she and Karl had found the bugs last night, but they still wanted to hear what was going on in her room and would hear what was said to the maid. As she reached for her coffee, she intentionally hit the vase of flowers, knocking it over and spilling water on the table.

"Oh dear, I'm so clumsy. Let's get some towels from the bathroom, and we'll refill the vase in there as well."

Hana took the vase into the bathroom as Juanita came in to get some towels. Hana put the vase in the tub and turned on the water. Quickly, the vase filled to overflowing—but the sound of the water splashing in the tub also masked their conversation. She closed the bathroom door.

"There, now they can't hear us. We'll be quick before they suspect anything. Is there something you want to tell me? What is going on here? Do you need help?"

"I cannot say, Señorita. Not safe. If they think I talk, they may send me away, or put me in jail, or not bring my family over. I have no papers here. I have to stay and work."

"Who is *they*, Juanita? Who is doing this? Is it Pastor Darwin? Is he keeping you here?"

Juanita was still for a moment, then said, "Nobody is making me do anything. I like it here. I work hard." She took the vase from the tub, emptied about half the water from it, and carried it back to the table, along with some towels to mop up the water.

"Here, let me help you with that. I want to help," Hana said, pointing at the vase and the cart, hoping Juanita would understand. Juanita just shook her head, looking both scared and sad. She finished up with the spill and took the wet towels over to the cart. Then she quickly wheeled the cart over to the door.

"Please enjoy your breakfast, Señorita Sinclair. Someone get you in about forty-five minutes for tour." Pushing the cart outside, Juanita closed the door behind her.

Hana sipped her coffee and thought about what had just transpired. Clearly, the girl was afraid of something, and it seemed that Pastor Darwin was at the heart of it. Were they making her live and work here because she was in the U.S. illegally? Was she afraid Darwin would turn her in if she told anyone she was being forced to live and work here? That could be it. But she also said that they might not bring over her family. This needed further investigation. Darwin was up to something...something besides his trade in suspiciously acquired artifacts.

Hana finished her breakfast and got dressed. Just as she was ready, she heard another knock at the door. Checking the peephole, she saw it was Karl and one of the conference center staff, a young woman. She opened the door.

"Good morning, Ms. Sinclair. My name is Brandie," she said, tossing her shoulder-length wavy blonde hair to one side. She wore a navy blue polo, tan slacks and white sneakers, and had a small radio clipped to her belt with a wire tucked under her shirt leading to an earpiece coiled in her left ear. "I'll be showing you around the facilities Pastor Darwin has built to the Glory of the Father and as a testimony to His holy favor.

"I took the liberty of collecting your assistant, Karl. We'll be starting here in the conference center, then on to the Diamond Ark Cathedral, the Biblical Hall Museum, and finish in the Administration building, where Pastor Darwin will be waiting to speak with you. Please, follow me."

Then she was off at a quick clip down the hallway. Hana glanced at Karl with an inquiring look. He just rolled his eyes and shrugged, then they both fell in behind Brandie.

It took over two hours for them to tour the entire campus. The grounds were certainly impressive. Hana noticed Hispanic landscapers trimming the hedges and mowing the grass, as well as Hispanic staff emptying trash cans, sweeping, vacuuming, and washing windows. She tried to stop to talk to some of them, greeting them in Spanish as she passed and asking how they were doing.

They were polite, but reserved, with the same cautiousness Juanita had shown. And each time she tried to stop, Brandie hurried them along, preventing Hana from attempting to continue conversations with anyone.

When they arrived at the Biblical Hall Museum, Hana was especially alert. This was the point of her mission, and she was watching for anything that might indicate Darwin had a hand in the theft at the Fielding Museum.

Darwin had amassed an impressive collection of artifacts and documents, that much was clear. They were all ensconced in glass display cases throughout the large space. The museum was divided into three wings, with six-foot walls creating a maze of twisting walkways lined with display cases. Black tile arrows periodically interrupted the white tile floors to direct visitors through the exhibits. There was an area for artifacts dating Before the Common Era, an area for Common Era artifacts, and a new area reserved for what was described at the entrance as "Heroes of the Faith." This area was the newest but was still incomplete. Empty display cases had placards describing items waiting to be displayed there. Apparently, Darwin expected to display a Gutenberg Bible, translation notes from fourteenth-century theologian John Wycliffe, and sermons from both John Calvin and Martin Luther.

And then she saw it. The display case dedicated to Galileo. It also was still empty, but had a placard for the letter from Galileo to Grand Duchess Christina, explaining that in this letter, Galileo had defended not only science, but that scriptural interpretation must be reevaluated where there are conflicts between the literal reading of Scripture and the evidence of how the world works as demonstrated by experimentation and observation.

"Do you know what the status is on filling the empty

display cases?" Hana asked Brandie, gesturing specifically toward the Galileo case.

"No, I'm sorry. I'm sure God has revealed to Pastor Darwin the items He wills for us to have and to display in His glory. And those items will be provided in due course."

"What happens to the new items when they are received? Do they go directly on display or is there a reserve of exhibits that rotates in and out?"

"Pastor Darwin has an expert curator on staff, Dr. Leon Becker. He and his assistants oversee the preservation and exhibition of the museum's treasures. But I'm afraid I don't know the contents of our full inventory. You would have to ask Dr. Becker, who isn't here today, or Pastor Darwin, who you'll be meeting with shortly."

While Hana had been talking to her, Karl had edged closer to a door marked *Authorized Personnel Only*. When one of the staff came out the door, Karl stepped back, keeping an eye on Brandie, whose back was to him, and placed his foot on the bottom edge of the door while he peeked into the room.

What he saw shocked him, but before he could react or signal Hana, an alarm sounded. The door was apparently on a timer if it didn't close promptly. Pulling his foot back, Karl let the door close and the alarm stopped. Brandie turned quickly to face Karl. She paused, her head tilted as she apparently listened to the radio earpiece, then she looked up at the black dome of a security camera in the ceiling.

"Well, that concludes the tour. Please follow me. Pastor Darwin is ready for you."

CHAPTER

NINETEEN

G unari Lakatos, the *voivode* or chieftain of the Roma clan based on the southernmost fringe of Les Pèlerins, France, landed at Chicago's O'Hare Airport with a contingent of Roma clansmen who were loyal to him without question, no matter what he asked of them. At the Arrival's curb, they got into two waiting white Chevy Suburbans, both driven by members of the New York City Roma clan.

When he determined that he had to go to Chicago to personally intervene, Gunari knew he had only a distant family connection with the Chicago clan, led by a man named John Boswell—but he did have closer associations with the New York and Miami clans, two of the larger Roma tribes in the United States after Chicago's, which was the biggest. So he had called in some favors and offered enticements to get some additional people to Chicago. People who he knew would be loyal to him.

Gunari hoped what he had to do wouldn't cause a rift between the clans, or worse, an inter-clan war. The Roma were chiefly guided by honor and duty, but also driven to power and wealth. Gunari would appeal to Boswell's sense of clan loyalty, and if that didn't work, he would try to buy his sons' freedom, if indeed Boswell was holding them as he suspected.

But if that didn't work, Gunari was prepared to use force. Nobody was going to harm his sons, his niece, or Father Michael, no matter what the deal had been. This matter was going to be put to rest his way.

JOHN BOSWELL ARRIVED at the safe house on the way to meeting Gunari Lakatos downtown. He wanted to personally check on the status of his "guests" before speaking to the other clan leader. When the Auxiliary Bishop of Chicago, William Loveridge, had called him and relayed the job description and the payoff, he should have known it was too good to be true or too dangerous. That's why he took the bishop's suggestion to contract outside talent for the job. He suspected it would get hot, but he hadn't thought it would get this hot or that the deal would start to unravel from both ends.

The bishop had called and wanted to know what had gone wrong. His sources in the police department described a witness who had been abducted and tortured but that had been found alive in the Chicago River. The Chicago police were beating down doors, shaking down the usual suspects and trying to come up with clues. Already several of his less-careful Roma black-baggers had been rousted and questioned. Fortunately, this job had been limited to a close circle of Boswell's confidants, so nobody who was questioned had known anything worthwhile.

But it worried him nonetheless. He figured the boys messed up to have had someone follow them to the heist in the first place. He also feared that the man the boys then abducted afterwards likely saw or heard enough to lead the police in their direction. The police knew he was head of the Chicago Roma. Once they ruled out the Italian mobs and the Russian Mafia and the more sophisticated gangs, they would circle back to focus on the Roma.

As Boswell entered the safe house, the guard at the door gave him the bad news.

"Hey, Boss. We had a little trouble, but we handled it."

"What kinda trouble?"

"There was this Roma girl and some Irish kid pokin' around. They walked through the neighborhood earlier today and we marked them. Then we caught them sneakin' around outside. She was tryin' to look in the basement windows."

"Roma girl, you say? What family?"

"Lakatos. Ain't they from Europe? Anyway, she has a mouth on her, that one. Now she's tied up downstairs with the boys, and that Irish kid, too. But she won't talk, even when we got a little rough with her."

"You got a little rough with her? What does that mean?" Boswell rushed past the man and down the stairs to the basement. Two other men were there, watching over the four people who were all duct-taped to kitchen chairs with black pillowcases over their heads. The girl's shirt was torn, hanging from her shoulder, and he could see bruises rising on the skin at the top of her breast visible through the rent in her clothing. He approached her and removed the pillowcase.

Kat turned to glare at him. Her eyes were red and teary, and another bruise was coloring her left cheek and darkening her swollen eyelid.

"Mother of God! What have you done? Don't you know who this is? This is Gunari Lakatos' favorite niece, Ekaterina. The only people he loves more are his own sons. *She* is the reason he owes me a favor, and he's on his way to Chicago right now to meet me." He turned to the two boys, grabbing the pillowcase from the closest head, which was Milosh's. "You two, what is Gunari Lakatos to you?"

Milosh didn't answer immediately. He turned and looked at Kat, and seeing her bruises, his voice grew cold and hard. "When my *baba* gets here, you'll be in big trouble."

"Look, boy. I apologize for how you have been treated. But now I've got to go meet your *baba* and make things right. And I can't have you four talking to Gunari before I do and making things even more difficult. So, I'm afraid you are just going to have to stay here a bit longer. But we'll take off the hoods, and nobody will touch you till I get back." Boswell addressed the others in the room. "Is that clear? They stay tied up, but nobody touches them till I return, or I will dump your miserable corpses in the river myself."

GUNARI SAT in the back seat of one of the two Suburbans and waited. When he'd called Boswell to notify him that he had arrived in Chicago, Boswell suggested meeting at a steakhouse on the river, at which point Gunari sent the other Suburban ahead to scout out the area and take observation positions. When he asked about the welfare of his team, or if he had any news of Ekaterina, Boswell had been evasive, which made Gunari suspicious. The boys had done a job for Boswell and he should have known their whereabouts until they were out of his purview and on their way back home to France. That he did not or would not admit to it made Gunari even more worried.

But he was also concerned about having to unwind the deal. That was bad business, and would make him look weak in the eyes of his American counterparts. He was coming to them hat in hand, but if things went badly, he was prepared to respond more forcefully. He was on their territory, but he was not without resources, and he had them well prepared.

The Miami team called in on Gunari's cell phone.

"A Lincoln town car just pulled up to the restaurant and three guys got out, one in a white suit. I'd say that's probably him."

"Thank you," Gunari replied. "Keep an eye on the place. We're on our way."

As the vehicle started up, his phone rang again. He looked at the caller ID and answered it quickly.

"Yes?...Okay, I understand. Do nothing more until I get there."

Gunari's Suburban soon pulled up to the restaurant. Gunari got out, taking two of his men with him.

Gunari was welcomed by the maitre d', who took him to a table in a reserved room. Boswell was already seated at the table, his two lieutenants standing behind him in black overcoats and dark sunglasses. Boswell did not rise to greet him, but rather gestured to the seat on the other side of the table. It was a breach of courtesy and an obvious power play, Gunari knew, but he graciously took his seat despite the slight in protocol. His two men stood behind him, mirroring Boswell's men.

Tension filled the room.

"Thank you for meeting me on such short notice, John," Gunari began. "I realize the circumstances are unusual, but then, everything about this job has been unusual.

"Before we talk about how to return the stolen items to the Vatican, though—and I cannot express to you the magnitude of my dismay that you agreed to steal such important artifacts from the Church—I want to talk to you about my family. I have asked whether you have any information regarding the whereabouts and condition of the team I sent to carry out your job, a team comprised of my two sons. And now my niece is missing, after she went looking for them. You were rather evasive when I spoke to you earlier, so I will ask you again directly. Do you or do you not know the present location of my sons and my niece and the friend who was traveling with her?"

Boswell was taken aback by the directness of his inquiry. This was not at all how he had anticipated the meeting going.

"Well, about that…"

CHAPTER
TWENTY

Their hands had been tied to their chairs so that none of them was able to reach the ropes that bound them. But when the four of them were arranged back-to-back, facing out in a cross so that they could not see each other directly, the positioning had placed their hands in proximity to the bonds of the person next to them. Ian was situated directly behind Kat, with a brother on each side of him.

It seemed to take him hours, working carefully on the knot with his fingertips, to try to loosen one of the brothers' bindings ever so gradually due to the tightness of the knots and the growing weakness of his fingers. He also had to work discreetly so as not to let the guards discover what he was doing.

Finally, he'd freed Milosh's right wrist from its lashing to the chair. Milosh bent his arm at the elbow and after another several minutes managed to loosen and clear his other wrist with his free right hand. Now both arms were unbound, but his legs were still tethered to the chair legs. The beginnings of a plan started taking shape.

"How long do ya think he's gonna be gone?" one guard asked the other.

"I dunno. Few minutes? All night? Why?"

"Cuz I'm hungry. How 'bout we order a pizza?"

"Yeah, I'm hungry too. I'll split it with you. Pepperoni and sausage? That okay with you?"

"Yeah, I'll call that place down the street. They deliver."

A short time later, the doorbell rang. One of the guards went upstairs to get the pizza, leaving the four hostages alone with the remaining guard.

"Hey, you guys ever think of getting *us* some pizza?" Milosh asked.

"No. I got no orders to feed you. My instructions were to leave you tied to the chairs till the boss gets back. And that's what I'm gonna do."

"But I gotta pee."

"Sounds like a personal problem."

"Then I'll just hop this chair over by you and pee," Milosh told him, and started trying to make the chair hop, pretending to strain against the ropes on his arms and legs. The guard got up quickly and came over toward Milosh, his right hand raised, ready to slap him.

"You knock that off, or I'll smack some respect into your head, and I don't really care who your daddy is. Didn't he ever teach you no manners?"

"No, but he did teach me how to untie knots," Milosh exulted as he launched himself up at the guard, catching him under the chin with his forehead. Milosh immediately yanked the chair up by the seat, pulling the chair legs from the loops of rope binding his ankles to the chair. He was now completely free. The guard staggered back, stunned by the unexpected blow. Milosh leapt forward, landing a fast, right-handed punch directly into the man's throat. Grabbing the guy by the ears and hair and pulling his head down, Milosh simultaneously brought his right knee up into the guard's nose. The blow rocked the man back again, and Milosh followed it up with a shin kick to the groin that dropped him to the ground gasping. Milosh knelt down on the man and bashed his head into the concrete floor a couple of times.

"That's for Kat."

Finally, Milosh pulled him onto a choke hold. Within a matter of seconds, the guard was motionless. Getting up, the young Romani quickly untied Shandor, and the two used their ropes to tie the guard to one of the chairs and put one of the hoods over his head. They were about to untie Kat and Ian when they heard the other guard starting back down the wooden staircase with the pizza. Shandor quickly resumed his seat, while Milosh hid under the staircase.

"Hey, why did you put the hood back on him? We're gonna get in trouble for…" The guard never finished his sentence. Milosh's hand shot through the narrow slats of the steps, seizing the unsuspecting man's ankles in an iron grip. With a fierce tug, he yanked the man's foot back.

The guard's expletive echoed through the stairwell as his foot was ensnared by the unknown assailant, sending him careening down the steps in a dizzying blur. The pizza went flying as his body collided with each step, his bones rattling like a bag of broken glass, until he finally crashed into a crumpled heap at the bottom of the staircase, pizza sauce and pepperoni slices splattering his torso and breath knocked out of him.

Milosh and Shandor sprang into action, charging toward the fallen guard with fierce determination. But their bravery was met with a chilling sight: the man had managed to pull out a deadly revolver from his waistband holster and aimed it at Shandor, the one closest to him.

Panic and fear washed over the boys momentarily until

Milosh surmised, "Hey, if he shoots us in the back, we were running away, and father will peel his skin off an inch at a time until he dies. Kat, Ian, we'll be back for you. Shandor," Milosh shouted, *"Run!"*

In a frenzied panic, the two boys raced past the man and up the stairs, their hearts pounding with adrenaline. Determined not to let them escape, the guard tried hobbling after them but the pain from his fall had taken its toll. His left lower leg had shattered, rendering him unable to give chase. He leaned his back against the wall and called out to the other guard, who didn't answer.

Then he stared menacingly at Kat and Ian. "You two are gonna wish they had untied you first. This ain't gonna go down well."

He took out his cell phone and made a call.

JOHN BOSWELL HAD JUST SPOKEN the words, *"Well, about that...,"* when his cell phone rang. He recognized the ring tone immediately: one of the guys he had left guarding the safe house. They knew not to call unless it was an emergency.

"Excuse me just a moment," he said to Gunari. He hurried into the restaurant kitchen and answered the call.

"This better be important."

"Somehow, one of the boys got loose, Boss. He jumped Lenny and knocked him out. I was upstairs getting some food, and when I came back down they jumped me, too. Knocked me down the stairs. I think my leg is broken. The two boys got away. They hadn't managed to untie the girl or her boyfriend."

"Sonofabitch!... Okay. I'll get some guys over there in a

few minutes. Be ready to move. The safe house is compromised."

"Sorry, Boss."

"Yeah, you're gonna be sorrier. Get on it. I'll deal with you later."

Boswell hung up and called the driver of the Suburban.

"There's a problem at the safe house. Gunari's two boys got away. Come pick me up behind the restaurant. *Now!*" He hung up and made another call. "The two Lakatos boys at the safe house got away. The girl and her friend are still there. Get over there and move them to the warehouse. Take the two guards I left at the house. One will need help; his leg's broken. I'll meet you there."

GUNARI WAS WAITING for Boswell to return when his phone rang. It was the driver of his car.

"Hey, the Chicago clan's ride just peeled out and went around the restaurant," the driver from his own car said. "Nobody got in out here. Want us to follow it?"

"No, stay put for now. Call the Miami guys and have them follow it. Boswell got a phone call and went into another room to take it. I'm gonna find him." He started toward the kitchen, taking his bodyguards with him, when the phone rang again. "Now what?" he muttered to himself.

"*B-Baba?*" Milosh sputtered when his father answered. "*Miro Divo, Baba,* are you really here in Chicago? We're in trouble. Where are you?"

"Yes, I am in the city now, my son, down by the river. I was meeting with John Boswell," Gunari explained as he entered the kitchen. "Where are you?"

"The guy we did the job for, his people were holding us

at a safe house just outside the city. Something must have gone bad." He explained everything that had happened after Kat came looking for them up to when he and his brother escaped.

Gunari heard the sound of the Suburban peeling away from the loading dock out back. "I'm coming to get you, Milosh. Tell me where you are now."

"We are at some tapas place a couple of blocks from the safe house. We ducked in and pleaded to use their phone since the guards took ours away."

"What are you doing in a topless place?"

"No, *Baba*, tapas. Tapas…like, Spanish food. Anyway, it's on Halsted Street."

"Alright, we will find it. We are on our way."

"I'm sorry, *Baba*. We couldn't get Ekaterina or her friend out."

"Do not worry, Milosh. We will get her. I brought a lot of help with me. Something about this stinks, and we are going to find out what it is."

CHAPTER
TWENTY-ONE

The next morning Michael sat at the defense counsel table in the moot courtroom of Loyola Law School and took in the surroundings. Anderson had explained that he was entitled to designate someone as his investigator, an expert in the case that sat at counsel table. Anderson wanted Michael close at hand in case an ecclesiastical matter arose and he needed his advice. It looked like everything he had imagined an American courtroom in a real courthouse might look like, even though this one was situated in a law school.

Dean Hastings was dressed in the customary black judge's robe, sitting at the judge's bench on an elevated dais, with the seal of the State of Illinois on the front and the seal of the United States on the wall behind her, and an American flag and an Illinois state flag on either side of the bench. On the judge's right side was her clerk's station, and on the left was the witness stand, adjacent to the jury box containing fourteen armchairs. On each jury seat were a steno pad and pencil.

On the other side of the room was a desk for the bailiff.

One of Bishop Sharma's security personnel, a tall, African-American man called Bram, was standing behind the desk, dressed in something that looked like an all-black version of the Swiss Guard uniform. He was holding an ornately carved, wooden baton tucked horizontally against his side, resting along his forearm. It gave Michael a chill, bringing to mind the formal inquisitions of ages past.

Sharma—along with another similarly dressed guard, Somchai, a short and wiry Vietnamese man—was standing at the counsel table nearest the jury. In American court tradition, the prosecutor, the agent of the people, sat closer to the jury. Michael sat farthest from the jury, with the defense attorney, Professor Tom Anderson, sitting between him, the prosecutor, and the jury: a physical representation of the fact that the defense attorney stands between the defendant and the power of the government.

Michael glanced over at Sharma. Rather than adopt the typical American courtroom attire, Sharma was dressed in the symbol-rich garb of a bishop: black cassock piped in red to represent the blood of Christ, with thirty-nine red buttons down the front to symbolize Christ's scourging by the Romans with thirty-nine lashes, and a matching black mozzetta, a short cape similarly piped in red with seven red buttons. Catholic vestments were intended to inspire reverence, either for the God who had ordained them or for their wearer's position as a leader in the Church. In this setting, however, Sharma's choice of clothing seemed more calculated to inspire ecclesiastic intimidation, if not fear.

As the clock crept toward nine o'clock, Dean Alice Hastings, the judge, motioned for the two sides to approach the bench. Professor Anderson and Bishop Sharma did so, standing close to the podium and speaking quietly with the judge.

Michael looked behind him at the area reserved for

spectators. Both sides were filled with people speaking quietly in small groups, sitting in their seats chatting with their neighbors, or reading the program that had been handed to them on arrival. A live television camera was positioned at the back of the courtroom, where it could capture a good view of the entire room. Several people scattered around the audience appeared to be journalists equipped with steno pads or recording devices.

Professor Anderson returned to the counsel table to speak with Michael.

"Well, Sharma is insistent that we hold the evidentiary hearing before the trial starts. I tried to convince him that this is just a demonstration project, and the exhibits are going to be admitted for the trial regardless of any objections, or there wouldn't be anything to demonstrate. I think he just wants another shot at embarrassing you in front of the cameras. Unfortunately, the judge is going along with it, so we have to do it his way."

"What does that mean?" Michael asked.

Before Anderson could answer, the judge rapped her gavel. The bailiff called out, "Be seated and come to order. The Honorable Dean Alice Hastings presiding."

"Greetings, everyone. Welcome to the retrial of Galileo Galilei. My name is Alice Hastings, Dean of Loyola Law School. I will be presiding as judge of this proceeding. Representing the defendant is professor and attorney Thomas Anderson, and representing the Vatican is the High Inquisitor, Bishop Vijay Sharma.

"Before we bring in the jury and the defendant, there are a few evidentiary matters that need to be cleared up. Then we will bring the jury in, introduce everyone, and have opening statements, and that should take us to the end of the day.

"Bishop Sharma, it's your motion. You may proceed."

"Thank you, Your Honor. May it please the Court, I have a number of exhibits, or rather copies of exhibits, that I wish to have marked as evidence. But in light of the theft of the actual exhibits that were supposed to have been on display here at the conference, and which would have authenticated the copies, I feel it is important to compel the custodian of the exhibits to authenticate the copies. I call Father Michael Dominic to the stand."

"Father Dominic, please come to the witness stand, remain standing and face the clerk of the court," Dean Hastings pronounced.

Michael looked at Professor Anderson and whispered, "Here it comes." Standing and making his way past the jury box to the witness stand, he turned to face the clerk, a trickle of sweat beginning to gather between his shoulder blades.

"Father Dominic, do you swear to tell the truth, the whole truth, and nothing but the truth, so help you God?" the clerk intoned.

"I do."

"You may be seated. Please give your full name for the record, spelling the last name."

"Michael Patrick Dominic. D-O-M-I-N-I-C."

"You may begin your inquiry, Bishop Sharma," the judge prompted.

"Thank you, Your Honor. Father Michael, you just swore to tell the truth—the whole truth—and yet on the very first question, you perjured yourself. How are we to trust you now?"

"I'm sorry, Bishop, I don't understand what you mean. There haven't been any questions yet."

"Oh, but there have. You were asked to state your name, and you gave us Michael Patrick *Dominic*. But Dominic is your mother's surname. And when a boy is born and the father is not known, it is the custom to have the boy take his mother's surname. But your father *is* known, is he not? He was known to your mother, and he has since acknowledged his paternity to you. Is that not true?"

Michael hesitated, sensing a trap. He spoke cautiously. "Yes...that is true."

"With the permission of the Court, I would like to approach the witness and show him a document," Sharma said, simultaneously showing the document to Professor Anderson.

"Your Honor," Anderson protested, "I object to the relevance of this document and this whole line of questioning. Furthermore, I was not given a copy of this document in discovery."

Sharma was prepared for this. "It was not necessary to give the document to Professor Anderson before the trial, Your Honor, since it is only being used for impeachment. I had no way of knowing Father Michael would lie so early in his testimony, and so could not anticipate needing this document. However, it *is* relevant for impeachment and is therefore admissible."

"Objection overruled. You may proceed, Bishop Sharma."

"Father Michael, where were you born?"

"In New York City, in the borough of Queens."

"And when were you born?"

"April 19, 1989."

"And your mother's name was Grace Dominic?"

"Yes."

Sharma made his way to the witness stand and handed a single piece of paper to Michael.

"Father Michael, I've handed you a piece of paper. Do you recognize this as a birth certificate issued by the State of New York?"

Michael looked at it closely. "Yes," he said apprehensively, as color drained from his face.

"And the child's birth is shown as being on April 19, 1989, with the mother identified as Grace Dominic?"

"Yes."

"And the child's name is listed as Michael Patrick Petrini. Because the father is Enrico Petrini, is that correct?"

Michael paused. "…Yes."

"And Enrico Petrini is also currently known as Pope Ignatius, is that correct?"

"Yes."

"So, the pope is your father?"

Pausing before answering, Michael looked down at his hands, then murmured, "Yes." There was a gasp from several people in the room. Apparently, the news from Malta hadn't made its way to every corner of America. The camera zoomed in on Michael.

"You look shaken, Father Michael. Don't tell me you have never seen your own birth certificate before?"

"Actually, no, I haven't. I've never had the need. My mother or Father Petrini always took care of the paperwork, like for school or my passport."

"But you have known this for some time now. Years, in fact. Yes?"

"Yes." Michael's eyes glistened as he looked down at his birth certificate, thinking about his father, who would almost certainly be watching the live feed.

"Yet you lied to conceal that fact from the world."

"*No!*"

"So you lied about your parentage for some other reason?"

"No, that was the name my mother gave me—Michael Patrick Dominic!"

"So your mother and your father also lied about your parentage? You are a whole family of liars."

"*Objection!*" Anderson protested, standing in outrage.

"I'll move on, Your Honor. Father Michael—well, at least we know your first name is correct—I'd like to ask you some questions about the documents that were stolen: the exhibits you brought from the Vatican related to the trial of Galileo. Do you know to which documents I am referring?"

"Yes," Michael responded, relieved to be moving on to something else.

"Those documents were placed on display in the Fielding Museum?"

"Yes."

"And you left two of your employees at the museum to watch over the exhibits on the first night?"

"Yes."

"And did you know that those two employees, Mr. Duffy and Ms. Lakatos, were romantically involved?"

"Well, not directly."

"Come now, Father Michael. Hadn't Mr. Duffy been sneaking down to Ms. Lakatos's office repeatedly of late?"

"How would you know that?"

"Father Michael, the question is not how *I* know but whether you as their supervisor knew—and you did, didn't you?"

"More or less."

"And the two of them were recorded on museum surveillance tapes sharing moments of intimacy before falling asleep in the cloakroom, instead of watching over the documents?"

Michael's cheeks reddened. "Yes"

"You also had two Swiss Guards available to take the overnight shift, is that correct?"

"Yes."

"But you didn't use them?"

"No."

"Nor did you take that shift yourself?"

"No."

"No, indeed. Instead, you went out to dinner with your girlfriend, whom you were photographed kissing in a restaurant around the corner." Sharma produced a copy of the newspaper photo from inside his sleeve and dropped it on the witness stand.

"I am a priest, Bishop Sharma, and she is *not* my girlfriend. We are just friends, and that wasn't even a kiss. It was clearly an accident."

"Yes, well, I imagine you were an accident, too."

"*Objection!*" Thomas shouted. "*Your Honor...*"

"Sustained," the judge ruled impatiently.

"I withdraw the question," Sharma said glibly. "It's not important now, anyway. What *is* important are these exhibits, or the copies of them. Did you prepare them yourself?"

"No, I had them prepared."

"By whom?"

"By Ms. Lakatos."

"And did you verify the copies against the originals?"

"I spot-checked a few, yes. Everything seemed in order."

"Was a manifest prepared of the exhibits that were transported from the Vatican to the museum?"

"Yes."

"And you verified that every document on the manifest that left the Vatican arrived here in Chicago?"

"Yes."

"Did you perform that verification personally?"

"Yes."

"Without assistance?"

"I was assisted by Ms. Lakatos."

"How did you conduct the verification?"

"I checked the documents, and she checked them off against the manifest. Then I signed it."

"So, you are confident that every document on that manifest was brought over from the Vatican from your collection in the Apostolic Archive?"

"Yes."

"And is this a copy of the manifest document, with your signature on it?" Sharma asked, again showing Michael a multi-page document.

Michael inspected it. Seeing nothing wrong with it, he relaxed and replied, "Yes."

"Very well, thank you. Your Honor, I would like to mark the copies of the documents as they are listed on the manifest for identification, having been assured by Father Michael—whatever his last name is—that they are complete and authentic copies of the documents that he allowed to be stolen by leaving a couple of lovebirds to oversee them while he went out to dinner and was caught 'accidentally' kissing a woman who apparently is not his girlfriend, if I understand his testimony correctly."

"The copies of the exhibits will be so marked," the judge stated, now annoyed that she had been persuaded to allow Sharma to engage in his theatrics. "May the witness be excused, Bishop?"

"Just one more question, if I may. Father Michael, do you know where Ms. Lakatos is now?" Sharma let the vague question hang in the air.

"No," Michael replied.

"Is she missing?"

"Well, I haven't heard from her this morning, though I expected to."

"Well," Sharma concluded with a mocking tone. "That is concerning."

CHAPTER
TWENTY-TWO

Hana sat alone on a comfortable, cream-colored leather couch in the lobby waiting area outside Pastor Gabriel Darwin's office, watching with keen interest the live feed from the retrial in Chicago on a large TV on the opposite wall.

Unfortunately, Karl was not with her. On their way over to the Administration building they had been joined by several security officers, two in uniform and two in suits. There had been a bit of a scene when they demanded that Karl would need to come with them to the security office to talk about why he had opened the private door in the museum, as well as other snooping activities he had been observed conducting while on campus—including disabling security monitoring equipment and possessing electronic security detection equipment in his bag.

Hana had objected strenuously to being separated from her "assistant." But the security officers then suggested they might cancel the interview and escort her off the property, so once Karl consented to go with them, she relented.

After Karl had been led away, Hana was brought to the

lobby, left on the couch and informed that Pastor Darwin would be with her shortly. While she was alone, she had the odd feeling she was being watched. Looking up, she noticed a dark camera dome in the ceiling to her right, presumably with a view of the entire waiting area.

And as it happened, Pastor Darwin was indeed watching a split-screen view from his office: on one side was the live feed from Chicago, and on the other, the live feed from the lobby. He still hadn't decided how to handle the interview with Hana, but when he heard that Father Dominic had been called to the stand as Hana was arriving, he decided that perhaps watching her reactions would give him some added insight into her personality and motivations.

As Michael was presented with his birth certificate, Hana teared up, especially when she saw him do the same on live TV. But when Bishop Sharma intentionally embarrassed the priest with questions about Kat and Ian, and Hana herself, she turned angry. By the time the questioning was over, she was ready to climb through the television and strangle Sharma herself. It was probably a good thing that she was here rather than in the audience in Chicago, as the courtroom cameras would almost certainly have caught her reactions. She wondered if Michael had had any inkling that this was coming and used the trip to Texas as a ruse to get her away from Chicago. Probably not. He wouldn't be that duplicitous with her.

Her musings were interrupted by the door opening and Pastor Darwin himself beckoning her into his inner sanctum. She straightened her skirt as she rose from the couch and walked past Darwin as she entered the office. The room was enormous. It easily took up half of the fourth floor of the Administration building, with windows on three sides. While the office was a completely open floor plan, the room had been artfully divided into several zones. Near the entrance was a large, wood-burning fireplace, in front of which rustic, rough-hewn chairs and a couch were arranged in a half-circle. On the opposite side, near the windows, Darwin's desk was a modern marvel of glass and chrome, with three large computer monitors arranged beneath the glass surface. The top of the desk was completely clear of objects except for a few stacked papers. To the side of it was a rolling book cart with a sloped easel on which rested a large edition of the Bible, above shelves filled with other reference volumes. In front of his desk was another assortment of chairs, couches, end tables and a coffee table that reminded Hana of the pictures she had seen of the American president's Oval Office. Off to one side were a large, black granite conference table with at least a dozen high-backed leather chairs surrounding it, a multi-directional speakerphone occupying the center, and a video projector and camera hanging from the ceiling directly above it. Over the window, she saw a drop-down projection screen. Clearly, Darwin could take video calls from the head of the table and include a remote panel of advisors if he chose.

The pastor gestured toward Hana to take a seat by the fireplace. Another large TV hung over the mantle was tuned to the trial, but the sound was off, and the proceedings seemed to be on a break, with people milling about in small groups while the bench was vacant. Darwin wore one of his bespoke white, three-piece leisure suits with a white shirt, white leather belt, and white patent leather shoes. He wore a large, gaudy gold ring on each hand, a gold chain with a dangling crucifix around his neck, and a gold chain bracelet on his left wrist.

"Thank you for being patient while waiting, Ms. Sinclair. I'm sure you can imagine the number of administrative responsibilities entailed in leading an organization this large," Darwin said, seemingly to excuse the time Hana had spent sitting in the lobby. She wasn't fooled. He had summoned her just as the trial was getting started and had left her in the lobby for the entire time Michael had been on the stand, presumably to watch her reactions. She now knew to be especially careful with someone of his guile.

"Yes, I'm sure it's a full-time job and then some."

"Well, I suppose you have a lot of questions, and so do I, but I hope you are not made uncomfortable by starting out with a question I ask of everyone with whom I meet. What is your position with respect to our Lord and Savior?"

"I'm not sure what you mean," Hana said, taken a bit off guard.

"Are you a Christian? A believer? A follower of Christ? A Catholic perhaps, since your boyfriend is a Catholic priest? Or perhaps something else?"

Hana caught the slight. She paused while she formulated a response. "Father Dominic is a good friend, Pastor, but we are *not* romantically inclined. To answer your question, though, I am open-mindedly and quite happily agnostic."

"I see. I only ask so as to know if there are any common assumptions we might be operating under with regard to the mission of the Catholic Church, and the church I lead in particular. But in regard to the other question, Father Dominic seems to benefit quite a bit from your friendship."

"I beg your pardon?!" Hana objected to the implication.

"No, no. No disrespect intended." Though clearly there had been. "I was referring to the use of your family's jet for his travels, access to your journalistic resources, and your other assets," Darwin suggested, leaving deliberately vague exactly which assets he was referring to.

"I assure you that my relationship with Father Dominic is entirely appropriate. Not that it's any concern of yours."

Darwin knew now he had touched a nerve. Time to back off a bit and come at her from a different direction. "Be that as it may. I suspect that Father Dominic sent ya'll down here to get information from me regarding my interest in acquiring a Galileo manuscript from the Vatican—specifically the Letter to Grand Duchess Christina—for the Biblical Hall Museum, and not just because you have an interest in my church for its own sake, or even for your own soul's sake."

Well, Hana thought, *he certainly is direct.* Should she admit it? What *did* he actually know?

"And why shouldn't a journalist like me have an interest in the empire you have built, seeing as how I have encountered it in the Holy Land and in Chicago, in my own recent travels, and you oddly turned up in both places at the same time I was there? One could say it started to strain the bounds of coincidence. Are you following me, Pastor Darwin?" Hana delighted in the double meaning. Two could play at this game, and she had avoided answering his question.

That fact was not lost on Darwin, nor were her implications. "Well, Ms. Sinclair, you certainly know how to turn a phrase," he laughed, letting her know he had caught her meanings. The game was afoot. "God in His infinite wisdom has directed my path, and yours, to intersect on these occasions, to some purpose yet unknown to us. I suppose we shall just have to wait on the fullness of His revelation."

"Yes, I suppose so." Hana decided to take a gamble. "But along those lines, what do you hear from that Israeli henchman of yours, Remi Shapiro?"

CHAPTER
TWENTY-THREE

I n an office in the Vatican, a man watching the live feed of the retrial in Chicago paused while the proceedings were taking a break. He found the examination of Father Michael Dominic most interesting. He took out his cell phone and sent a cryptic text to a special phone number.

"Matthew 25:21," the message read.

A few moments later, a reply came back.

"Exodus 22:18."

The man texted back. "Matthew 6:10."

The man then sent a text to a different number. This message read: "Ms. Lakatos's return flight is cancelled. Please make arrangements to let her know." He deleted the texts and the message history from the phone and returned it to his pocket. Then he got up from his desk and took a walk.

∽

FATHER NICK BANNON sat in a chair next to Pope Ignatius, who was lying in bed propped up against a cascade of pillows. The two men were watching the live feed of the retrial from Chicago. At the break after Michael's testimony, Nick waited for the pope to speak first.

"Well, if there was anybody left in the world who had not heard that I had a son, they certainly know now."

"Shall I prepare Bishop Sharma's excommunication, or will a transfer to the Diocese of Antarctica be sufficient?" Nick joked.

"From your lips to God's ears," the pope replied. "No, I don't think Sharma is the one we have to look out for. He may be a snake, but he's not the head of the snake. He wouldn't have acted so brazenly without cover. The question is whether it's his boss, or one of the other cardinals who is thinking they are going to replace me soon."

"There is no shortage of those, to be sure," Nick agreed, "but I could come up with a short list of candidates for Sharma's benefactor."

"As could I," the pope groaned and rolled toward his left side, his right hand clutching his left bicep. Nick quickly rose to his feet and put a hand on the pope's shoulder.

"Shall I call for the doctor?"

"No, Nick, it will pass. You know there is nothing the doctors can do at this point. No sense in feeding the vultures any more meat than they are already getting today. And no calling Michael. He has enough on his plate without worrying about me. There is still time. Not a lot, but enough."

"As you wish. Is there anything I can do for you?"

The pope was about to answer when the phone beside his bed emitted a staccato buzzing sound. Nick recognized it as the ringtone originating from the pope's reception desk, which another assistant was covering while Nick was attending to His Holiness.

Nick picked up the receiver. "Yes?"

"Cardinal Caputo is here to see the Holy Father."

"Hold on." Nick put the phone on Hold and turned to the pope. "Speaking of snakes, Cardinal Caputo is here to see you. Do you want to grant him an audience?"

"I suppose I should. Help me to the desk and turn off that TV."

When the assistant admitted Cardinal Caputo to the office, Father Bannon met him at the door and escorted him to where the pope was sitting at his desk in a wheelchair. The cardinal knelt and kissed the pope's ring, then rose to stand before the desk.

"Holy Father, I just watched the beginning of the retrial of Galileo in Chicago. If you ask me to, I will recall Bishop Sharma immediately," Caputo blurted out. Then, realizing that he should have let the pope speak first, he became quiet, hoping the slight would be overlooked.

"Why? What did Bishop Sharma do?"

"Were you not watching?"

"I have many important matters that require my attention, Boris. That is not particularly one of them. I suppose, then, that you did have the time to watch?" the pope asked, leaving Caputo to assume that he had not watched the morning session.

"Well, yes, since Bishop Sharma is my chief prosecutor, I felt I was obliged to assess his performance in such a high-profile situation."

"And apparently, he did something that caused you enough concern that you had to come to me and ask if he should be recalled? What has your chief prosecutor done?"

"I regret to have to be the one to bring you the news, but he raised the issue of Father Dominic's...um...parentage, as well as the theft of the exhibits, the faults of the staff that were left at the museum to watch over the exhibits, and the woman that Father Dominic was photographed supposedly kissing, all on the live feed from the conference. I assure you I had no idea Sharma was going to pursue that line of questioning. I have no idea what got into him."

"I see. Yes, well, that is regrettable. Yet all of those things were already in the news, so it doesn't seem like any fresh harm was done. And it would not do for *me* to ask him to tone it down. It would sound like I'm trying to censor him. No, I will leave Bishop Sharma's fate to your discretion. You are his superior. I would not want to interfere with how you supervise him. He is your responsibility." The pope was fairly confident Caputo got the gist of his meaning. Sharma's behavior would be attributed to Caputo. It was for Caputo to rein him in or let him run. It was a test for this particular cardinal.

"Yes, Your Holiness. I'm so sorry to disturb you. I should have asked, but…how are you feeling?"

"Thank you for your concern, Boris. This old body is tired, but there is much work still left that the Lord has called upon us to do. And we should be about it now. Thank you for coming." The pope gestured to Nick to see the cardinal out. Caputo knelt and kissed the pope's ring again, and the pope made the sign of the cross over him before he rose.

"The Lord be with you, Cardinal Caputo."

"And also with you, Holy Father."

～

WILLIAM LOVERIDGE, the Auxiliary Bishop of Chicago, looked at the text on his phone.

Flight cancelled? he mused. *Well, I guess that means she isn't going home.* He typed out a text message to a number in his contacts that had no other identifying information attached: *The smallest of the packages you are holding is no longer needed. Please dispose of it promptly.* That should do it. The reply came back a few moments later.

And the others?

He had no instructions about the others, and he really didn't want to text back to the person who gave him the instructions, so he improvised: *Whatever is easiest for you, but don't make a mess.*

There is a complication. We have guests from out of town.

Again, the bishop didn't know how to respond. He thought for some time about getting further instructions but didn't really want to have anything more to do with this, so again, he decided to let them take care of things their way.

Not important. Dispose of the packages as soon as possible. The buyer wants the order cancelled.

A response came back right away: *There will be an additional charge to cancel the entire order.*

He replied: **Understood. Make it happen. I have been assured that cost overruns will be covered.**

As you wish.

What I wish, thought Loveridge, *is that I had never gotten mixed up in this at all.*

As CARDINAL CAPUTO walked back to his office, he was surprised that the pope didn't seem to be aware of the controversy stirring around him on account of his son, his liberal policies, and his health, or surely he would have been monitoring what happened at the trial, especially with his son being so badly and publicly mistreated.

Clearly, the Church was in need of new leadership. Leadership with a cleaner reputation and, ideally, more conservative leanings.

~

"Now, help me get back to the bed, please, Nick. Caputo can be exhausting. I need to rest."

Nick wheeled the pope back into the bedroom and helped him settle in.

"That one bears watching," the pope continued. "He is so conceited that he doesn't realize how much he is giving away. He would not have come unless he needed to distance himself from Sharma. I expect he'll be making Sharma the scapegoat for whatever else he has planned. But we need someone in his inner circle who can warn us if something is coming. Give Commandant Scarpa a call and ask him to assign Sergeant Koehl to the DDF for a little while. Oh, and please turn the TV back on. Let's see what else Bishop Sharma and his benefactor have in store for us."

CHAPTER
TWENTY-FOUR

T he preceding eighteen hours had been some of the most frustrating Gunari had ever experienced, and Boswell was going to pay for that frustration.

Yesterday at the restaurant, they had just begun to discuss the whereabouts of his sons and niece when Boswell had taken a call, immediately leaving the meeting without so much as a goodbye.

Gunari and his soldiers made their way to the northern suburbs of Chicago to pick up Milosh and Shandor after the boys escaped and called him. The boys guided him back to the safe house, which he and his men hit with the fury of a hurricane—but to no avail. The house had been abandoned. Kat and Ian had been taken somewhere else.

Gunari spent the next several hours trying to gather information. He sent out his people to beat the bushes, going into bars and hangouts in neighborhoods populated by Roma. In America, Roma tended to live in ethnic enclaves, often in the same apartment buildings rather than in rural tent camps as his tribe did in France. While wary of strangers, the common bonds of language and extended family—as well as buying food and drinks and spreading around the possibility of monetary reward—slowly opened the hearts and willingness of the locals. Soon, bits of intelligence began trickling in from the New York and Miami Roma whom Gunari had recruited.

Gunari continued to call Boswell every fifteen minutes or so, just to let him know he was still out there...still hunting him. He wanted to get inside the man's head. Maybe John would come to his senses, he thought, and turn over Ekaterina and Ian, and negotiate the return of the exhibits. Hopefully, Boswell would realize that was his only viable exit plan. Anything else wouldn't end well for him.

The night and early morning passed with no progress.

JOHN BOSWELL HAD RALLIED his troops and evacuated the safe house. Everyone was moved to a warehouse near the river that served as a holding area for an import business which, while it did maintain legitimate pursuits, also covered for the import and export of more questionable products.

The floor of the warehouse was a maze of pallets stacked with boxes bundled in plastic wrap. On the second floor, which was a smaller section of the building, Kat and Ian sat on chairs, still tied to them and pushed up facing the wall so that they could not reach each other's bindings.

Once everything was secure, Boswell sent home to sleep as many people as he could, while keeping a sufficient number on site for security. He knew Gunari was looking for him and would spare no resources to find him. That meant it was just a matter of time. When the time was right, Boswell would contact him and arrange another meeting, but he first needed a plan and a separate place to meet. A neutral location, but secure, with a number of escape routes. Someplace he could see coming the forces Gunari would have arrayed against him. A place where he could arrange his own security.

He did not have such a spot readily at hand, so he spent some time trying to locate places that would fit his needs. Also, he wanted his people rested and alert after the events of last night, so while he needed to speed things up, he also had to buy time. With every minute that passed he had to assume that Gunari was that much closer, that much angrier. He had turned off the ringer on his cell phone, but still it buzzed annoyingly every fifteen minutes or so, displaying Gunari's number on the screen, as a constant reminder that he was stalking him.

Boswell had two things Gunari wanted to be returned: his family and the exhibits. This gave Boswell a little bargaining power. But he had offended the French clan leader and at least partially reneged on their arrangement, which diminished his position. He just wanted a clear exit strategy out of this mess. But for the moment, he couldn't see one. Waiting for a better location or a strong strategy would eat up time he didn't have. Better to see what opportunity might come out of a negotiation.

He was just about to call Gunari and begin the negotiations to reconvene their meeting when his phone buzzed again. He glanced at it, expecting to see Gunari's number, but was surprised to see a different one. Still, it was one he recognized.

"Hello, Excellency," Boswell answered, knowing who it was.

"We have new instructions, John. The merchandise needs to be secured but the packages you are holding are no longer of use to the buyer and should be disposed of immediately."

"That may be a problem. We have another interested party, one from across the pond, that has a strong interest in both packages. I have been trying to reach a resolution."

"That doesn't matter to me or to the buyer. Get rid of everything. No exceptions. And make it clean. Nobody wants this coming back."

"At this point, I don't know if I can make it clean. I might need help."

"I'll see if there are any resources available, but you will likely need to take care of this on your own. You understand what is at stake?"

"Yes, but I'm not sure you do. The other interested party is not without assets. There will be ramifications either way. Fallout is unavoidable at this stage. The acquisition team is no longer under my control. All I have is the merchandise and the follow-up team from the other interested party."

"Yes, I understand, and I believe the buyer does, too. Clean up your mess. I will get back to you about assistance as soon as I can."

The line went dead. Boswell set down the phone. He was dismayed at the instructions. This had not been anticipated as part of the transaction. But it also gave him the glimmer of an idea. A way out.

Nothing like a common enemy to unite forces. *The enemy of my enemy is my friend.* If he could convince Gunari that he himself were being used and coerced, then maybe Gunari could help him get out of his current predicament.

He picked up the phone, scanned his recent calls list, and tapped Gunari's number.

TWENTY-FIVE

Karl had been walked back to the museum by the guards and the two men in suits, then led into what he assumed was a makeshift interrogation room, one that looked like it had been a storage closet at one time.

The only things in the room now were a gray metal table and two metal folding chairs, one on each side of the table. Karl had been brought in, asked to sit in the chair furthest from the door, and then the four guards left, locking the door behind them. Karl waited a few moments for them to come back, then got up to check the door. It appeared that the knobs had been reversed, making it so that the keyholes were on the inside of the closet instead of the outside. He took a mental inventory of what he had in his pockets. A lock pick set was not among them. It was still in his room with his other belongings. Also, they had taken his camera. Poor planning on his part, but he hadn't anticipated being abducted before Hana's interview. He had expected to be at the interview with her.

He looked through the peephole in the door. It was also

reversed. One could use it to see into the room but not out of it. It was odd that a storage closet even had a peephole, much less one intended to look into the closet from the hall.

He checked his phone. There were no service bars. The room seemed to be blocking all incoming cellular signals, with no other way to contact anyone on the outside.

After about forty-five minutes, Karl heard the faint sound of footsteps approaching. Getting up, he put his finger over the peephole and waited. There was a pause, which he figured was when someone was looking into the blocked peephole. Then there was a knock, just two quick raps, and a voice from the other side of the door said, "Please return to your seat. We are not here to play games."

Karl really wasn't in an advantageous position and didn't want to compromise Hana, reasoning it would be better at this point to go along with the program. He took his seat.

He then heard the door being unlocked, and the two men in suits came in. One of them relocked the door with a key. They apparently didn't want their "guest" making a break for it.

Karl took a good look at the two men. The first one in the door was taller, lean and muscular. His tie was loosened. He had a guarded wariness that marked him as probably being, or having been, a soldier. Karl noticed the bulge under his suit coat where a shoulder holster would be, and the clip of a sheathed folding knife on his belt. He probably had other weapons on his person and was clearly dangerous.

The other one had the look of an accountant, wearing bifocals with a gray fringe to his balding head. He had several pens in his shirt pocket but no sign of a weapon, as far as Karl could see. This man took the seat across the table from Karl. While he had come in second, he seemed to be in charge, and spoke first. The other man leaned against the door, listening in silence.

"Well, sir, like the proverbial cat, your curiosity may have gotten the better of you. You may call me Mr. Jones. My associate here is Mr. Smith. Please tell me your name."

"Karl Dengler."

"Your full name?"

"Karl Gustav Dengler"

"And your birthdate?"

"Sixth February, 1994."

"And your social security number?"

"I don't have a social security number."

"You are not an American?"

"No."

"Where is your passport?"

"In the suitcase in my room."

The bespectacled man nodded to Mr. Smith, who unlocked the door, stepped outside, and immediately returned with Karl's suitcase and backpack, depositing them on the floor. He relocked the door.

"Your passport was not in your suitcase," Mr. Jones said stoically. "That was the first time you have lied to me. I hope it will be the last. Shall we proceed?"

Karl nodded. "As you wish." Clearly, they had retrieved the things from his room and gone through them. Fortunately, there was no identifying information in them, at least that he could recall.

"How long have you worked for *Le Monde*?"

"I don't work for *Le Monde*. I work directly with Ms. Sinclair."

"Yes, well, that explains why *Le Monde* hasn't heard of you."

So, they had been checking up on him. He needed to be

careful. Mr. Jones had let him know that fact deliberately. *How much did they know?*

Mr. Jones's coat pocket buzzed quietly. He took out his phone and glanced at the text message.

"You do not seem to have much of a presence in social media, Mr. Dengler. No presence at all, in fact. Most curious. That makes you very different from nearly everyone else of your generation. Why is that?"

"Just not a social media kind of guy, I suppose."

"There's that. Or maybe there's another reason. Something to hide, perhaps? Some particular reason to be invisible?" The man seemed to be talking to himself more than to Karl. He tapped out a message on his phone and set it on the table face down.

"Why does your phone work in here and mine doesn't?" Karl asked.

"Let's just say I have a special phone. But I'm the one asking the questions. Your passport, Mr. Dengler...you wouldn't happen to have it on your person, would you?"

"No, I'm afraid not." He had, in fact, left it on the plane when they arrived in Dallas. However, he did have Swiss Guard identification in his wallet. A fact he really didn't want this guy to find out, at least not until he figured out what was going on.

"Well, before we get to the unpleasantness of having Mr. Smith look for it on your person, I'd like to ask a few more questions. You are probably wondering what this is all about. You were instructed that there was to be no photography within the museum. The tour guide swears she never saw you raise your camera to take a picture inside the museum. Instead, you spent most of the tour on your phone, with your camera hanging over your shoulder. We looked at your camera, Mr. Dengler. It was affixed with a right-angle attachment and was set to link wirelessly with a cell phone app. You took a lot of pictures...very unusual pictures: security camera positions, door sensors, locks, motion detectors, as well as many shots of the most prized exhibits, the oldest and rarest. And then you were caught looking through a doorway that you should not have been near and may have seen things you were not invited to see. So, I ask you, Mr. Dengler: what *did* you see?"

Karl was silent.

"All right, if you aren't willing to discuss this like a civilized person, we may just have to discuss it in other ways. I'll give you one more opportunity to be forthcoming."

Karl remained silent. He was hoping these people were the type he suspected they might be, and that they had followed the protocols he suspected they had.

Mr. Jones's phone buzzed again. He picked it up and read the text.

"It seems, Mr. Dengler, that you are something of a ghost. Since you are not American, we checked you out through Interpol and a few other databases, but you are not in any of them. That's highly unusual. You should have pinged somewhere."

Karl waited.

Then Jones's phone rang with an incoming call. Picking it up, he answered, "Jones..." There was a pause while someone was speaking. "I see." Another pause. "You're kidding me? Which security flags?" Pause. "Okay, I'm standing by."

Jones set the phone down and looked at Karl. "Who are you, really?"

Karl just smiled.

The phone rang again. Once more he answered it. "Jones..."

Karl heard a loud command, "Put us on speaker!" Jones

lay the phone on the table and tapped the speaker button. An authoritative voice filled the room.

"Mr. Dengler, are you there?"

"Who is asking?"

"Mr. Dengler, I am the Deputy Director of Operations for the Central Intelligence Agency. I have on the line with me Colonel Scarpa, Commander of the Vatican Swiss Guard. Mr. Jones, am I to understand that you are holding their Sergeant Karl Dengler?"

"Yes, although we had yet to establish his bona fides."

"And how is it that he came to be in your care?"

"He was on a tour of the public-facing facility, and may have seen part of the operations here."

"I see. Sergeant Dengler, have you been mistreated in any way?"

"No, sir. Mr. Jones and I have been having quite the cordial conversation while I waited for him to trip the security flags trying to figure out who I am. I knew that would alert Colonel Scarpa."

Colonel Scarpa's voice came on the line. "Why is it always you, Dengler? I've had a short conversation with the CIA's deputy director here. This is a few steps above your pay grade, but we'll get it sorted. You just sit tight for now. Answer their questions. I'll be back in touch as soon as possible."

"Yes, sir," Karl replied.

"Jones?" The deputy director came back on. "You may continue your discussion with Sergeant Dengler, but only with the utmost professionalism and decorum. There are going to be many eyes on this, and it needs to be handled carefully. Recognize that Sergeant Dengler has a special form of diplomatic immunity. We'll deal later with the fact that we didn't know he was in Texas. I have been assured by Colonel Scarpa that you will have his complete cooperation." Karl caught the dig at Colonel Scarpa and knew he hadn't heard the last of this. Scarpa knew he was assigned to guard Michael in Chicago, but Karl hadn't called in the trip to Texas.

The call ended. Jones slowly picked up the phone from the table and arched his eyebrows.

"Curiouser and curiouser, Sergeant Dengler of the Vatican Swiss Guard," Jones said with emphasis. "I guess it's going to be that civilized discussion after all. So, tell me. What did you see?"

Karl frowned. He didn't want to tell this guy anything. But...since Karl now knew to whom he was talking—the CIA, along with the cooperation of his commandant of the Swiss Guard—he finally acceded to revealing what he'd seen during his and Hana's tour of Darwin's compound. He was curious to see their reaction, anyway.

"As Hana and I were walking through a corridor with our tour guide Brandie in the lead and me trailing behind, a door opened. A brief glance inside showed a lot of activity in the room behind it. Intrigued, I placed my foot as a door jamb to get a good look inside before the alarm tripped.

"Imagine my surprise, then, when I saw boxes marked 'Holy Bibles' being packed with M67 fragmentation grenades. Which begs the question: what would a Christian ministry be doing with hand grenades?"

CHAPTER

TWENTY-SIX

With a *rap-rap-rap* of her gavel, Judge Alice Hastings called the court to order. Michael resumed his seat next to Professor Anderson. He noted that a third chair had been brought to the defense table. Tom leaned over and gave Michael a friendly elbow in the ribs.

"I've got a surprise for you," Tom said just before being interrupted by Judge Hastings.

"Be seated and come to order. Now that the preliminary matters are concluded, I have the honor of formally introducing the participants in our legal exercise. My name is Dr. Alice Hastings, Dean of Loyola Law School, and I will be presiding over this trial. I'd like to introduce our jurors at this time. We have twelve volunteers, some from the law school, some from Loyola University, and a few from the community at large." She went on to name the twelve jurors and their positions in the school or the community, including Auxiliary Bishop Loveridge, Monsignor Abernathy from Holy Name Cathedral, and the Chaplain of Loyola University, Father Murray.

"Now, representing the prosecution, from the Vatican we have Bishop Vijay Sharma, Deputy Prefect of the Dicastery for the Doctrine of the Faith and Chief Inquisitor. Bishop Sharma has extensive education, training, and experience in canon law. However, to level the playing field somewhat, the matter today is being decided under the common law of England and the United States, using Federal Rules of Evidence. Defending the case will be Loyola's own Dr. Thomas Anderson, an expert on medieval legal systems and canon law who writes on the impact of historical cases on modern jurisprudence. The defendant could not ask for better representation.

"Finally, I would like to introduce the defendant himself, Galileo Galilei, who is being portrayed by none other than Professor Emeritus Dr. Luigi Bucatini, who holds a PhD in the philosophy of science from Harvard University and recently retired from his endowed chair at the University of Padua in Italy. Galileo and the impact of his discoveries on the fields of science, engineering and theology have been a keen interest of Professor Bucatini for most of his career."

The audience applauded as Bucatini—attired in full period garb appropriate to a financially struggling scientist and philosopher—entered the room through a side door, made bows toward the bench and the defense table, then feigned a scowl at the prosecution as he ambled over to his seat next to Professor Anderson.

Michael realized he was staring with his mouth open, completely surprised by this turn of events. He knew Luigi as the kindly old newspaper vendor down the street from the Vatican, whom he saw many mornings on his daily run. And while he knew that Luigi had been a philosophy professor at the University of Padua, he had no idea he was such a credentialed scholar.

Luigi leaned back, stretched an arm out behind Professor Anderson and gave Michael a friendly punch to the shoulder.

"Surprised?" Luigi almost giggled.

"You are full of surprises, my friend."

Dean Hastings continued. "Galileo Galilei stands accused of heresy, and heresy is not a modern criminal offense, therefore when the case is wrapped up, I will give you the law which the parties have agreed applies to the case. We will be proceeding under modern rules of evidence and procedure. With introductions out of the way, we will now proceed to opening statements. Since the prosecution bears the burden of proof, it will go first. Bishop Sharma, you may proceed."

Sharma rose and slowly walked to the center of the courtroom, focusing his attention on the jury.

"Ladies and gentlemen, I want you to forget everything you have ever heard about Galileo. Yes, he is famous—or should I say, infamous. And around such figures there becomes attached a great body of legend and myth, only tenuously rooted in reality, and which can only distract you from the truth. So forget what you know, or think you know, about Galileo. As jurors, you must decide the case based only on the evidence before you. You will be exposed to exhibits and facts that have perhaps not been seen in centuries. And you will have a chance to weigh this evidence against the charges that were leveled against him.

"In addition, I want you to forget all you know, or think you know, about the Catholic Church. The Catholic Church is not on trial here, although to hear some people speak, you might think it was. Indeed, ladies and gentlemen, there are people out there, and perhaps in this very room, who would like to put the Catholic Church on trial for her many crimes throughout history, real or imagined, using Galileo as the vehicle. But we have neither the time nor the tools to accomplish that mission, nor is this the forum for it. Many people, even some people within it, hate the Church, and that bias can cloud their judgment. As jurors, you have agreed to hear this case as free from bias as humanly possible. We all, each of us, have our own biases. I need all of you to look inside yourselves and at least acknowledge if you have any ill will or grudge—indeed, any disagreement with the Catholic Church whatsoever—and agree that to the best of your ability you will set those feelings aside for the duration of this trial. You are certainly entitled to your feelings. I am not trying to change them, but both Galileo and the Church need your most unbiased deliberation in this matter, and both are entitled to it.

"This includes the Inquisition. As a disciplinary arm of the Church, the Inquisition has a storied history, especially as depicted in the popular media of today. But we must weigh the actions of the times and the motivations of the actors against the times in which they lived and not against the values or principles of the present day. What we might do today, from a different perspective and with different information, is an unfair ruler with which to measure the past. So I want you to forgive me for wearing the title of Inquisitor. I did not choose it. It came with the job. But the job of a prosecutor is an important one, and I am not ashamed to be one. Without people to enforce the rules, laws would mean nothing, and we would have anarchy.

"But now, ladies and gentlemen, fellow investigators of the truth—for that is what you are—let me speak of the charges. Science is not on trial here, no. And the Church is not on trial either. What *is* on trial is a man—and he is on trial not for following science, but for breaking his word and defying the Church. At the time of Galileo's discoveries, the questions he raised and the positions he took, while they have eventually proven true, were revolutionary. The Church, if it changes at all, moves very slowly. And Galileo was not a patient man. He wanted the world to change in accord with his opinions immediately, as he was so convinced of the rightness of his positions. But the rest of the world was not ready for so rapid a change. Even science itself says that before a different position can be accepted, it must be thoroughly tested.

"In 1616, when Galileo was most vociferously advocating his revolutionary discoveries, he was brought before the Church, before Cardinal Bellarmine who was an agent of the Inquisition, and before many other Church officials. After listening to his impassioned pleas, they formally admonished him not to advocate, teach, or defend the heliocentric model of the universe until further notice. This was to give the Church and the scientific community time to catch up and verify Galileo's findings. The man himself agreed to this injunction, and there will be documentary proof provided to you in that regard."

At this, Tom and Luigi exchanged confused glances and turned to Michael. In a whisper, Tom inquired, "Are you aware of any proof of the actual injunction? I was not aware it had ever been found."

"I don't remember seeing any actual injunction," Michael replied, "and nobody who's looked at the exhibits has mentioned it."

Sharma continued. "But that alone was not Galileo's crime. He went on to write, in a letter published and widely circulated, that should the Church have a disagreement with one of his opinions, it ought to change the way it interprets Scripture. That, ladies and gentlemen, is heresy, plain and simple. Christ himself gave to the Church its authority, its holy chrism, to be free from teaching errors on matters of faith and morals. If the Church was wrong about the interpretation of Scripture, that would invalidate its authority. Indeed, it would invalidate the very nature of the Church itself. No, this case is not about the Church being against science or even being slow to adopt new and revolutionary scientific claims. Instead, it is about one man who thought he was smarter than all the other scientists and churchmen of his time and more insightful than the Church itself.

"And for those things, Galileo is as guilty today as he was then."

TWENTY-SEVEN

T om turned to Michael and whispered, "That was not at all what I was expecting. Are you sure there wasn't any mention of a written injunction?"

Michael shuffled through the pre-marked exhibits another time, looking for one with too many pages or some other indication that the injunction had been missed.

"Mr. Anderson," Dean Hastings called out, "you may proceed."

"May we have just a moment, Your Honor?"

"A very brief one, Mr. Anderson."

"Thank you, Your Honor."

Michael went back to the list of documents on the transit invoice. He checked them against the invoice, one by one. Tom turned to his own exhibit list which he had prepared for his trial notebook from the exhibits he had received. There was nothing in there about an injunction.

"Mr. Anderson, the jury is waiting…"

"Yes, Your Honor." Tom turned to Luigi. "Have you ever heard that the injunction had been found?"

"No, not that I am aware of."

"Oh, jeez," Michael exclaimed softly. "Here it is, on the transit invoice. But I swear that I didn't hear about or even see this entry either when we packed the exhibits in Rome or when we unpacked them at the museum."

Tom grabbed the invoice, looking at where Michael indicated the entry was.

"You signed the invoice at both ends. They are going to say we had it and lost it. I'll bet Sharma has a copy. I'm going to have to ask him for a copy of his. If he'll even give me one at this point. He is going to say he got it from us. How could this happen?"

"Mr. Anderson, it's time," the judge called out.

Michael said, "Kat read me the invoice as we checked it against the exhibits. I saw what we had, she checked off the list, and I signed it. She either missed it, both times, or skipped it for some reason, but I know I didn't see it. I need to talk to Kat."

"Where is she?"

"I don't know. She had to go take care of some family business and I haven't heard from her."

"Find her. We need to know what happened." Tom turned to the Court. "Your Honor, there seems to be a problem locating one of the exhibits to which Bishop Sharma referred."

"Well, Mr. Anderson, as I understand it, your side provided all the exhibits and verified them at the museum. We will have to deal with that later. The jury would like to hear your opening statement now. Please proceed."

"Yes, Your Honor." Tom stood, took a deep breath, and turned to the jury.

"Integrity. Integrity is going to be the touchstone of this case. Integrity and trust. A man is presumed innocent until and unless he is proven guilty in a court of law. Galileo comes to us innocent. We do not have to prove that he is innocent. But not only that, the prosecution has to prove his guilt beyond a reasonable doubt. Those two concepts, the presumption of innocence and the burden of proof, combine to create a third, implied concept, which is that Galileo is due the benefit of a doubt. If there is a question, an ambiguity, any uncertainty in any of the evidence, you must go back to the presumption of innocence and the burden of proof and ask yourself: of the two ways of looking at the evidence, one favoring guilt and one favoring innocence—unless the prosecution has proven that the evidence favors guilt beyond, yes, *beyond any reasonable doubt*—then you are required to take the interpretation that favors innocence.

"Let me give you an example. The other day, my little boy was going to go out to play, and when I let him get up from the breakfast table, I told him, 'Don't slam the door on the way out.' Because he always slams the door when he leaves. And he got up, grabbed his jacket and headed out, and then BANG, I heard the door slam. Boy, I tell you, I was mad. I had just warned him not to do that. I ran out the door, onto the porch, and stood there looking for him. And BANG, a little gust of wind slammed the door behind me. I hadn't slammed it; I just hadn't closed it yet. Now, I didn't *see* my son slam the door. I have evidence that the door might have slammed itself. But the boy has a habit of slamming the door. How do I proceed? Do I punish him? If it were a criminal case, I couldn't, because there are two ways to interpret the evidence: one that he slammed it, and one that he didn't. And I haven't proven beyond a reasonable doubt that he did slam it.

"That's how this works. If the evidence against Galileo has more than one way to look at it, and both ways are reasonable, the prosecution must prove not just that their position is more likely, but that the other ways are not reasonable. If the other ways are reasonable and possible interpretations, then the presumption of innocence says you *must* take Galileo's side. If there is any doubt, perhaps a question or an uncertainty, then Galileo is entitled to the benefit of that uncertainty. You start on Galileo's side until and unless the prosecution convinces you there is no other reasonable alternative.

"Now, back to trust and integrity. I don't trust the prosecution. And you shouldn't either. Galileo deserves that. You have to critically evaluate every piece of evidence they bring to you. Every piece of evidence needs to stand or fall on its own, regardless of any endorsement by the prosecution. I know he's a priest. A bishop, even. You would think that you could trust him. You want to trust him. You are supposed to be able to trust him. He holds a position of trust.

"But don't do it. And as much as I would like you to, don't trust me either! Nothing the lawyers say is evidence. Our job is to present the evidence or challenge the evidence, but not to *be* the evidence. We will try to convince you to see the evidence a certain way, using every trick of rhetoric and psychology we know. See through it. Weigh the evidence yourselves.

"Each and every one of you on the jury is important. Your opinions are important. And we need each of you to evaluate the evidence separately and independently. The prosecution only gets to win if all twelve people, independently, are convinced that he is guilty.

"Which brings me back to the evidence in this case, and what Galileo is charged with. Galileo has already been vindicated by history. He is charged with one thing—heresy. Heresy is holding beliefs contrary to the accepted doctrine of the Church. What beliefs did Galileo have? That the Sun, and not the Earth, is the center of our solar system, and that the Earth and the other planets revolved around the Sun. This was not some crackpot idea. Galileo did not invent the telescope, but he refined it and adapted it, and pointed it at the heavens, and he recognized the signs he saw there and what they meant. Galileo did not invent the idea that the Sun is at the center of our solar system. That idea was known as far back as the ancient Greeks. It was written about by Copernicus a century before Galileo's writings. It was recognized by Galileo's contemporary Johannes Kepler.

"And, as it turns out, Galileo was right. And the Church, which operates its own Vatican Observatory, would never claim that Galileo was wrong. So, what was Galileo's crime? Being right before his time? The prosecution would like to shift your focus from Galileo's proven discoveries to his conflict with the Church. He wants you to believe that Galileo was guilty of the heresy of believing that God left the truths of the universe open for any to behold, therefore challenging the doctrine that the Church alone was privy to the truth; and that whatever the Church said about Scripture was absolutely and indelibly true, regardless of whether it disagreed with the evidence of our God-given senses. But the Church has changed on that, too.

"Galileo argued that where scientific observation and literal interpretation of Scripture conflict, that we should look for a poetical or theological interpretation of the words since the Scriptures are concerned not with the physical matters of this world, but with the spiritual matters of the next. The Bible is a book about salvation, not science. And today, the Church agrees with that, too, and has moved to a 'historical-critical' interpretation of the Bible rather than a purely literal one—which you will note is a position championed by St. Augustine of Hippo Regius, one of the most revered Fathers of the Church.

"The prosecution would like you to put on your seventeenth-century hats and decide this case like seventeenth-century citizens, deferential to the authority of the Church. It is his position that in a conflict between the Church and an individual, the Church should win every time. Because in his mind the Church can never be wrong. History disagrees. But more importantly, in this room, this courtroom, the Church does not enjoy that veneer of infallibility. Instead, Galileo enjoys the presumption of innocence and must be proven guilty *beyond a reasonable doubt*—with facts, not fiats."

Tom returned to his seat and glanced over at Bishop Sharma, who had a smug grin on his face. He was up to something.

Tom whispered to Michael. "Find Kat. I've got a bad feeling about this."

TWENTY-EIGHT

S itting alone on a park bench under the thinning canopy of silver maple trees on the south side of the Chicago River, just east of North Columbus Drive, Gunari had to admit, Boswell had chosen the location for this meeting wisely.

Gunari could hear the traffic of upper and lower East Wacker Drive behind him, the split-level roadway amplified even further by the additional level below. He had been instructed to get out of his car alone on upper Wacker and walk down the metal stairs to the Riverwalk two stories below. While he had tried to position his people in as many vantage points as possible, he knew Boswell would also have the area well covered. He was aware he could be seen from every direction, including from across the river. There could even be snipers, as there were many places for them to hide. So, he sat alone on the bench and waited.

Fifteen minutes later a large craft pulled up to the landing: a sixty-foot Schaefer 600 motor yacht. Gunari could see several people on the boat, including Boswell, who was standing on the bridge deck holding a cell phone to his ear.

Just then, Gunari's cell phone rang. It was Boswell.

"Hello, John. I have to tell you, I'm not comfortable getting on your boat. It's bad enough I have to be sitting on this bench by myself, and so exposed."

"Oh, Gunari. Don't be so worried. I can see you have a lot of people with you. As you probably suspect, we've had this area under surveillance for hours. We've marked everyone who has come into the area and remained in place. I know where your people are and how many you have here. But I understand your concerns. Look, we need to speak privately. I'll have everyone get off the boat but me. You can come on board and verify that the boat is empty, then we'll go for a little sightseeing trip and talk, just you and me. That's as fair and neutral as I can make it."

"I still don't like it, John. This is your turf. You have all the advantages, especially on a boat. I suggest you just return Kat and her friend to me right now or there will be consequences."

"Kat and her companion are nearby. But right now, despite all those advantages you think I have, they're the only things keeping you from killing me, and I can't give them back to you, as much as I might want to, until we have an agreement. I know you're a man of your word, Gunari. I'm sorry the circumstances have played out this way. But there are some things you just don't know that I need to share with you, and when you've heard them, well, I think you might see things differently. At least, I hope you will."

There was silence on the line as Gunari contemplated what to do. If he had the man killed now, he might not be able to get Kat and Ian back at all. Boswell clearly had the advantage.

"Look, Gunari, I can tell you are not comfortable with this, so I'll tell you what...call out a few of your men. I'll give you my boat crew as collateral. You can hold them while we talk. These are good men. Family. People I care about and don't want to lose."

"Okay, but I'm not just holding them here where you have people to rescue them. They come off the boat, get searched, then go for a ride in one of my vans. No phones, no weapons, no tracking devices. They leave all that on the boat. Anyone comes ashore with any of that, and the deal's off, your men are forfeit and you are next. I'm not kidding around here. You have no wiggle room, John. You'll be lucky if I don't strangle you with my bare hands."

"All right, calm down now. Let's stay objective and remember what's at stake here. Are we good?"

"No, we are not good. But I accept your plan. Send your people out."

Several men came out on deck and made a show of putting their cell phones on the table. A couple of them went back inside the cabin and returned, holding their jackets open to show there were no weapons under them. They climbed from the boat to the landing and walked toward Gunari, who dialed a number on his phone and gave instructions to his people. A like number of men appeared from the places along the Riverwalk where they had been stationed. The men from the boat walked over to a picnic table near where he was standing and sat down. His men took up overwatch positions. When he was satisfied, Gunari got up and walked over to the boat.

"Come on aboard," John called down to him. "Careful getting on, it's a bit wet. You can inspect the cabins. There are two decks: the one you came aboard on, and one below. I swear there is nobody on board but you and me."

Gunari climbed aboard the boat and went inside the main cabin. The Miami crew had provided weapons for Gunari and his people, and Gunari took out a Glock 42 he'd tucked in his waistband and carried it down by his side. He inspected the entire boat carefully, on both decks, but found nobody else on board. Returning the pistol to his waistband, he joined Boswell on the bridge.

"Satisfied?"

"More or less," Gunari replied.

"Look, I know you have no reason to trust me at this point. I'm grateful that you are being accommodating. I realize it looks like you have no choice, but I also know you could kill me now and then try to get your people back from my men. Or you could try to take me hostage here on the boat. I see you're armed and I know you have a lot of people nearby. But we are still family, Gunari, and that still means something or you would not be here. I respect that. And you know it. Are you ready?"

"Let's get on with it."

Boswell had been keeping the boat at idle, holding its fenders against the landing. He put the throttles in reverse and gave the boat a little gas to steer the bow into the channel, and once the boat was headed out, he gently pushed the throttles forward and the boat pulled away from shore. He guided the craft under the FDR Bridge then angled it across the river, coming to a stop against North Pier.

"Okay, this is far enough."

"What's going on?" Gunari asked, reaching for the grip of his Glock but not pulling it out.

"A gesture of good faith. Look on the shore."

Gunari turned to look, and he now saw Kat and a young man, whom he presumed to be her friend, Ian, sitting on a wooden shipping crate on the far side of the dock. A few yards away, a couple of men stood smoking cigarettes next to a beat-up old van, keeping watch over them.

"Your niece and her friend will join us shortly if our discussion goes as I hope it does. But I wanted you to know they are here, and I am willing to give them back to you. I apologize for how this went down. I feel like I've been caught in the middle. But I want to make it up to you."

"You want to show me good faith? Have them come aboard now. We both know they are not armed. And you already know that I am. Your safety will not be any more compromised with them aboard than it is now."

Boswell considered it for a moment, then waved to the men on the dock. They appeared to say something to Kat and Ian, both of whom got up and started walking toward the boat.

"Before she gets here, I have to tell you that she got smart with one of my men and he smacked her. They didn't know who she was at the time. When your two boys escaped, they'd already taken their revenge on the guard. He won't be the same. But I'll deal with him myself when this is over."

Gunari's eyes flinched in anger. "By God, if he hurt her…" He left the threat unspoken.

Kat and Ian got on the boat and came up to the bridge. Gunari noticed that she had a purple bruise on the side of her face, apparently from when she was hit.

He wrapped her in a big hug, then held her back and took a good look at her face.

"Are you alright, Ekaterina?"

"Yes, Uncle. It just looks worse than it is. It will be gone in a few days."

"And your friend?"

"*Voivode*, this is Ian. He works at the Vatican Archive along with me. He's okay, too."

Gunari reached out his arm and shook hands with the young man. "Good to meet you, Ian." Then he turned to Boswell.

"All right, John. I accept your apology. Take us upriver. Then we can talk.

Boswell headed the boat back the way they had come.

"So, Gunari," he began as they motored up the river, "this job, the guy who retained me, he is an old friend. I grew up with him. He's in a kind of special position now. One I did not expect to be getting assignments from. He's protected some of my people when they needed it. And I owed him. It sounds to me like he's getting orders from someone else in his organization, which on its own is surprising. Normally I would not divulge this information or identify a client to anyone, but he changed the contract after the job was done, then tried to add an extra condition.

"He said he had orders from his buyer. I assume he's talking about the person who was supposed to gather the merchandise. Anyway, he knew about the boys and Ekaterina and her friend. I don't know how. Maybe he has a mole in my organization, it wouldn't surprise me. But what *did* surprise me was when he ordered that we tie up the loose ends, all four of them.

"No!" Gunari said reflexively.

"That's when I pushed back, of course. If this had been some other job, some other subcontractors, well, then maybe, and for a whole lot more money. But I couldn't take down your boys or these two. I just couldn't. I needed time to figure out what to do. And then it hit me. We don't need to be on opposite sides of this. We need to be on the same side, Gunari. I wish I had known your niece was here in Chicago. She kind of walked into a mess."

"That's all right," Gunari said. "At first I didn't know she was here, either." Boswell glanced over at Kat, who was sitting with Ian at the back of the bridge. "But she wasn't over here for the job or the boys. She was actually here with her boss, bringing exhibits here from Rome for a conference. If I had known what you needed my sons for, I would not have sent them. Ekaterina's boss is an old friend of mine. He has history with the boys, and he did right by them and me. More than once, in fact. He is a man of honor and integrity. I would never have allowed the boys to work against him."

"This job was very compartmentalized," Boswell said. "They were never told what they were taking, just how to find the merchandise and where to take it when they were done. Don't blame them. Anyway, I have orders from the client to eliminate both of them and these two. That's why I'm giving them back to you. If I don't have them, well, I can't eliminate them. We'll have to make it look like you came and snatched them back before I had a chance to deal with them. Then it's on you to get the four of them away. But to be honest, I am worried about them. My client's organization is huge—global, in fact. If someone even higher up has exposure and wants them gone, there might not be any safe place on earth."

"My God. Who *is* your client?"

Boswell's phone rang. He looked at caller ID.

"Well, speak of the devil."

CHAPTER
TWENTY-NINE

Young Viggo Pisano had been watching the proceedings in Chicago from the very beginning, but now that the judge had called for a break, he needed to accomplish certain duties that required him to leave his office before he had to make a dash for school.

Pushing a cart from office to office once a week, it was his responsibility to collect DDF documents for shredding that had been secured in special containers. Each office had a locked metal box with an insertion slot. When a document required shredding for confidentiality's sake, it was placed into the locked box through the slot. For each box, Viggo had one key, and the department prefect had the other. It was Viggo's responsibility to open each box, remove the documents, and place them in a large envelope, seal it shut, and label it showing the office it came from and the date he picked them up. A special safe was situated next to the shredding apparatus to store the pending envelopes. After thirty days, he would feed the envelopes stored in that safe into an industrial shredding machine.

It was a cumbersome and time-consuming procedure,

but the DDF prefect had instituted it after a set of very important documents had been inadvertently destroyed in an office shredder. Now, individual shredders were prohibited, and the thirty-day delay in shredding acted as a physical safety backup. If any mistake was caught within thirty days, the documents could be recovered from the folders in the safe.

He tended to do his weekly collection rounds late in the day after everyone had left, so as not to disturb anyone. Though it was forbidden, he found himself perusing the documents before he put them into their envelopes and sealing them. He found the process tantalizing, learning much about what was going on throughout various Church departments from his readings. Things he had no business knowing about, but found too compelling to stop the practice.

As he made his way through the offices collecting the documents and filling his envelopes, he noted there was still a light on in the prefect's office. He imagined that the prefect might also be watching the proceedings from Chicago, since his Chief Deputy, Bishop Sharma, was leading the prosecution there. He moved on down the hallway, stopping at Sharma's office. Like the janitorial staff, Viggo was entrusted with master key access.

Once in Sharma's office, he opened the shredding box. He had emptied it right after Sharma left for Chicago, but routine was routine, and he always checked every office. So he checked Sharma's office, too, expecting it to be empty as it had been when he cleared it out last week—which is why he was surprised to see a couple of pages now sitting there. Viggo took them out and inspected them.

As he was reading what he found, he nearly fell back into a chair as he tried to take a seat.

The first document was a handwritten copy of the

injunction read to Galileo in 1616. Except this one had a bunch of strikeouts and insertions, like it was a draft of a document in process. It was written on modern paper, in what appeared to be bright-blue ballpoint pen. Viggo turned to the second page. There were blank spaces for the signatures of Cardinal Bellarmine and Galileo. Viggo was baffled as to what to make of it. He looked further among the documents. The remaining page was a letter addressed to the prefect. He read the letter and was shocked to his core. Now he knew exactly what the draft injunction was intended for.

The letter read:

Your Eminence,

I am writing to explain my conduct in the upcoming trial in Chicago if things do not go according to plan. I have become aware that a restorationist in the Secret Archive is having an inappropriate relationship with a fellow employee. This information came to me through the confessional. The restorationist is a ward of the prefect, a gypsy who has a checkered past. She was implicated in several high-profile forgeries but was never charged. Father Dominic seems to have intervened on her behalf with the Art Squad. I have used her indiscretions to coerce her into doing a bit of work for me, recreating the missing injunction of Galileo before Bellarmine in 1616. It is my intention to use this recreated document to change the focus of the trial and win it for our side. I have made arrangements to make it appear that the injunction was lost in the archives and just recently found in preparation for the conference. I hope to embarrass Father Dominic with this information in order to discredit him and draw attention to the rank nepotism that got him his position, to the detriment of both Dominic and his "father." Should my plan be discovered, this letter will absolve you of any knowledge of the plot. I did not inform you of my intentions before-

*hand and am only writing now to prevent my actions from
implicating you. Hopefully, I will be successful and there will be
no need for this letter.*

Veritas vos liberabit,

Bishop Vijay Sharma

Deputy Prefect

Dicastery for the Doctrine of the Faith

It was not signed in the space above Sharma's name, but
that might not be expected on a document that was found
in the shredding box. Viggo held the document in his hand,
trembling. Was there another signed copy somewhere? Was
this really from Sharma, or had someone written it for him
to deflect blame away from the prefect if the trial went
sideways?

Sharma could not have put these documents in the
shredding box. He was in Chicago, and Viggo knew the box
had been empty right after he left. If things went badly for
Sharma in Chicago and his fraud was revealed, Church
authorities would certainly search his office and find these
documents in the shredding container. Viggo would be
questioned about his habits in collecting the documents and
it would be discovered that he had already emptied the box
after Bishop Sharma left. Meaning someone here would be
in trouble for those documents. So that person would try to
retrieve them first, and if they were missing, would figure
out that Viggo had collected them, as was his job, but might
speculate that he had read them, too. Which he had. And he
could be in real trouble then.

There wasn't time to figure out what to do. He had to be
in class in less than an hour. He took his cart and returned
briskly to his office, grabbed his backpack, stuffed the
controversial documents inside, and anxiously headed off
to school.

~

PROFESSOR AARON PEARCE stood at the front of the classroom in the John Felice Rome Center mentally preparing his lecture. His Reformation and Counter-Reformation class was one of his favorites, and he had a good group of engaged students. As he was about to start, he noted that Viggo Pisano, one of his students who worked in the Vatican, had come in a few minutes late, looking rather harried, which wasn't really like him. He was usually early.

As he lectured about the Galileo retrial—being a current topical event—Aaron had coincidentally commented on the injunction revealed during Bishop Sharma's opening statement. Given that the document—if it existed at all—had disappeared some time between 1616 and 1632, since it wasn't present at Galileo's trial for heresy, it seemed odd to him that it had only surfaced now, after some 400 years, just when the prosecution needed it for a high-profile re-enactment. Aaron also commented that he knew the prefect of the Secret Archive pretty well, and if a document of such importance had been rediscovered in his domain, Father Michael would have made a major announcement about it, not hidden it so that it could be revealed as surprise evidence. It posed many questions which Aaron hoped Thomas Anderson would raise during the trial.

After the lecture, during which Viggo had been uncharacteristically silent, his young student had lingered behind until all the other students had left the room.

"Professor Pearce, may I ask you a question?"

"Sure, Viggo. What's up? You don't seem yourself today."

Viggo chose his words carefully, looking slightly embarrassed. "So...what if you had done something wrong, but by doing so, you discovered really important information in the process?"

"Well, normally, I would say that you should keep that information to yourself since you are not supposed to have had it in the first place and that you should go to confession and discuss with your confessor how to make amends for your sin."

"What if it *is* my confessor about whom I learned the important information?"

"Well, that certainly complicates things, yes. Perhaps if I knew a little more about the specifics of your case, I could give you a better answer. I promise I will hold it in the strictest confidence."

Viggo took a deep breath and let it out. "Part of my weekly duties in the Dicastery for the Doctrine of the Faith is the collection of documents destined for shredding. But... um... sometimes I read them before I shred them. I *know* it is forbidden, but I can't help myself. I see them when I take them out of their shredding boxes in the offices. The text is right there, I scan it almost automatically, and often it is so interesting I just can't look away. But I was in Bishop Sharma's office tonight, and I found these." He took the documents out of his backpack and showed them to Aaron. "I think they mean that the injunction that Bishop Sharma has for the trial is a fake, and he had it made by someone in Father Dominic's office. He's going to use it against Father Dominic to make him look bad."

Aaron looked closely at the documents. Like the young novitiate, he couldn't believe his eyes.

"You're right, Viggo, this is very serious. Do you know whether it was Bishop Sharma who left these in his shredding box?"

"That's the thing. I emptied his box right after he left for Chicago. I checked it again tonight, mostly out of habit.

And because he hadn't been here, since I had already emptied the box, he *couldn't* have put them in there himself! Somebody else had to have done it."

"Viggo, I have to say, this smacks of conspiracy at a high level. I'll tell you what. I was leaving tomorrow to go to Chicago myself and see…well, to see somebody. Let me try to catch an earlier flight. I'll take these to Michael, to Father Dominic, I mean, and see what he thinks. If they're fakes, he deserves to know."

CHAPTER

THIRTY

Pastor Darwin was surprised that Hana had inquired about Remi. Clearly, she knew more than he assumed she did. Truth be told, all he'd heard from Remi was that he had not been successful in getting the letter out of the museum. The rest Darwin had learned from the news and from staff at the Jewel Ark Chapel in Chicago.

So, what to tell her about Remi, his acquisitions agent? Perhaps the truth would serve him well in this situation.

"Actually, I've heard very little from Remi. He is an independent contractor, after all. He accommodates me from time to time in locating items I desire, and assists in the negotiation for and logistics of acquisition. But since he is his own boss, I do not always hear from him until he has progress to report."

Hana observed him carefully. She knew Darwin had a tell when he was lying, something she had picked up when dealing with him in Jerusalem. A slight twitch to his eye that he probably wasn't even aware of. But she didn't see it now. He seemed to be telling the truth. And she also noticed he wasn't dropping his Gs in speech, presuming that he intentionally came off as a good old boy only when it served him.

"So you didn't tell him to get you Galileo's letter to Duchess Christina from the exhibits at the museum?" Hana knew it wasn't there but wanted to see if Darwin was aware of that.

"I did ask Father Dominic to sell me that letter. Though he denies it, I still believe the Vatican has the original, or at least an early copy. I asked him to bring it to Chicago. It was not among the exhibits I saw at the museum, though I understand it has already been alluded to in the trial." Darwin nodded toward the far end of the room, behind her. Hana turned to see one of the wall monitors silently displaying the trial, captions running across the bottom. "I asked Remi to assist me in acquiring it. I did not tell him how to accomplish his task. I am a results guy. The means he uses to accomplish his missions are his to answer for."

"Is that true for the other artifacts in your museum? You pay people for results, and you don't care how they get them? Isn't that being deliberately ignorant, from legal and ethical standpoints?"

"My goodness, darlin', that sounds so accusatory, like I'm setting up plausible deniability or something. But I do deny it. I am not responsible for what people do in my name if I don't tell them to do it. I didn't even hint about what means I was willing to accept. It's not my fault if people choose to sin in accomplishing their purpose—even a good purpose—on my behalf. Was God responsible for the Crusades? For the Salem witch trials? For Catholic missionaries bringing disease to the Native Americans? No, He was not. Sometimes people make poor choices in their pursuit of the good. And that is not the fault of the good;

it's just a fact that people are not perfect. We have to accept that and forgive it."

Somehow, Darwin made it sound like he was completely innocent of the lies, deceit, and theft he inspired in Remi and others. *Could he really be that deluded?*

"But you could, if you chose to, dictate that the people working for you, or inspired by you, *must* act morally in your name!"

"I could involve myself in a great many things, but that would impair my ability to focus on the things I am called to do. No, Ms. Sinclair. I determined a long time ago that I could not be responsible for the rest of the world. I serve Christ, but I am not Christ. That is not my role. I need only answer for myself."

"So, you did not tell Remi Shapiro to break into the museum and steal a copy of the letter to Grand Duchess Christine?"

"I have already said as much."

Hana watched him closely. No tell. He really believed he had done nothing wrong, and that Remi was acting on his own, even though he had done so in Darwin's name. He had completely rationalized it for himself. His conscience was clear.

Hana shifted to a new tack. "I have had some interesting conversations—or in some cases lack of conversation—with the staff here. Can you tell me where you get your employees?"

"That also seems vaguely accusatory, Ms. Sinclair. But I have nothing to hide. I get the majority of my staff for both the conference center and the rest of the compound from an employment agency here in Dallas. They assure me that everyone I employ is in the United States lawfully. I pay them for a certain number of employees. They handle the HR services for them—payroll, benefits, tax withholdings and such. I provide room and board so that I have full staff coverage for the guests. I think it makes us more of a family, and a more effective team. Also, the staff is always welcome to attend services here at the cathedral. We have a special staff room where services are transmitted on a big screen. They get to see and hear me as if they were in the front row. Better seats, I must say, than most people who come to the cathedral have. There are only so many front-row seats, and they are reserved for my most faithful supporters, o' course."

"So the staff can come and go as they please?"

"You bet. However, I don't see to their transportation needs. If they wanted to go somewhere, they would have to get there on their own. But there is little need to leave. They have food and lodging and various activities right here at the cathedral and the conference center. We have Bible studies, musical groups, sports teams, children's groups, teen groups, movie groups... They play frisbee and golf on the grounds. There's a fitness center on the first floor of this building, and a thrift shop. I don't prevent them from leaving. And I make it possible for them to live full lives without ever having to leave the compound."

Hana was somewhat taken aback by his answer. Once again, he had managed to take her question and completely turn it around. She had imagined him with a staff of indentured servants smuggled into the country illegally and indebted to him for their every need. He made it sound like he was a beneficent father looking out for his employees like they were not-so-distant relatives working for the family business. Again, he seemed completely sincere. Had she jumped to conclusions because she didn't like the guy? No. She was sure there was something going on here that didn't add up. Her journalistic senses had never failed her. There was one more approach to take. When all else fails, follow the money.

"So, running an operation like this must be vastly expensive. How do you manage it?"

"Ah, the old 'follow the money' approach, is it?" Hana tried hard not to let show the heat she felt going to her face. "Well, that's fine, too, honey. We have some very generous donors. Each Jewel Ark Chapel becomes self-sufficient within three years of inception. The conference center is self-supporting on conference fees alone. We sell advertising on our cable TV channel, which broadcasts every service here at the cathedral, as well as replays of services from some of the Jewel Ark Chapels around the world, as determined by local ratings and reviewed by our program directors, and in-house-produced Bible studies and documentaries. Some of the Jewel Ark Chapels are so successful that they tithe a portion of their proceeds back here to support our ministry. While there are some perks of recognition for our highest regular donors, nobody is required to pay anything to participate in any of the programs or activities here at the cathedral. We freely give, and the people we serve give freely as well. We support them spiritually, and they support us financially.

"Some people might call my lifestyle extravagant: the big house, the fancy cars, the private jet. But you know what? I'm hardly ever at the big house, I spend so much of my time here. The cars are comfortable, but I don't really drive much. I have a driver so I can focus the time spent moving around working on the next thing that needs my attention. The plane, well, you must know how much I travel and arranging all those flights to out-of-the-way airports all over the world. As you know yourself, travel by personal aircraft is so much more efficient. And when I'm not using it, the plane is flying medicine and relief supplies to desperate areas of the world.

"Ms. Sinclair, there's a good portion of the world that is sick from preventable diseases, hungry from mismanaged food distribution, thirsty for clean water, poorly clothed and unhoused. And the people we send out, funded by our ministry, are making a real difference in their lives. Here in the U.S., darlin', we live in the lap of opulence, relatively speaking. And we put on a feel-good show for wealthy patrons, so that we can inspire their generosity and repurpose their money so that we can make a difference in the lives of so many hurting people. That's our real calling. So you can think I'm one of those crazy, rich hypocritical televangelists, and to an extent, maybe I appear to be, but that's not all I am."

Darwin glanced at the clock on the wall. "I'm sorry, Ms. Sinclair, but I'm out of time for this interview. I hope you got what you came for. Actually, I hope you got more than what you came for. Brandie will take you back to the conference center and arrange your transportation back to the airport. I'm sure your assistant will be able to join you shortly."

Hana was startled to see Brandie practically materialize through a side door at the mention of her name. Darwin must have had some subtle way of summoning her.

"Oh, and Ms. Sinclair? Do tell Father Dominic that I'd still love to acquire that letter if we can come to terms, one way or another."

Hana was swept away by the ever-smiling Brandie before she had a chance to recover enough from his self-promotion to say or ask anything.

· · ·

As HANA WAS BEING LED out of the office, Mr. Jones was just coming in through another door.

"That was remarkable," he said with genuine admiration. "I almost believed you myself."

"The question is, whether she believed me."

"Well, that doesn't matter. You gained for yourself, as you said, 'plausible deniability.'"

"What about her 'assistant?'" Darwin asked, making air quotes around the word.

"We're taking care of it. Don't you worry about a thing."

CHAPTER
THIRTY-ONE

After the phone call with the CIA Deputy Director and Karl's boss, the Swiss Guard found himself questioned by Mr. Jones yet again, though with more civility. When Karl didn't immediately answer yet another in a series of questions that had been put to him by his interrogators, Jones gave an exasperated sigh and sat back hard in his chair. He was about to make a biting remark when his phone buzzed. He looked at the screen.

"I'll be back in a moment. Meanwhile, keep in mind that cooperation your boss made clear you would be giving us."

He got up and left the room with Mr. Smith, leaving Karl alone again.

Karl waited a few moments, got up, and checked the door. Locked again. Back to the waiting game. He wondered if he was really going to find out what was going on here, and why they were loading hand grenades into crates of Bibles.

Another hour passed before Smith and Jones returned.

"Okay, Mr. Dengler, so you have seen things you were not supposed to have seen. If you have not yet surmised, this is an intelligence operation of the United States government. It is classified, and you don't need to know details beyond what I'm going to read you in on now.

"As I said, the CIA has co-opted Mr. Darwin's operation. He does not know it. But if he suspects, which I sincerely believe he does not, then he keeps his mouth shut and his eyes closed. I run this operation. We expanded his reach by building the Jewel Ark Chapels around the world. The chapels are CIA outposts, staffed by Darwin's people and ours. His provide aid, ours collect intelligence and carry out operations in country. I understand you have had encounters with both. You are not to discuss those with anyone without specific permission from me. This facility is the intelligence collection center and point of coordination for the overseas operations. We bring people in to staff this place though a front, an employment agency. They are actually witnesses against the cartels under our protection. You may or may not be aware that the Catholic Church and the CIA have had a long-standing intelligence sharing agreement. The pope, the Vatican secretary of state, the prefect of the DDF, and your boss, Colonel Scarpa, are privy to the details. The pope, however, would not allow us to run operations out of Catholic facilities, so we had to make other arrangements. Hence, we took over running Darwin's shop. It's good for him, and it's good for us.

"So, before you leave here today, you are going to sign a rather comprehensive non-disclosure agreement. I can assure you that if we find out you've violated this agreement, there will be severe consequences."

At this point, Karl had had enough of being bullied.

"If you think you can scare me or threaten me, gentlemen, you are sadly mistaken. I'll sign your damn form when I am told to do so by my superiors. And I'll obey orders from my chain of command. But until then, it's not likely we'll find common ground. If you hurt me, my commandant reports to two people: the Chief of the Swiss Armed Forces and the pope. And I don't think you want to piss off either of them. Meantime, I think we are done here for now. I'm going outside to call my commandant, and then I'll be in my room at the conference center when you want to come over and talk like civilized people."

Karl started to get up from the table. Mr. Smith moved to intervene, putting his right hand on Karl's shoulder and pushing him back down. As if expecting it, Karl instantly trapped the man's hand at the wrist, pinning it to his chest. Smith tried to pull back and go for his weapon in his shoulder holster, but his right hand was immobilized by Karl's grip. He tried to grab it with his other hand, but Karl leaned forward, putting pressure on Smith's wrist in a martial arts move that guaranteed intense pain. Smith swung his left fist to hit Karl, but Karl blocked the blow with his left forearm. His right hand still clutched Smith's right wrist and he twisted it. Karl's left hand jabbed into Smith, smacking him down onto the table in an armlock.

Karl looked up at Jones, who had produced a small pistol from his pocket and was holding it to Karl's temple.

"You have made your point, Sergeant Dengler, but I'm afraid that while you might be very well skilled, you are simply outnumbered, and in something of the same boat. Our boss reports to the President of the United States.

"So, tell you what. You let go of Mr. Smith, and I assure you that he will cease hostilities against you. You will sit down—civilly, as you say—and we will call your commandant and have him instruct you to sign this NDA. Then we will take you to your transportation and you will be delivered to the airport, never to return to this facility again. We have already gathered all your belongings from your room."

"And if I don't?"

"Then I will have a lot of paperwork to do to justify pulling this trigger. But it will be Mr. Smith's and my own word against yours, except you won't be able to tell your side of the story, sadly. Don't tempt me, Sergeant Dengler. I've been a field agent for decades, and it wouldn't be the first time I've pulled this trigger."

Karl looked in his eyes and saw he was speaking the truth. Grudgingly, Karl let go of Smith, maintaining arm control at the elbow for as long as possible before releasing him completely. Smith started to go for his gun, but Jones stopped him.

"No. I gave him my word. You've been doing this too long to let him get to you. For now, let it go."

Karl sat back down and waited. Mr. Jones dialed a number on his phone.

"Jones here. Dengler isn't signing the NDA, and actually, I can't blame him. We didn't get off on the right foot here. Can you patch me in to his commandant and have him get it from the top?"

After listening for a moment, he ended the call and set the phone on the table. Five minutes later it vibrated with an incoming call. Mr. Jones picked it up and listened. He handed it over to Karl.

"Sergeant Dengler, Colonel Scarpa here. Sign the damn form and get back to your assignment. Understood?"

"Yes, sir."

Karl signed the form, after which Smith and Jones walked him outside the museum and across the grounds to the parking lot, where a car was waiting. As they arrived, Karl could see Hana and their tour guide Brandie walking over from the conference center.

"So, how did the interview go?" he asked Hana.

"I'll tell you on the plane. What happened to you? Are you okay?"

"Yeah, I'm fine. They just had some questions about how I liked the tour. Let's get out of here."

"I agree. We are so done with this place."

CHAPTER
THIRTY-TWO

L eaving the courtroom, Michael stepped out into the hall to try getting in touch with either Kat or Ian, but neither was answering their phone. He came back in and sat next to Tom Anderson.

"I can't reach them. I'm really starting to worry. It's not like them to be out of touch this long."

"Try not to worry about them. It won't do much good anyway, and I need your head in the game. Sharma has got to be up to something, and I need you paying attention."

"Okay, I'll do my best. I just hate not knowing what's going on. I haven't heard from Hana or Karl for a while, either."

At that moment, Lukas came into the courtroom from the back door, holding his cell phone in his hand.

"I just heard from Colonel Scarpa, Michael. I can't tell you what happened, other than that Karl and Hana are all right and are on their way to the airport to get back here. Scarpa only gave me the barest account of what happened, and then swore me to secrecy. I'm not sure I was even supposed to tell you that I've been sworn to secrecy.

Anyway, they are fine and on their way here, so that's one worry off your mind."

"Thanks, Lukas, That is good to hear."

The sound of the rapping gavel made everyone look up at the judge. "Please take your seats and come to order. Bishop Sharma, you may call your next witness."

"Thank you, Your Honor. The prosecution calls to the stand Mr. Galileo Galilei."

Luigi stood and walked toward the witness stand. Once there he remained standing. After he was sworn in, the judge said, "You may be seated, Mr. Galilei. Remember we are recording these proceedings, so please, let the person speaking finish before you answer. It gets very confusing if two people are talking over each other."

"Understood, Your Honor."

"Bishop Sharma, your witness."

"Thank you, Your Honor. Mr. Galilei, would you characterize yourself as a good Christian man?"

"Yes, I'd like to think so."

"Do you believe in Catholicism?"

"Yes, of course."

"So you are not a follower of Martin Luther?"

"No, I am not."

"You are not a Calvinist?"

"No."

"And you are not a follower of Huldrych Zwingli?"

"No." *Where was this going?* Luigi as Galileo wondered.

"But you would admit that you were influenced by the prevalence and severity of dissent against the Catholic Church at the time."

"Not consciously, no."

"So you accept the authority of the Catholic Church?"

"Yes, I do."

"When did you first become aware of the telescope?"

"That would have been in 1609. And in 1610, I set about improving the device using it to observe the heavens."

"Did nobody ever tell you that God did not mean for us to view the heavens with anything other than the eyes he gave us?"

Galileo rolled his eyes. "Yes, there were those who took that position. Some even refused to look through the telescope, afraid they would see an illusion and be deceived."

"Yes, just as you were."

"I was not deceived!" Galileo smacked his palm down on the witness stand.

"I'm sorry, Mr. Galilei, there was no question pending. Your Honor, I move to strike from the record the non-responsive statement Mr. Galilei just made."

"I will strike it this time, Bishop Sharma, but please curtail the editorial comments in your questioning and save them for argument, so the witness will not be confused and think you are asking a question. Please proceed."

"Thank you, Your Honor. Now, Mr. Galilei, there are a number of things that you observed though the telescope that are not visible to the naked eye, things that make you believe in the truth of the heliocentric model conceived by the blasphemer Nicolaus Copernicus, whose work has been banned by the Church as heretical."

"Objection!" Tom shouted.

"Grounds, Mr. Anderson?" the judge asked.

"It is an improper question with false premises. It cannot be properly answered."

"Overruled," the judge said, turning to Galileo. "Mr. Galilei, you may answer."

"I did see such things, as did anyone who was willing to look through the telescope. And at the time Copernicus's work had not yet been condemned or banned."

"These things that you saw—the imperfections of our

Moon, the appearance of moons around Jupiter, the appearance of phases of Venus, the tides on Earth—these things have explanations other than reliance on a heliocentric system?"

"Yes, but—"

"No buts," Sharma interrupted him. "Please, Mr. Galilei, if I ask a 'yes-or-no' question, do me the courtesy of giving it a 'yes-or-no' answer. If Mr. Anderson would like you to explain, he can ask you a question. But if you insist on explaining every answer you give, we will be here until next week. Now, these other explanations, some of them are consistent with the model of the universe as described in the Holy Scripture?"

"Yes," Galileo answered with a scowl, bristling at being prevented from responding more fully.

"And as you made these so-called 'discoveries,'" Sharma said the word with smug disdain, "you wrote about them and made yourself very well known for the novelty of them?"

"I suppose that is accurate, as far as it goes."

"So, is that a 'yes'?"

"Yes," he sighed.

"See, Mr. Galilei, that is not so hard, to say 'yes' or 'no.' Now, at some point, about 1615, you became aware that there was considerable dissent against your views, especially coming from many of the most learned men of the Church; is this true?"

"Yes."

"And then, also in 1615, one of your followers had occasion to dine in the court of the Duke of Tuscany and represented your discoveries, and there were objections raised that your interpretation of those discoveries was contrary to Holy Scripture. And your—should I say, 'disciple'?—tried as best he could to explain your position regarding that apparent conflict, and he wrote to you and explained how he had tried to defend your position. But then you felt it was important to even more fully explain yourself, and you wrote a letter to Grand Duchess Christina, wherein you stated that in areas where Holy Scripture appeared to conflict with your new scientific discoveries, that the Church must be wrong about the interpretation of those passages, and you preferred a more poetic or theological interpretation rather than a literal one."

"Yes."

"And this letter was copied extensively and distributed, and was widely read and very critically received?"

"It did seem to stir up quite a controversy," the witness replied.

"And so it should, since it directly challenged the authority of the Church to correctly interpret Scripture. And so you took it upon yourself to travel to Rome and, shall I say, take the temperature of the room to see how you were being received?"

"Yes, and to meet with the pope to discuss my discoveries."

Sharma paced slowly back and forth in front of the witness stand and the jury box, occupying the space like a Roman orator.

"Yes, you thought very much of yourself that you presumed you would be permitted to have discussions with the pope, didn't you?"

"Well, I wouldn't put it that way."

"No, of course *you* wouldn't," Sharma said demeaningly. "Nevertheless, before you could speak with the pope, you spoke to a number of other people, and were then summoned before Cardinal Bellarmine, whom you knew."

"Yes."

"And in front of many witnesses, Cardinal Bellarmine

told you that you were not to hold, teach as fact, or defend the heliocentric model of Copernicus," Sharma shook his finger at Galileo, "and that Copernicus's work, and the works of several others in that same vein, were being added to the Index of Forbidden Books."

"Yes, that is what I was told."

"And, as I understand it, you had reservations about that, because you wanted to continue to do your research and make your observations?"

"Yes, I wanted to continue the work, even if it was only as an academic exercise."

"And so those members of the Holy Inquisition who were present insisted that you therefore be formally enjoined from those activities."

"I do not remember any such formal injunction."

"Yes, that is what you said at your original trial, but we aren't there yet. Memories are such feeble things the older one gets, aren't they? That is why we write down important things. Correct?"

"Yes, and it is why I asked Cardinal Bellarmine for a certificate or letter, explaining what I was allowed to do and what I was not."

"Indeed. And you kept that letter, but you did not keep a copy of the injunction?" Sharma crossed his arms, waiting as Galileo paused before answering.

"As I said, I do not remember receiving an injunction."

"So then, shortly after that time, you did speak to the pope, and then you returned home, with the understanding that you could continue to do your work, to explain the appearances, but not to hold, teach or defend those appearances as fact?"

"Yes."

"And then in 1623, your friend Maffeo Barberini was

elevated to the papacy, taking the regnal name Urban the Eighth?"

"Yes, that's right."

"And you saw this as your opportunity to reverse the injunction and proceed more openly with your work and your writing?"

"As I said, I had no injunction, but in a manner of speaking, yes, so I could openly proceed with my work."

"And once again you came to Rome and spoke to the pope. You know, in all my years as a priest and as a bishop and as the Deputy Prefect of the Dicastery for the Doctrine of the Faith, I have never had a private, personal audience with the Holy Father. And yet you have had extensive talks with two of them?"

"So it would seem." Galileo said, nodding.

"Nevertheless, you then returned home and began work on a book, as you were under the impression from your discussions with the pope that you were allowed to explain how your discoveries appeared to fit the Copernican model, but not that they proved the correctness of it. Yes?"

"Yes."

"And the pope: he explained to you his position, that no matter what you thought you saw through your telescope, it was within the power of God to make the universe to appear that way when observed thusly, and yet in reality to be in perfect conformance with the description of Holy Scripture?"

"Yes."

"And this is not a foreign concept for you? It is the same concept by which we see the wafer and the wine, once consecrated, become the actual body and blood of our Lord Jesus Christ, even though they retain the appearance of bread and wine. You accept this doctrine without question?"

"Yes, transubstantiation is one of the most sacred tenets of the Church."

"And yet you cannot accept that the very same God could make the universe to appear one way through your telescope, and yet be in reality exactly the way Holy Scripture describes?"

Galileo looked shocked at Sharma's analogy, his eyebrows raised and jaw dropped.

"I...I had not thought of it in those terms, actually."

"Then you proceeded to write your book, which you styled as a dialogue between three people, not unlike the dialogues of Plato. You wanted to be so clever."

"That is how I wrote it. I cannot judge my own cleverness," Galileo said with a shrug.

"And of the three people who starred in your escapade, there was Salviati, the academician who argued for you and Copernicus. There is Segredo, a neutral but intelligent layman, and there is Simplicio, who ineptly argues for Ptolemy and Aristotle, and in whose mouth you put the pope's words?"

"Yes."

"And that was your folly, was it not? Your cleverness, making his name so close to 'simpleton'?"

"I suppose that was part of it."

Sharma walked right up to the witness stand and spoke directly to Galileo.

"Yes, and while you were told that you could explain your position neutrally, not advocating for its correctness, anyone who read this dialogue could see through that thin veil to the force of your argument in favor of Copernicanism and the weakness of the arguments you presented against it."

"Looking back now, I can see how it could be read that way. It was not my intention when I wrote it, but I may have been overeager in my characterization of the arguments on that side."

"So you said at your trial." Sharma stepped back, his point made. "Now, I would be remiss not to admit that once you finished the book in 1630, you submitted it to not one, but two different censors, one in Rome and one in Florence, due to the outbreak of plague?"

"Yes, and it was ultimately approved by the censor in Florence."

"And it was published, and copies were distributed, and it ultimately reached Rome. And you were subsequently invited to appear before the Inquisition and answer for yourself?"

"Yes, that is correct."

"It took some time for you to get to Rome. You claimed to be ill."

"Not claimed. I *was* ill! I had been in poor health for some time. That is why it took so long to write the book."

"Be that as it may, during the trial, you were confronted with the notes from that meeting with Cardinal Bellarmine, which recorded that you had been formally enjoined not to hold, teach or defend Copernicanism."

"Yes, but I still had a copy of Bellarmine's letter that said I could pursue the work nonetheless."

"And because the original injunction you signed had gone missing by that time, the prosecutor was forced to make a plea bargain with you such that you avoided being found guilty of the harshest form of heresy?"

"I suppose from your point of view, that would be correct. I am not convinced that there ever was a formal injunction. Cardinal Bellarmine did not mention one in his letter. It only came up because it was mentioned in the notes of some anonymous scribe."

Sharma had been facing the jury, watching their reactions. He spun and pointed at Galileo, his right arm extended from his shoulder to his spindly index finger.

"So, you deny that you were formally enjoined not to hold, teach or defend Copernicanism?"

"I have no memory of any such injunction."

"So you deny it? Say as much!"

"Fine, I deny it! I was not so enjoined. I would think if I had been subjected to such an extreme stricture that I would have remembered it and challenged it."

"And history has borne you out, for no such document has ever been produced, has it?"

"Not that I have ever seen."

"Yes, you answer so very carefully, Galileo. '*Not that you have seen,*' you say. Indeed. Not that one does not exist. You saw the invoice for the exhibits brought to the museum, did you not?"

"Yes, just today."

"And on that invoice, there is an entry for the very injunction of which we speak, is there not?"

"Yes, there is, but the exhibits were stolen, so I have not seen a copy."

"Yes, that is a shame. If only their security had been given more attention. To have such an important historical document lost, it's almost unforgivable. Fortunately, I took the injunction from the exhibits myself before the rest were stolen, so as to properly safeguard this irreplaceable treasure."

Aghast, Tom Anderson and Michael looked at each other. Michael was utterly dumbfounded. Sharma had taken the injunction? How could he have done that?! And why? Could it be that it was only so that he could have this dramatic moment? Could he have been behind the theft of the rest of the exhibits to prevent us from discovering his deceit or to hinder the presentation of our defense? *No,*

Bishop Sharma is a prince of the Church! Michael argued with himself. *He could not be so unethical. There must be some other explanation.*

Bishop Sharma went over to his briefcase, took out a document secured in a transparent plastic case, and carried it with obvious ceremony to the witness.

"I want you to look at this document very carefully. You are familiar with your own signature? You have placed it on so many documents in your lifetime, you would recognize it on sight, would you not?"

"Yes, I would recognize it."

"Then look here, on this document, which I would like marked as the Prosecution's Exhibit One. This document is entitled *'The Injunction of Galileo Galilei, 26 February 1616'*; is that your signature at the bottom of the page?"

Luigi looked very carefully at the document, his eyes wide. He trembled to behold it. There at the bottom, was a signature that was identical to those he had seen of his namesake, Galileo Galilei.

"It certainly appears to be, yes."

CHAPTER
THIRTY-THREE

Michael was startled by a soft buzzing sound coming from his pocket. He tried to discreetly pull out his phone and look at the number. The caller ID showed *Gunari Lakatos*. Michael felt his chest tighten. If Gunari was calling, it likely had something to do with Kat and Ian. Michael tapped Tom on the shoulder and motioned to his phone.

He whispered, "I've got to take this. It's Kat's uncle."

Michael got up from the counsel's table just as Luigi confirmed Galileo's signature on the injunction. The courtroom paused, expecting Michael to say something, but he hurried for the door and left.

"Hello, this is Father Dominic," he answered once he was in the hallway.

"Michael, this is Gunari. Don't worry, Kat and Ian are fine. At least they are fine *now*. So are Milosh and Shandor."

"Wait, what do you mean 'fine *now*?' And what do Milosh and Shandor have to do with anything? And how are you involved?" His questions tumbled out in a rush.

"Michael, wait. We don't have time for questions. I will

fill you in on everything later. Right now, you have to go to confession at the Holy Name Cathedral."

"What, *now?!*"

"Yes, now. And please, don't interrupt. I am told the cathedral is a couple of blocks away from the law school. But you'll need to hurry. The noon Mass will be starting shortly, so there is little time. Go into the second confessional on the right, from the priest's side. Turn on the occupied sign. Someone will come into the penitent's booth. They will have information for you. Hurry, please! Go now. "

Michael started walking toward the law school exit while composing a text to Tom. *"Something has come up. Have to run. Back shortly. Explain later."* He hoped he would have something to explain.

Michael had seen the cathedral on the way into the law school. It was a short walk and he covered it quickly. Going in the main doors, he was momentarily awed by the beauty of the architecture. He had always marveled at the ingenuity and grandeur people were capable of when trying to imitate the glory of God and inspire His followers.

He looked around for the confessionals. The pews were beginning to fill with people for the noon Mass. Those who had come early to pray were seated throughout, mostly with heads bowed. He looked around. Somebody here was waiting for him, or maybe several somebodies. He went around the right side, found the door that led to the priest's side of the confessionals, entered the second one, and waited.

∾

BACK INSIDE THE COURTROOM, Sharma looked to see the reason for the pause in the courtroom and saw Michael heading for the door, phone in hand. He looked at the jury and made eye contact with the Auxiliary Bishop, who responded with the slightest of shrugs. Sharma then looked at his security staff. Bram nodded, waited until Michael had gotten through the door, then got up to follow him.

Bram kept a discreet distance from Michael all the way to Holy Name Cathedral, waiting for the priest to enter. He paused at the door, then went inside. He saw Michael go into the second confessional. Fortunately, the lighting in the cathedral was dim, and Bram went to a far pew and sat down near a couple of old women, then put his head down as if in prayer while keeping a close watch on the confessional door.

A FEW MOMENTS LATER, Michael heard the confessional door open and close. Someone stepped inside and sat down. Michael waited a few seconds, unsure how this non-confession meeting was supposed to proceed. The other person said nothing. Sliding the privacy panel open, Michael greeted him in the name of Christ, the traditional beginning of the rite of confession.

The confessor began. "Bless me, Father, for I have sinned. This is my first confession. These are my sins. I conspired with a prince of the Church to have the Galileo exhibits stolen from the Fielding Museum. I arranged for professional thieves to be brought in from overseas to keep my own people uninvolved. My people took the thieves and their relatives into protective custody when it appeared that the thieves' mission might have been compromised. I then negotiated with the thieves' father to return them to their family. The father has convinced me that it would be wrong to keep the exhibits or to sell or destroy them because they are precious historical artifacts, and because he has a relationship with you, and would not want you to be harmed by this. I'm not taking any chances. I'm giving them only to you, in person, tonight. If you want the exhibits back, Father, meet me at the cement factory on Peoria Street, off Chicago and Halsted streets. Go to the river at the bridge at eight p.m. and wait. Come alone, or the deal's off. We will contact you there."

There was a buzzing sound in the penitent's booth. The man paused a moment.

"You were followed, Father. Take a different way out. Be careful. You're being watched."

Michael heard the door open, and the person was gone.

∾

"OBJECTION, YOUR HONOR."

"Grounds, Mr. Anderson?"

"Foundation, hearsay, and authentication."

"Bishop Sharma?"

"Your Honor, the document would be admissible for impeachment, and for refreshing the witness's recollection. Recollection refreshed requires no foundation, or authentication, even if it was hearsay. But if you want me to cure those imagined defects, we need only have Father Petrini— or *Dominic* if you wish—testify again. I acknowledge that this document was not under consideration when we took care of the preliminaries this morning."

"Perhaps that would be best," the judge concurred. "But I think he stepped out. In which case, this might be a good time to take our noon recess. Ladies and gentlemen, we are going to take our lunch break a few minutes early today. Please be back ready to go by one thirty. We'll have the doors open at one fifteen. Court stands in recess." She rapped her gavel soundly.

KEEN ON SITUATIONAL AWARENESS, Bram noticed near the front of the pews a man dressed in a black hoodie and sunglasses get up, walk to the second confessional and go inside. There was no light above the third confessional booth. Bram got up and started walking over. When he was nearly there, another man stood up from a nearby pew and stood in his way. He tried to go around him, but the man stepped in his way again. Clearly, this was no accident. Bram reached into his pocket and removed a seven-inch long wooden dowel, a Japanese martial arts weapon called a yawara. Grasping it firmly in his fist, he thrust the end of it toward the man's solar plexus, intending to knock the wind out of him so he could get to the confessional in time to hear whatever exchange might be taking place.

In that time, however, a second man had come up behind him, and as Bram was attempting to hit the man in front of him, the guy behind him pulled out a leather coin purse shaped like a sap and smacked him hard on the side of his head. Bram stumbled, then his world shrank to darkness.

In the dark shadows, the two men opened the door to the third confessional and lifted their victim inside. Then they walked out the front door and took up positions across the street at either end of the block, waiting to see if Father Dominic was followed as he left.

HAVING RETURNED TO THE COURTROOM, Michael entered just as the last of the spectators were leaving, and both Tom and Bishop Sharma were packing up.

"What's happening, Tom?"

"Breaking for lunch."

"Well, I have some good news."

"I have some bad news, but I could use the good news. You go first."

Michael leaned in close and whispered, "Kat and Ian are okay, and I'll be getting the exhibits back tonight. Now, what's the bad news?"

"You're going back on the stand after lunch," Tom answered.

CHAPTER
THIRTY-FOUR

B ram woke up to at first a gentle, then more vigorous shaking of his shoulder. His head hurt. He opened his eyes slowly. Wherever he was, it was dim, but not dark. He was in a very small room, no bigger than a closet. He was seated on a small bench, dark paneling all around him. There was a screen in front of him, covered in a decorative wooden grill. He turned his head and looked at the person shaking his shoulder.

Memory came flooding back: following the priest, the confessional booths, someone blocking his way, being hit from behind. A confessional booth. They must have knocked him out and left him there. He quickly glanced at his watch. It was twelve forty-five. *Damn!* He had been out some forty-five minutes.

When Bram tried to stand his world rocked and rolled; fortunately, he caught his balance on the door frame. He looked at the man who had been shaking his shoulder. It was a priest, probably someone from the cathedral.

"Are you all right? Do you need a doctor?" the priest asked. "I can summon an ambulance."

Bram swayed in the doorway, taking stock of his condition. He reached up and gingerly touched the side of his head. There was a significant lump, but while the pain was substantial, it was not sharp like a skull fracture, which he knew from experience. But it was likely that he had a concussion.

"I'll be fine. Excuse me. I have to go."

He brushed past the priest, heading for the door while still unsteady on his feet. He needed to get back to the law school and speak to Bishop Sharma. He would be worried. He had probably called a dozen times.

Bram was still thinking slowly. Of course, Sharma had probably called and texted. He reached into his pocket for his phone. Gone. Whoever hit him had probably taken it.

When he reached the law school, the doors to the courtroom were locked. Bram went looking for Sharma. He found him in the cafeteria. As he staggered in, Sharma got up and helped him to a chair.

"What happened to you?" he whispered harshly to his security aide.

Bram explained the sequence of events.

"Someone must have needed to tell him something, urgently, and with certain confidentiality. Which doesn't bode well. Something's up. But right now we need to take you to a doctor. We need to make sure you're fit for duty. I can't have you going down when I might need you the most. I will call the judge and ask for a recess in order to take you in, which will also give me time to make some calls."

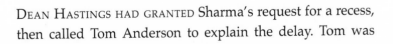

DEAN HASTINGS HAD GRANTED Sharma's request for a recess, then called Tom Anderson to explain the delay. Tom was relieved, as was Michael, that it was likely he would not be going back on the stand today. The jurors had been called and told to return at three o'clock instead of one thirty.

Michael was unaware of the altercation that occurred outside the booth, but instantly assumed that Sharma's security man had been injured in relation to following him. It only made sense. Did the man he had gone to meet have anything to do with it? He considered it likely, even probable. They had warned him he had been followed. He had slipped out of the confessional through the back door that led to a private hallway accessible only to cathedral staff and clergy. The priests could enter the confessionals from the inside, to prevent parishioners from knowing which priest was in each booth and shopping for the most lenient confessor.

"Tom, the man I met with told me I was being followed. I wonder if it was Sharma's man who followed me."

"I think that's possible, if not likely. His man left shortly after you did, just before we took an early lunch recess."

"But why would he be following me?"

"You rushed out, everyone saw that. And Sharma doesn't like surprises sprung on him. I still think he has something in store for us. He isn't done with his own surprises."

"Yeah...I can't wait."

～

CHICAGO'S AUXILIARY Bishop William Loveridge was having lunch with two other of the jurors, a monsignor and the chaplain, in a small cafe a couple of blocks from the law school when his phone rang again. The first time, it had been the dean, telling him there had been an emergency and that the trial would not be resuming until three o'clock.

He informed the dean that he was with two other jurors and would pass along the information. They had agreed that even with the additional time, there was insufficient opportunity to get any work done back at their offices. Instead, they would use the time to take a more leisurely lunch and discuss the latest gossip from Chicago and Rome.

But when Loveridge saw the familiar number on caller ID on the second call, he excused himself and went outside.

"You should not be calling me during the trial. It is improper. In a real case, I would have to report this to the judge."

"Relax. It is not a real case and you will do nothing of the sort. You are only there at my invitation anyway. My assistant Bram followed Father Dominic to the cathedral right before lunch. Dominic took someone's confession, or at least spoke to them in the booth. I want to know who that was. Do you have any way to find out?"

"No, there are no cameras inside the cathedral, and the outdoor cameras only come on after hours."

"What about the priest at noon Mass? Might he or someone else have seen who went in there?"

"I would have to call and find out."

"Do so, discreetly. Bram was jumped by people keeping watch while the person Dominic met was in the booth. I need to know who those men were. And by the way, please tell me that the other project assigned to you has been completed."

"Uh...no." Loveridge paused. "There has been a complication. My people have guests from out of town who have interfered with the project you requested. I have been told they no longer have access to the personnel but that they are dealing with the inventory."

"You idiot! Must I do everything myself? That personnel matter was critical. They could spoil everything I have planned. You should not have failed me... There will be consequences."

"What do you mean, 'consequences?' I did everything I could! I don't handle things like this, especially personally."

"Pray, my friend. Pray this all works out. Now I have to go and fix your mess."

The line went dead.

BISHOP SHARMA SAT in the waiting room of Northwestern Memorial Hospital Urgent Care, only a few blocks east and south of the law school, making plans and placing phone calls. He should have known better than to rely on other people to get things done. Other people were unreliable. They did not share his passion or his attention to detail. Well, contingencies had to be dealt with. But at the same time, he had to report to his boss about what was going on. The man hated being in the dark.

Sharma dialed a number from memory. "I have been watching the trial," said the voice at the other end once the call was connected. "You have made your points well, but I do not think you have gone far enough. Tell me you have something better planned."

"Yes. Father Dominic will be going back on the stand, and I have a surprise planned for him."

"Good, good. I will be looking forward to that. But I suspect that wasn't the reason for your call."

"No, there has been a complication. That personnel matter you requested has not been handled yet. My resource had difficulty getting his assets to accomplish the task. Apparently there has been outside interference. And my man here was jumped while keeping the priest under surveillance. Dominic met someone at the cathedral. I am trying to find out now who it was, but there seems to have been counter-surveillance in place."

"That is most disappointing. But this mission cannot fail. There is too much riding on it. I do not want to get involved at this level, but I will if you cannot handle it. Is this too much for you? Tell me now, while there is still time to do something about it. I have other resources, but I'm hesitant to deploy them. There would be certain costs to me and to you…"

"No, I will take care of it. I will not disappoint you."

"Good. Your future depends on it."

THIRTY-FIVE

At two forty-five, the doors to the courtroom were opened and people began flowing inside. Father Michael, Tom Anderson, and Luigi Bucatini had been huddled together in a spare classroom going over strategy for the afternoon session.

Tom thought it likely that the delay would prevent Michael from having to take the stand today and that they would instead finish with Galileo. They would put Michael on the stand in the morning, and then present closing arguments, and the jury could deliberate in the afternoon and deliver their verdict, if they reached one, before the end of the day and culmination of the conference. The court clerk had texted both Tom and Bishop Sharma to let them know the doors were open. Now they filed in and took their places at the counsel tables.

Bishop Sharma, Bram, and the bishop's other assistant, Somchai, came in shortly after. Bram had an egg-shaped bruise on his right temple, an angry red and purple swelling. He glared in Michael's direction, as if to blame the priest for the actions of the people he had gone to meet. He sat next to Bishop Sharma and waited for the judge to come in. Sharma began arranging documents on the counsel table, ready to be selected as necessary during the questioning.

Promptly at three o'clock, Judge Hastings came out and took her seat on the bench.

"Please, remain seated and come to order. The retrial of Galileo Galilei shall resume. Does either counsel have anything to bring before the Court prior to continuing testimony?"

Tom Anderson stood. "Your Honor, may it please the Court. Mr. Bucatini was not expecting to have to stay past today and may have to rearrange lodging and flights if he needs to stay an additional day—which could be done if absolutely necessary, but it would be a significant inconvenience. Father Dominic is staying for the entire trial and would be amenable to taking the stand in the morning if necessary. I would propose that we put Galileo back on the stand for the remaining time we have and see if we can get him finished."

"Bishop Sharma, your position on that proposal?"

"Your Honor, I have no objection. I would love to see Galileo finished." His voice dropped at the end, somewhat menacingly, and he smiled at Luigi, but not in a particularly friendly way, as he let the dual meaning of his statement sink in.

"Very well. Mr. Galilei, please resume your place on the witness stand, and I remind you that you are still under oath."

"Yes, Your Honor," Galileo said as he seated himself in the witness box.

"Bishop Sharma, I believe he is still your witness. Do you have further questions for him?" the judge inquired.

"Briefly, Your Honor. Just a few." He rose and walked

around the counsel table, using the courtroom as his stage. He knew the eyes of the world were upon him...well, not the whole world, but the world that mattered to him. If they were not going to get to Father Michael today, he needed to finish strong with this witness. "Mr. Galilei, before the break, you admitted that you recognized your signature on the injunction that was read to you at Cardinal Bellarmine's residence in 1616. Is that correct? You did say that you recognized your signature?"

"Yes, that appears to be my signature."

"Do you have any reason to doubt the testimony of your senses?"

"Only that I have no recollection of ever having seen this document before."

"Yes, well, that is why we write things down, is it not? So that a record can be made that is not subject to the frailties of memory?"

"Yes, I suppose so."

"Now, speaking of things we write down to preserve a record, you do recall what happened at your trial, do you not?"

"Yes, of course."

"Good, then for the benefit of the jurors who were not there, let us make reference to another document that bears your signature." Bishop Sharma went over to the counsel table and selected one of the documents he had laid out. He showed it to Tom and then turned to the Court. "Your Honor, may I approach the witness?"

"You may approach the witness, and you do not need to ask permission from now on. In over thirty years of being a lawyer, I have yet to see trial counsel attack a witness. If you promise me you will not attack anyone on the witness stand, you may approach at will."

"Thank you, Your Honor. I assure you that *I* will not

attack a witness." He slightly emphasized the "I" as he said it.

Sharma took the document over to Galileo. "Now, I would like to direct your attention to the bottom of this document as well. Do you see your signature there?"

"Yes, that is mine."

"It appears as similar to the previous one as any two signatures made by the same hand?"

"Yes."

"And do you recognize this document as one you have seen before?"

"Yes."

"What is this document, Mr. Galilei?"

"It is my confession, which was made by me before the Holy Office at the conclusion of my trial."

"And you read this document in open court, word for word, while swearing to the truth of the contents while placing your hand upon the Holy Bible?"

"Yes."

"Then would you be so kind as to read for me the second sentence of the first paragraph, which begins '*But whereas....*'"

"'*But whereas, after an injunction had been judicially intimated to me by this Holy Office—*'"

"Stop there," Sharma interrupted him. "You admitted it. Swore to its correctness, out loud and in writing, that you had been so enjoined."

"I...I suppose so, but they were going to torture me if I did not so affirm."

"Are you saying that this is a false confession? Did you lie to the Church?"

Luigi as Galileo recognized the trap that had been laid for him. He could either say he had lied under duress, but lied nonetheless, or accept the language of the confession, which admitted the truth of the injunction Sharma had produced. He couldn't admit to lying; that would throw into doubt everything he had said before and anything he might say yet. So it was better to accept the documents as they stood and hope that Tom Anderson had some way to rehabilitate the case. "No, that is not what I am saying."

This wasn't looking good.

"I thought not," Sharma said smugly, retrieving the document to read it aloud himself. "That sentence goes on to say, '*I must altogether abandon the false opinion that the Sun is the center of the world and immovable, and that the Earth is not the center of the world, and moves, and that I must not hold, defend, or teach in any way whatsoever, verbally or in writing, the said false doctrine, and after it had been notified to me that the said doctrine was contrary to Holy Scripture, I wrote and published a book in which I discuss this new doctrine already condemned, and adduce arguments of great cogency in its favor, without presenting any solution of these, and for this reason I have been pronounced by the Holy Office to be vehemently suspected of heresy, that is to say, of having held and believed that the Sun is the center of the world and immovable, and that the Earth is not the center and moves...,'*" Sharma stopped. "Those are the words you spoke, which were written down and signed by you, are—they—not?" Sharma emphasized each word with a pause.

"They are."

Sharma paused again for effect. There was total silence in the courtroom.

"They are indeed." He went on, "You were told not to defend your heretical ideas, either verbally or in writing, and then you wrote a book that did exactly that."

"But I had permission from the pope."

"Do you have any proof that you had permission from the pope? Do you have an indulgence or a pardon? Did the pope ever come out and say to the Holy Office, 'Oh, wait, I gave Galileo permission to write that book?'"

"No."

"Certainly not. Before you gave this confession, you had the expectation that your sentence would have been much lighter, given your conversations with the prosecutor and the letter you presented from Cardinal Bellarmine."

"Yes. I was surprised by the change in direction."

"Do you know why there was such a change in direction?"

"No."

Sharma went back to the counsel table and picked up another document, holding it in his hands. "Would it surprise you to know that the pope was getting daily summaries of the proceedings?"

"No, it would not. My understanding is that he was quite upset about the language in the book."

"Yes, that is my understanding as well since you put his argument in the mouth of your fool, Simplicio. Would it also surprise you to know that it was the pope himself who directed your sentence?" Sharma asked, waving the piece of paper he held over his head for emphasis.

Luigi paused. There had been intimation of that by several scholars, but never any proof. Did the DDF have this record also? It seemed to, if that was indeed what the document Sharma was holding purported to be. No need to make this any worse. "I would not have suspected that of my friend," Luigi's Galileo said.

Sharma put the paper down, having gotten what he wanted. He picked up the injunction again. He knew he had him now. Time for the coup de grâce.

"So, you would agree that the crime for which you were convicted was not that you had been right all along but that you had disobeyed a direct order of the Church, an order which you had sworn to obey, both orally and in writing, signed by your own hand. Further, after you published your book and were confronted with your disobedience, you freely and willingly confessed your guilt, not just for believing something contrary to the Holy Scripture and the teachings of the Church, but for breaking your promise not to hold, defend or teach that doctrine, verbally or in writing. And this confession was also written down and signed with your own hand. So, I ask you, Galileo, did you lie when you spoke and signed the injunction, or when you spoke and signed your confession?"

And that was it. Sharma had played him superbly. Luigi had walked right into it. He was trapped, painted into a corner. It didn't really matter that he had been right about the science. He had broken his word, and Sharma had very cleverly reframed the trial to get him to admit exactly that.

Galileo responded slowly, in a near whisper. "I...made a mistake."

"Yes, you made many of them. And the Church was right in chastising you for them."

Bishop Sharma turned to the judge, "I have no further questions for this witness."

CHAPTER
THIRTY-SIX

"Mr. Anderson, do you have questions for this witness?" the judge asked.

"Yes, Your Honor, thank you. Mr. Galilei, are you an honest man?"

"I like to think so."

"Do you get to tell the pope what to do?"

"No, certainly not."

"So, it is not your fault that you do not have any proof that Pope Urban the Eighth told you that you could write your book?"

"No, I did not even think to ask for it. I expected it would be well received."

"Now, you spoke to him about your book shortly after he was elected, correct?"

"Yes, I went to congratulate my old friend and, since he had been a supporter of mine, to seek his permission to write about my findings."

"And he gave you that permission?"

"Yes, with the caveat that I not take sides in the presentation of arguments, just present the premises for each side so that people could see how an argument could be made for both sides, to show that the truth could not be determined merely from the arguments."

"And that is what you attempted to do?"

"Yes, although I might have been overly enthusiastic about the scientific side of the arguments."

"But those scientific arguments turned out to be correct."

"Yes, all but the tides. I was wrong about where the motion of the tides came from."

"So, you are willing to admit where you were wrong? Do you think it is important to admit when you were wrong?"

"Yes, I think that is part of having integrity."

"And that would be true of organizations as well as individuals, would it not?"

"Yes, I think that applies equally to both."

"Now, when you got that permission from the pope to write your book, that was about nine years before the book was eventually published?"

"Yes, there was a lot going on during those years, and I was not in the best of health."

"Now, the Counter-Reformation was also going on at that time, was it not?"

"Yes, it was."

"So, the Church, and the pope himself, were under a lot of pressure from both progressive and conservative factions challenging and supporting orthodoxy and the authority of the Church?"

"Yes."

"So, looking back, it is not so surprising that nine years after you received permission to write your book, that the pope's feelings about it might have changed?"

"Yes, that is quite possible."

"Now, you didn't just rely on the pope's permission alone. You also sent your manuscript to two different Church censors who reviewed it for orthodoxy prior to publication, one in Rome and one in Florence?"

"Yes, initially in Rome, but because of an outbreak of plague, it could not be completed in Rome, so the Roman censor's concerns were communicated to the censor in Florence, and all those concerns were addressed before the book was ultimately approved."

"So, not only did you have permission from the pope to write the book, you had permission and approval from an official censor of the Church to publish it?"

"Yes."

"If there had been some formal proscription against you that prohibited you from writing and publishing your book, you would think that the pope and the censors would have checked with the Holy Office to make sure before they gave their approvals."

"Yes, that is the case. Not only did I not sign," he hesitated, then continued, "or remember signing any formal injunction, but I expected that the people who gave me permission also would have been aware—or have made inquiries with the Holy Office to become aware—of any proscriptions against me, given the controversial nature of the material and infamy attached to me at the time."

"This injunction that you were accused of violating, was it actually produced at your trial?"

"No, not to my recollection."

"But you signed a confession admitting that it existed."

"I took it on the authority of the Holy Office that it existed. I assumed they wouldn't lie about it. And as I said, I was seventy years old, and in poor health. If I hadn't made the confession as they provided it to me, they would have tortured me until I did. They told me as much."

"So, the Holy Office threatened to torture a sick old man to get him to sign a confession they wrote?" Anderson asked, staring at Sharma with contempt.

"Yes."

"Well, I can certainly understand why you signed it. I would have."

"Objection! Relevance," Bishop Sharma shouted. "It really doesn't matter what Mr. Anderson says he would have done, only what Galileo did."

"Your Honor, I think it matters what anyone would have done under those circumstances."

"Sustained. Ladies and gentlemen of the jury, please disregard Mr. Anderson's statement. Only what the witness says is evidence," the judge instructed.

Anderson continued. "Now, the Church eventually admitted that you were right, did they not?"

"Yes, they took my book off the banned list in 1835, and then I was found not guilty in 1992."

"So, the Church eventually moved from its previous position?"

"Yes, it moved."

"It seems very slowly, however."

"Oh, yes."

"So does it seem fair to you to hold a man accountable for breaking a promise that he was forced to make under threat of torture? Or to publish a treatise that he received the permission of the pope to write, and approval from the Church to publish, and whose premise both history and science have proven to be correct, a fact that the Church concedes?"

"No, it does not seem fair to me."

Tom Anderson thought about stopping there. It really was a good place to stop. It had good jury impact, but he wanted more.

"So, the Church admitted that it was wrong?"

"Yes."

"Do you think the Church might eventually admit it was wrong about other controversial topics? Women deacons? Married clergy? Things that do not impinge on the Church's authority over faith and morals but, rather, uphold just the history and tradition of the Church?"

"I suppose that's possible."

"Thank you, Mr. Galilei. I have no further questions."

Tom sat down at the counsel table. Michael looked at him quizzically, whispering, "What was that last part about?"

Tom muttered back, "I'll tell you later."

Dean Hastings addressed the jury. "Thank you so much for your patience. That's all we have time for today. Tomorrow we will start up after morning Mass, promptly at nine o'clock. I'll have the doors open at eight forty-five. For now, you are excused. Counsel, remain behind, please."

When the jury and spectators had left, the judge addressed the lawyers. "What is your vision of the morning tomorrow? I'd like to give the jury as much time for deliberation as possible, but I don't want to shortchange your closing arguments. Are you ready to proceed with those first thing in the morning?"

"I would be happy to," Tom replied.

"Well, I would not be," Sharma rebutted. "I think it is most important to put Father Dominic back on the stand, in front of the jury, now that Mr. Anderson has made such a big deal about the records we used to confront Galileo."

"Very well." The judge turned to Michael back at the counselor's desk. "Father Dominic, you are also ordered back tomorrow at nine o'clock," she said, a little too committed to her role as judge, before realizing her faux pas. "Well, what I mean is, we would appreciate it if you were also here by nine to continue assisting us in this re-enactment... Thank you."

"I'll be here," Michael responded, without much enthusiasm. There was a lot to do between now and then. Hopefully, he would have the exhibits back.

THIRTY-SEVEN

As soon as Hana and Karl were aboard the plane after Darwin's people had dropped them at the private air terminal in Dallas, Hana turned to Karl. "Okay, what the heck happened back there?"

"Hana, I don't want to talk about it."

"What do you mean, *'I don't want to talk about it?'*"

"Just let it go," Karl said, holding a finger to his lips. He rooted through his backpack and on a small, spiral-bound notepad scribbled: *Can't talk. Might be listening devices. They had my backpack too long.*

Hana read the note, frowned and—indicating that he should follow her lead for the benefit of their eavesdroppers—continued, "Well, I want to talk about it. I think Darwin is up to something, but I don't know what it is. I don't think he has the exhibits. Maybe because he didn't think of it, or more likely that somebody else got there before Remi Shapiro did. But I'm usually a pretty good judge of people. If he had the exhibits, he would have let on that he did. He'd be too proud of having them. No, I don't think he has them, but it's not because he doesn't want them. That man thinks he's entitled to anything he wants. And I really don't buy the image of saintliness he tried to portray. It was like he was reciting a script."

"What did he say?"

"Oh, a whole bunch of stuff about how he doesn't get to enjoy the riches his church brings in; it's all work, work, work, putting on a show for the rich so that he can actually help the poor. Oh, please. He says this while wearing a suit that costs more than most families make in a month." She paused a moment, in thought. "We should call Michael and let him know we're on the way back to Chicago."

Karl tapped the note again and said, "I'm sure he knows," then winked.

Now Hana's curiosity was really piqued, but she nodded. "I'm going to take a nap then. It was a long morning."

Karl turned and looked out the window. How much could he tell her without violating the CIA's non-disclosure agreement? He knew she was a dogged reporter. When she latched on to something, she was relentless. And, as his cousin, she expected the relationship would entitle her to a little more inside information than anyone else might get, except maybe Lukas.

That was another problem. What could he say to Lukas, his life partner as well as a fellow soldier? That would be even stickier. Karl thoroughly expected that he was being watched and listened to, and probably would be for a while, to see if he was good to his word. He would have to be very careful going forward.

WHEN THE PLANE landed at Chicago's O'Hare Airport and taxied to the private air terminal, Hana and Karl hopped into a ride-share vehicle and headed for the hotel. Traffic coming down Highway 90 was heavy, and they looked enviously at the train moving quickly between the lanes of opposing traffic. They stopped at their hotel long enough to drop their bags then walked over to the law school.

They arrived at the courtroom just as everyone was filing out, but the doors were closed before they could get inside. They waited in the hallway for a few minutes while the participants talked to the judge and were there when they came out. As soon as Michael cleared the courtroom door, Hana stepped up to him. She wanted to wrap him in a big hug, but reporters swarmed the area about the case and she greeted him with just a sympathetic smile instead. As Bishop Sharma and his entourage filed out past them, Bram glared at the group, and Hana marveled at the bruise on the side of his face.

"What happened to him?"

"I'll tell you over dinner. We're all going to grab some food and talk. Luigi is leaving for Rome early in the morning, so we're taking him out to thank him for participating. Also, we have something to do tonight," Michael said cryptically.

"Luigi? And where are we going?"

Michael grinned. "Yes, my Roman newsstand friend, but I'll explain later. Tom made reservations at one of those Brazilian steak houses. It's only a few blocks away so we can walk."

Lukas and Karl hung back a moment as the group went through the doors out of the law school and onto the street. Pulling him into a bear hug, Lukas whispered into Karl's ear, "I missed you. Everything okay?" Karl replied pointedly, "Right as rain, *schatz*. And I missed you, too. Let's not get left behind. Did I miss anything?" Lukas looked Karl in the eyes, long and penetratingly, looking for a clue as to why Karl had used one of their distress codes. *"Right as rain"* was something they said to let the other one know there was danger that could not be spoken out loud.

"Well, okay, then. Yes, let's not get left behind. I get your point. And I wouldn't be surprised if some of Bishop Sharma's group put in an appearance, even though they weren't invited."

Karl knew now that Lukas understood, and would be going to the front of the group—the point position of a tactical formation—while he took up the rear guard. He also understood that Lukas was concerned that they were being followed by Sharma's security people. Great...now he had two groups to worry about.

OUTSIDE THE LAW SCHOOL, Bishop Sharma took Bram aside. "Keep an eye on them. We need to know what they are up to. I'll talk to Bishop Loveridge and see if we can get any action against the girl, but you have permission, and direction, to dispose of her if she ends up meeting with Father Dominic. I can't have her unraveling everything that has been done. It's going too well so far. Understood?" Bram nodded. "Good. Take Somchai with you, and don't get caught. Here," Sharma said, handing Bram a small package from an outside pocket of his trial bag. "I sent Somchai to get you a new phone. Keep in touch."

Bishop Sharma stepped into the ride-share vehicle that was waiting at the curb. Bram motioned to his counterpart, and they turned to follow Michael's party. Somchai crossed the street, pulled out a gray hoodie from his bag, and put on a pair of sunglasses. With the hood up, he was just another anonymous person walking the streets of Chicago. Somchai put in a pair of wireless earbuds, and, looking at his phone, tapped the speed dial button for Bram's new cell phone. Bram answered, and now they were able to communicate. Since Bram was more identifiable with his new bruise, Somchai took the lead on their surveillance. He could see Michael's group about a block ahead. He put the phone in his front pocket and started after them.

Bram held back, staying on the other side of the street. He was watching Michael's group, but mostly he was watching to see if anyone was observing Somchai. They had been burned by counter-surveillance once on this mission. He wasn't going to let that happen again.

Michael's group made it to the steak house. Somchai went around to the back of the restaurant.

"I'm out back," he reported to Bram.

"Good, hold your position there. I'm out front, down the street. Father Dominic's group picked up a tail. A man and a woman just went into the restaurant. She's wearing a black pantsuit and what I suspect is a blonde wig. The man is in a dark gray suit with a white shirt and striped, gray tie. They came behind you from just past the law school. There may be a vehicle following as well."

A dark Crown Victoria slowed down just as they were entering the restaurant. Bram looked back at it.

"Clearly, we aren't the only ones following Dominic tonight."

CHAPTER

THIRTY-EIGHT

ichael, Tom Anderson, Luigi Bucatini, Hana, Karl and Lukas were escorted to a reserved table behind a red velvet cordon in a quiet corner near the back of the restaurant. Karl and Lukas sat diagonally across from each other, their backs to the walls so they could observe the restaurant.

Shortly after they were situated, a young couple was seated near them, the man in a gray suit, and the blonde woman in a black pantsuit with oversized jacket. Hana perused the wine list and chose for the group two fine bottles of red that would go well with their meal.

The authentic Brazilian food just kept coming, family-style. The servers brought skewers of meats and seafood fresh off the rotisserie or the grill: medallions of filet, ribs so tender the meat fell off the bone, deeply smoked sausages made in-house, and huge prawns, among other specialties. Just as soon as diners had finished one delicacy, another server appeared with something even more sumptuous. The side dishes were served from a buffet in the center of the restaurant, including several varied offerings of potatoes. Michael was particularly impressed by the mashed red potatoes with roasted garlic butter, sharp aged cheddar and chives. Hana teased him about being a meat and potatoes boy at heart, while she returned with a second helping of the prosciutto-wrapped grilled asparagus, drizzled with extra virgin olive oil and a Balsamic reduction, and sprinkled with aged Parmigiano Reggiano.

As the meal was winding down and diners were declining tempting offerings from the dessert cart, Tom brought the group back on task. He tapped very lightly on his wine glass with his fork, gathering everyone's attention.

"I want to thank Luigi for coming all the way from Rome to Chicago to endure the abuse he received today. While the conference paid his expenses, his participation in today's spectacle was entirely voluntary, and I can't imagine how much money it would have taken to adequately compensate him for what he had to go through. I wish I was going back to Italy with you, Luigi."

"Please, professor, it was no trouble. I just hope I was equal to the task. Bishop Sharma was a formidable adversary. I'm afraid he scored more points with the jury than I anticipated. Still, your questioning was just as impressive."

"Thank you, my friend. I just wish I knew what he has in store for young Michael tomorrow. I will be prepared to head off what he did to you this morning," Tom said to Michael, "but I just can't imagine that is all he has planned. You could decline, you know. This is just an exhibition, after all."

"I understand," Michael said. "But I think I'm going to have to play along. It might only be an exhibition here, but I agree that Sharma is up to something. Something that I think he intends will have more effect back home than here. At least I think we'll have the exhibits back."

"Well, I hope so. That might take some of his sting away."

"Speaking of the exhibits, I'd better get going. I have to meet someone about getting them back. Luigi," Michael said, standing up and holding out his arm for a handshake, "you never cease to impress me. Safe travels, my friend."

Luigi did not take Michael's hand but got up and gave Michael a hug. "*Amico mio*, please, be careful. I agree that Bishop Sharma is not to be trusted. Something about that injunction bothers me, but I can't put my finger on it. It certainly looked authentic to me, and I have seen a lot of documents signed by Galileo. Still..." he paused in contemplation. "Mention me to the Holy Father when you next see him. I will pray for him. Perhaps he could say a prayer for me?"

"I will, of course, and I'm sure he will." Michael turned to the group. "I'll touch base when I get back."

Karl, Lukas and Hana all spoke over one another, each saying essentially, "Where do you think you're going all by yourself?"

"My instructions were to come alone. If I take anyone with me, the deal is off. I need to get those exhibits back, for the trial's sake and for my father's sake, as well as my own. I'm willing to take the risk."

"Well, *we* are not willing for you to take that risk," Lukas said assertively. "That's the whole reason we're here —to protect you from this kind of risk. If our boss found out that we let you go off to meet some unknown person in an unknown place with no protection, we'd get an earful, if not outright dismissal. Besides, we like you, Michael. We don't want anything bad to happen to you. So we need to figure out a different plan."

Michael thought about it. "I'm sure the location is already staked out by their people. If I show up with you, they'll just leave and I'll never see them. I need those exhibits back for tomorrow. So, yes, I have to arrive alone. I'm going to hop in a ride-share. But the meeting is under the bridge where Halsted meets the river. I don't want to know where you are."

"Okay, but you need to give us a few minutes' head start," Karl said. "And Hana, I need you to stay here and watch to see if anyone follows Michael when his car leaves. Lukas and I have to get there ahead of him."

"But I wanted to come!"

"We'll go scout things out and let you know when it's safe. We can't worry about protecting both of you. The two of us are barely enough to protect Michael. Especially when he's going separately and alone."

The entire team left the restaurant and stood out front, saying their goodbyes. Karl and Lukas got into a ride-share and took off toward the river. Hana watched as they left. The couple from inside the restaurant came out, and a dark-colored Crown Vic picked them up from the corner, then turned in the direction Karl's ride-share had taken.

Bram spoke quietly into his wired phone mike, "Two of the party just left in a ride-share. Be ready to move. I'll give you directions when Dominic leaves."

Somchai replied, "I have a cab waiting out back."

Tom, Luigi and Hana stood out front for a few minutes until Michael's ride-share arrived, at which point he left. They started walking toward the corner and saw a cab leave from behind the restaurant and turn to follow Michael's vehicle. It stopped briefly down the block where another tall man got in, then it resumed going in the direction Michael had taken. Hana took out her phone and called Karl.

"You were right. A dark-colored sedan followed you

after it picked up the couple who sat near us in the restaurant. When Michael left, a cab came from behind the restaurant and picked up a tall man down the block, and went in the same direction as Michael's car. I couldn't tell from this distance, but it might have been that tall guy Bishop Sharma had with him at the museum."

"You did great, Hana, thanks. I wonder if whoever's in the sedan is related to the people we are going to meet, or somebody else? I guess we'll have to wait and find out. We'll be in touch."

∾

MICHAEL GOT out of the car at the entrance to the cement factory. The gate was secured with a loose loop of chain and a rusty old padlock, leaving a gap of about two feet between the sides of the gate. It would keep out cars, but not people.

Michael walked inside and looked around. There were several cement trucks parked in the lot. A conveyor system ran from the water's edge to huge tanks and containers elevated on a system of struts above the yard. Two large barges were tied up at the river's edge, one heaped with sand and the other with cement. Michael surmised that the barges brought in the components in quantities that would be difficult to truck through the streets of Chicago, and that they were mixed with water from the river and dispensed into cement trucks for delivery to numerous construction projects throughout the city.

But now, the yard was empty. Everything was shut down, and only a couple of dim, incandescent bulbs in iron cages lit the doorways to the offices. Michael saw the bridge on the right side of the yard, and in front of him the black void of the river. He headed to his right, spying the beginning of a path toward the river along the wall of the bridge. While he could not see anyone else, he felt as if there were a million pairs of eyes on him. The hair on the back of his neck stood up, and his flesh broke out in goosebumps. He shivered, but not from the cold.

When he got to the river, the space under the bridge was empty as well. He stood and waited. A few moments later, a sixty-foot yacht that had been tied up on the far side of the river and down a ways sprang to life, its motor roaring as it leapt across the space between them and came to a stop in front of him. He heard a voice he recognized from the confessional call him from the bridge.

"Come on, Father, get on board. Quickly! There are a lot of people watching."

Michael hesitated, not sure he should leave his protection behind. Karl and Lukas would have a fit if he got on that boat. Two figures emerged from the cabin a deck below and also called to him to get on board.

"Father Michael…" he heard Ian's voice call out, "Come on, it's safe." Then he saw Kat coming out, reaching a hand out to him so that he could get across to the boat.

Suddenly, Michael felt more than saw a shape coming at them from his left. The man dove at Kat, hitting her just below the shoulder and taking her off the boat and into the water between it and the dock. He was stunned, motionless, unsure what to do.

"Kat!" Ian screamed, diving into the water after her.

Another man came out onto the deck and followed Ian into the water. Instantly, it seemed, Karl and Lukas were at Michael's side. Two more men arrived. Water splashed everywhere as people came to the surface and were dragged back under by combatants. One of the men on the dock pulled a Glock from his waistband and, looking at the fray for a moment, picked his entry point and jumped in. There was the muffled sound of a gunshot underwater, then another.

Then the splashing stopped.

CHAPTER
THIRTY-NINE

Slowly, several heads bobbed to the surface of the river between the boat and the wharf. The man from the boat was holding an Asian man dressed all in black. He appeared to be unconscious, but Michael could tell he wasn't from the sputtering breaths he took while spitting out river water.

John Boswell and the other deckhand reached down and pulled the three men into the boat, and started tying up the assailant. Michael could see that the victim's foot was bleeding, but otherwise, he seemed unharmed.

Karl held at gunpoint another man who had come out onto the wharf from the shadows.

Lukas looked back and, seeing Karl guarding their backs, yelled to the boat, "Do you have any other people up here?"

Boswell looked up, recognizing the man Karl was guarding as one of his own, and replied, "Yeah, he's one of mine. He's no danger to you."

Karl lowered his weapon but did not put it away.

Michael called down to the wharf, "Hey, where are Kat and Ian?"

"Over here," Michael heard Ian say from the water on the other side of the boat. Boswell and his deckhand leaned over to get Ian. They saw him treading water, holding Kat to his chest by the forehead while keeping her mouth above water.

"She's breathing, but she's out cold. Take her up first," Ian quietly told the two men as they reached over the side of the boat.

They pulled Kat's limp body out of the water and laid her on the deck. Michael knelt at Kat's side, joined moments later by Ian, then said a silent prayer as he searched for a pulse. She was so cold. Boswell took off his jacket and gave it to Ian to cover Kat. Ian draped it over her upper body and covered her head. Michael started to pull it back, but Ian stopped him with a whispered. "Wait."

Michael was confused. *She was okay, wasn't she?* Tears started pooling in the corners of his eyes as he turned to look at Ian questioningly.

Boswell called up to Karl, Lukas, and his last man on shore. "Hey, you three, get in the boat, quickly. We're getting out of here." They scrambled down rapidly. When they were safely aboard, the deck hand took the boat down river at a good clip, then veered left at the first fork, heading north in the canal.

BRAM WATCHED from the barge as his partner was taken away, apparently alive but captured and possibly wounded. They had anticipated there could have been people watching, but perhaps not this many. They considered it worth the risk to accomplish Bishop Sharma's order to eliminate the threat to their mission. He dialed his phone.

"Yes? What is it?" he heard Bishop Sharma answer.

"We followed Father Michael to a cement factory at the river. Some people came by boat to meet him. The girl was among them. Somchai made an attempt on her and they both went into the river. He was captured by the people on the boat, and may be injured. They took the girl out of the river but she was limp. The priest got in the boat and prayed over her. They covered her face with a jacket. I think she might be dead. They took off down the river. I am unable to follow them."

"Okay, get back here. We'll have to wait to see if we hear from them or from Somchai. There is nothing more you can do from there."

Bram climbed off the barge and walked through the gate and back to the main street, where he called a cab. A few minutes later, the cab picked him up, driving him past an empty Crown Victoria parked nearby.

As soon as they gained some distance from the bridge, Ian pulled the jacket down and helped Kat roll to her side. She started coughing violently, spitting out the water she had inhaled. Michael was so relieved.

"Oh, God, that was so hard, not coughing," she sputtered.

"What kind of a stunt was that?" Michael asked, a little annoyed. "I thought she was dead."

"When I got Kat away from the guy who attacked her, we were down below the boat, and we came up on the far side. I told her to play dead, in case there was anyone else who was going to try to attack her. If they thought she was dead, they would leave her alone. If it fooled you, maybe it fooled anyone else who was watching."

"You came up with that, in the water, that fast?"

"Yeah, I guess so. I told Mr. Boswell and the mate that she was out cold, so they wouldn't panic, but you were too far away, and I didn't want anyone else to hear."

Kat sat up, and Michael took both of them in his arms. "I'm so glad you're both okay. I was really worried."

"We have a lot to tell you. But how's the trial going?"

"About like this did. Sharma really beat me up today over the theft, and you two, and that sham 'kiss' with Hana, and who my father is. And he beat up Galileo pretty good, too. He had a copy of an injunction signed by Galileo that was on the invoices for the exhibits, but which I never saw. That was pretty damaging." He looked at Kat. "I need to talk to you about that later. So, do you have the exhibits?"

"Yes, we're going to get them now. The plan was to pick you up and take you to them. At least, that was the plan before I was attacked," Kat said.

As the deckhand drove the boat, Boswell came back to speak to Ian, Kat and Michael.

"Michael, I'm John Boswell, chief of the Chicago Roma. Your guy, Lukas, tells me that the man who attacked Kat is one of Bishop Sharma's security people. Any idea why he would be after Kat? Do you think they somehow knew you were going to get the exhibits back?" Boswell asked.

"Maybe," Michael replied. "One of them might have followed me to the confessional at the cathedral. Court was delayed after lunch because of an emergency with one of Sharma's assistants. And he came back with a big bruise and a bad attitude. But that was the really tall one, not this guy."

"Yes, that makes sense. The men I had watching the confessional for my safety did rough up a tall guy who resisted them when they prevented him from getting to the confessional booth next to mine. I didn't make the connection. Thought he might have just been a vagrant or something. He had a hoodie on, not court clothes or a uniform."

"It just doesn't make sense to me why Sharma is so keen to keep me from getting the exhibits back. He already has made most of his points from the fact that they were stolen in the first place. And he already has copies of them all anyway. Would it be such a big deal if I got them back? And why would he have Kat attacked?"

Kat took a deep breath and looked down. "I think I might know."

CHAPTER
FORTY

Professor Aaron Pearce tried to sleep on the flight, but it had been no use. He had to forfeit his business class seat on a later flight in order to get a coach seat on this flight, and he ended up in a middle seat between a generously overweight man on the aisle, and a young mother with a colicky baby by the window.

To make matters worse, behind him was a young boy whose solution to boredom was to play air drums to the music on his headphones, with the back of Aaron's seat serving as the bass drum. The youngster was seemingly oblivious to the looks Aaron sent between the seats when he could. The flight had significant turbulence, and both the baby and the mother had gotten sick. There was no way the mother could make it past both him and the portly man before making a mess, which mostly landed on the man but spattered on Aaron, who did everything he could not to lose his own dinner.

When he got off the plane in Chicago, just after midnight, he headed for the men's room with a small overnight duffel that he kept ready in his car and a

messenger bag with his school materials and other documents. He did his best to clean up and would make a point
of going to his hotel to complete the job before trying to see
Hana or Michael. He'd tried calling both from the airport in
Rome to let them know he was coming, but the call went
straight to voicemail, so he gave up and stuck the phone in
his messenger bag. He would just surprise them both.

Leaving the terminal, Aaron crossed over the vehicle
lanes to catch the train into the city. He considered taking a
cab or a private car, but the train was so much cheaper, and
given the way he still smelled he would probably be repel-
lent to cab drivers—so the train it was.

In his fatigued state, he had not become aware that
somebody was following him from some fifty feet behind,
using other pedestrians on the sidewalk to shield him from
view.

It was Remi Shapiro.

Remi had come to the airport on the train himself and
was walking to his terminal when he was surprised to see
Aaron walking past, having recognized him from their
recent encounter in the Middle East. He wondered at the
coincidence of the professor being here at the airport—even
being in Chicago for that matter—knowing Father Dominic
and Hana Sinclair were here as well. It might be a stretch,
but there was a chance he was bringing Michael the letter
Pastor Darwin had ordered, since it was not among the
exhibits at the museum. Given that possibility, he decided
to follow Aaron and see what it was he might be up to.
Perhaps Remi could still be of service to his paymaster
after all.

Aaron, seeing that the next train was delayed, went back
into the terminal and stopped at a coffee kiosk, setting his
bags on the floor in order to get his wallet out. Remi
stepped behind a magazine rack outside the adjacent news-

stand next door, watching from a safe distance. A man pushing a cart full of luggage went past Remi, and as he passed Aaron, the edge of the cart caught the side of Aaron's messenger bag and started pulling it away. The escaping bag having caught his eye, Aaron abruptly turned and went after it.

"Oh, hey, you snagged my bag there," Aaron called as he went after the man pushing the cart, who stopped and looked.

"Oh, sorry, man. Didn't see it."

"No worries. Just an accident, but I can't afford to lose that." Aaron retrieved his bag from the front of the cart.

"Well, good luck with that. Sorry again," the man said, resuming his trek through the terminal.

That's it! Remi assured himself. *I'm certain he has the letter... I just need to get that bag now.*

As Aaron finished getting his coffee and resumed walking toward the terminal, Remi fell in behind him again. He tried to think of some way to get Aaron to put his bag down, or a way to somehow grab it away from him and take off with it, but convenient circumstances hadn't materialized. He knew he needed to act fast when he saw Aaron heading in the direction of the elevator to the overpass bridge for the train station.

Remi was wearing a hoodie and jeans, the better to blend in with the American crowd. He put his hood up and walked a little faster trying to catch up with Aaron. When Aaron got to the elevator, the train car was at the upper level, visible through the glass walls of the elevator shaft. A couple of other people were already waiting for the car, and a few more were heading in that direction, clustering right behind Aaron. Remi blended in with the small group.

He waited until the elevator arrived and the doors opened and Aaron entered. Stopping just shy of the doors,

Remi reached past the person in front of him and grabbed the strap of Aaron's messenger bag. As Aaron started to turn back to face the doors, Remi used his shoulder to shove the person between himself and Aaron directly into Aaron's body, giving a strong yank on the strap at the same time. Coffee went flying, and the person fell into Aaron, who let the bag go in order to brace himself against the person falling into him.

Remi pulled the bag toward himself, easily clearing it from the closing doors. He then turned and began walking at a normal pace away from the elevator. Aaron shouted in protest and tried to stop the doors from closing, but the person in front of him had not fully regained his balance, so Aaron could not get to either the doors or the button to stop them from closing.

Remi briskly crossed the terminal and took the service stairs down a level. He did not want Aaron to come back down and search for him. He had only a minute or two to disappear. He came out in the baggage claim area and walked back in the direction of his concourse. He paused in an alcove that used to hold a pay telephone, took off his hoodie and stuffed it into his carry-on bag. Now his appearance was different than when he was at the elevator in case Aaron caught a glimpse of him. He was pretty confident he'd kept his head turned away enough that he probably wasn't recognized. Opening Aaron's messenger bag, he took out all the documents he found, then put them in his carry-on bag without taking time to inspect them.

He needed to keep on the move, and as he headed into the security checkpoint, he hoped he could get through before Aaron contacted airport security. Now that he had what he wanted—the documents—he dropped Aaron's messenger bag in the empty alcove.

He made it through security without any more trouble

than usual—for a military-age male traveling in America on a Middle Eastern passport. Luckily, he was not randomly selected for extra screening, as was frequently the case on so many other trips to this country.

As he boarded his plane, he made plans for his arrival in Dallas. He would take a cab to the Diamond Ark Cathedral, check in with Mr. Jones, then see Pastor Darwin and give him the good news. He might even up his fee in light of the difficulty of obtaining this treasure for him.

Minutes later, Aaron came back down the elevator and looked around. He really didn't expect to see the thief; he was probably long gone by now anyway. But from what he understood, thieves often went through the purses and bags they stole looking for valuables, then dumped the incriminating parcels after taking what loot they found. Aaron checked the trashcans and alcoves on the level he was on, then went down to the lower level and looked around the baggage claim.

There, in an old phone booth alcove, he found his messenger bag, his school materials—and more importantly, his phone—still inside. The only thing missing were the copies of the letter and the draft injunction. He wondered to himself, *Who would want those?* Was this a random theft, or had he been targeted? Who knew he had them and that he was coming to Chicago? Only Viggo, actually. Had someone gotten to him? Or was he just being paranoid?

Aaron decided not to risk the train now, having been accosted once already, and went to the cab stand instead. He thought to himself, *As soon as I get to the hotel, I'll get in touch with Hana and Michael and get this sorted out, right after I take a shower. And then I'm getting some sleep.*

CHAPTER

FORTY-ONE

I t was after midnight when Michael finally got back to his room at the hotel. He placed the exhibits next to the bed, stowed in their original travel cases. He tried to fall asleep. He needed rest to be ready for the day that was to come, but the events of the last several hours kept swirling in his mind. He texted Hana to let her know the exhibit materials were okay, and that he would catch her up in the morning. He had a lot to tell her.

They had taken the boat up the North Branch Canal on the east side of Goose Island and pulled into the Weed Street Boathouse. There in the parking lot, a space away from the old brick smokestack—a testament to its industrial history, now surrounded by retail shops rather than factories—Gunari waited with his men and some of Boswell's crew in the beat-up old van with the exhibits in two backpacks. The telescope had already been sold to an international antiquities dealer, something they would have to deal with later. Somchai, now conscious and securely trussed and gagged, was hauled out of the boat and unceremoniously dumped in the back of the van as one of the men kept watch over him. Whenever he got too restless or agitated, the man kicked him in his wounded foot. When the pain subsided, Somchai was more compliant. The man repeatedly checked his captive's bonds to make sure he was not using his agitation to cover an attempt to loosen them and escape.

Kat, Ian, Boswell, Gunari and Michael gathered together next to the smokestack.

"Well, Father Michael, I'm afraid we owe you an apology, and an explanation," Gunari began. "A few weeks ago, John contacted me and asked for some help with a job. Something too complicated and high profile for his local boys. I owed him a favor, and he's family—distant, but still family. So, I loaned him my boys, though I didn't tell him who I was sending. And I didn't ask for details; sometimes it's better not to know. I just put the boys in touch with John and sent them on their way."

Boswell took over from Gunari's explanation. "I was hired by someone here in town, a prominent person I'm reluctant to reveal at the moment. He hired me to acquire the exhibits from the museum. I don't know why. As Gunari said, we don't ask questions if we don't need to know the answers. We were to hold the exhibits until we got further instructions. The boys went and did the job, and we put them up at a safe house in Lincoln Park, just a ways north of here. Everything seemed fine, but there was too much heat from the cops. Whenever there's a big crime and they don't have a clue as to who might be involved, they start looking at the 'usual suspects.' Since we Roma fall into that category, they started shaking us down pretty hard. The boys at the safe house were nervous. I was staying away so as not to draw attention to things, since the cops were keeping tabs on me.

"Anyway," he continued, "Ekaterina and Ian somehow

managed to figure out the approximate location of the safe house. Our lookout spotted them walking down the street. He recognized her as Roma. That worried him, so he put the safe house on alert, and when these two came back later that night, we were ready for them. Also, the boys, Milosh and Shandor, went from being guests to hostages. My men thought maybe the boys had tipped someone off or screwed up and got tailed. Anyway, my men took Ekaterina and Ian hostage as well. They overreacted. I'm sorry for that."

Kat interjected, "At the museum, I recognized a signature Milosh leaves at his big jobs. I knew when I saw it that the boys were involved. I was sure they didn't know the exhibits were Father Michael's—Uncle Gunari never would have approved that. So I called him and tried to find out where the boys were. He didn't know, exactly. Apparently, they had missed their regular check-ins. He wouldn't tell me who hired them. I told him I was going to look for them. Ian and I were able to hack the cell phone location system. We had to use a computer at one of the SixG Cellular stores, but we figured out about where the safe house was from the cell tower data. I guess Uncle Gunari didn't believe we would find them, so he decided to come to Chicago himself. That was when I knew the Roma here were involved."

Boswell continued. "So, Gunari is on his way here, and we arrange to talk when he arrives. But then everything goes haywire. The boys escaped but weren't able to take Kat and Ian with them. We got further instructions to get rid of the exhibits and the assets who took them, as well as Kat and Ian. Now, I knew I couldn't do that, so I had to work out a plan. I got hold of Gunari again, and we worked out a deal. He was pretty angry over how everything was going, and I don't blame him. But then again, he was trying to undo a deal I had already made with someone else, and that would have repercussions for me since we Roma frown on interfering with another clan's business. But when my client turned on me, I felt free to change sides. I wanted to make sure you got the exhibits back personally. By contacting you in the course of a confession, I figured you could not tell anyone the details.

"But, we were worried about my client. You were followed to the cathedral—by Bishop Sharma's people, as it turned out, but they could have been my client's. So we set this up to flush out and ditch anyone who was following you. They might have had people on foot and in cars, but they probably wouldn't have a boat. We didn't expect that they were going to try to take out Kat, but we had people on the boat and on the shore for protection. You were also apparently worried about being followed, because you brought two people of your own, despite being told not to. Which again is why we brought the boat. We were planning to bring you, and only you, here to get the exhibits, which are now here in the van.

"We'll put you and your people in a ride-share and send you back to your hotel. Gunari and his boys will go home, as will the New York and Miami clans he brought for reinforcement. I assume your people will be able to protect you and the exhibits until you return to Rome? At this point we're stepping back from this mess."

Michael looked from Boswell to Gunari, to Kat, and back to Boswell. "Well, that is quite the story. I almost wouldn't have believed it if I hadn't been involved myself. It would really help to know who hired you, John. I feel like there is still this unknown enemy out there, and I don't know what to prepare for if I don't even know who it is. And I still don't know why they wanted Kat out of the picture so badly."

Kat looked down at the ground but kept quiet. Ian put

an arm around her shoulders. Boswell pursed his lips, thinking.

"Michael, come over here," he said, taking the priest far enough from the group not to be overheard. "I'm invoking the seal of the confessional again. This is between you and me. You can't tell anyone, but I can't leave you in the dark like this, either. It's not fair to you, and I've wronged you enough already. So this is maybe a little bit of penance.

"The guy who hired me is Bishop William Loveridge. We go way back. Grew up together, he and I. He's helped me and my people over the years, so I owed him. And you don't usually tell a bishop 'no.' So, I took the job. Had to. I'm sorry you were hurt by it. If I had known we were stealing from the Church, I never would have done it."

"Thank you, John," Michael said, putting a hand on his shoulder. "In the name of Christ, I absolve you of your sins. Your penance is accepted, go and sin no more."

As they walked back to the others, Michael contemplated the import of the revelation, feeling stunned... *If Loveridge had hired John to have the exhibits stolen, what would be in it for him? How would it help him? It wouldn't. But it would help Sharma. That must be it! Sharma must have had Loveridge, someone local, arrange to have the exhibits stolen to improve his chances at the trial, and to embarrass me and probably the pope. And now Loveridge is on the jury—a vote Sharma could certainly count on to go his way.*

CHAPTER
FORTY-TWO

The red-eye flight from Chicago to Dallas got Remi to the conference center at the Diamond Ark Cathedral a little before six in the morning. He went to the room that was reserved for him there when he was in town. He really wanted some sleep, and a shower, but he knew his best time to get a few minutes alone with Pastor Darwin would be first thing in the morning before his appointments started.

Darwin was a workaholic. Remi suspected that he wasn't really happy at home, and preferred to spend his time at the cathedral instead. Remi knew Darwin routinely arrived at his office promptly at six o'clock, and spent the first hour in private preparing himself for the day. Remi took the envelope of documents he had removed from Aaron Pearce's messenger bag at the airport and headed over to the Administration building.

Remi wasn't the only person who knew Pastor Darwin's schedule. Mr. Jones also took advantage of Darwin's routine to check in with the pastor and discuss the operations of his empire.

Darwin had come to rely on Mr. Jones for a great many things. Jones had largely overseen the expansion of the Jewel Ark Chapels outside the United States, the kind of growth Darwin himself had never envisioned, assuming his ministry would largely be confined to the United States. But the overseas chapels and their associated field missions— schools, hospitals, shelters and food pantries—had grown exponentially and rapidly under Mr. Jones's leadership.

Yet Jones was the most humble of servants, never seeking credit for the scope of the empire he had helped build. He'd insisted that Pastor Darwin was the vessel God had chosen as the public face of the ministry, and Jones was content to wait to receive his reward in heaven.

So, Remi was a little irritated, but not surprised, to see Jones entering the Administration building just as he was approaching it. Seeing him coming, Jones waited for him just inside the doors.

"Hello, Remi. How was your trip to Chicago?" Mr. Jones already knew a fair bit about Shapiro's trip. He and Pastor Darwin had talked about his attempts to get that copy of Galileo's letter to Grand Duchess Christina.

"I think I got it!" Remi enthused. "I ran into Aaron Pearce at the airport in Chicago. He's a friend of Father Dominic. I recognized him from my earlier Middle East trip. I overheard him say he was taking something important to a friend in Chicago, and I knew Dominic was there without the letter, so I figured he'd sent for the letter and had Aaron Pearce bring it to him. But as it happened, Pearce wasn't very careful keeping his bag with him, and I ended up with it, thinking I'd do them the favor of getting the letter to Pastor Darwin more expeditiously." Remi gave Jones a conspiratorial smile. "I haven't even opened the envelope yet." He proudly held up the large envelope he had taken from the messenger bag for Mr. Jones to see.

"You know, Remi, someday you are going to get yourself in real trouble that even I won't be able to get you out of. Until then, let's see if you've got the goods." He reached out for the envelope.

Remi pulled back reflexively. He wanted to see Pastor Darwin's face when he produced the letter. He was afraid Mr. Jones would take his treasure and present it to Darwin himself as though he had been involved in its acquisition. He hesitated.

"Come on, Remi. If it's really the letter you think it is, I'll let you take it right up there and give it to Pastor Darwin personally. But you do realize that your contract with us supersedes any work you do for Pastor Darwin on the side, right? I let you do that because it generally doesn't interfere with the work you do for me, and I know there have been some slow periods, but—you still work for me first, and him second. Let me see the envelope."

Remi reluctantly handed it over. Mr. Jones broke the seal and pulled out the few pages that were inside. He looked at them, reading them over. Remi fidgeted with anticipation.

"Well?" Shapiro asked. "Is that it?"

Jones's face revealed the answer before he spoke it. "I'm sorry, Remi. No, it isn't the letter you were looking for. It has nothing to do with that. But don't worry. You're in luck because, by chance, these papers happen to be important to me. I will make sure you get paid appropriately. Go to your room, and I'll let Pastor Darwin know you're back."

Remi frowned deeply, his chest tight. He had so been looking forward to coming though for Pastor Darwin. His disappointment was palpable. Remi turned around and headed back to the conference center, his head down and shoulders slumped, curious as to what papers had made Jones so pleased and only a little grateful that all was not lost.

Jones, on the other hand, waited until Remi was out of sight, then left the Administration building and returned to his office in the Biblical Hall Museum. Once inside, he found Smith sitting at his desk.

"Hey, something big just fell into our laps. I need you to get me the phone number for Aaron Pearce, an associate of Father Dominic's. And I need it now."

CHAPTER
FORTY-THREE

J ust before six in the morning, Aaron called Michael. The priest had finally gotten to sleep a couple of hours before, after wondering what he was going to tell the pope about the last twenty-four hours.

"Hey, buddy, did I wake you?"

Michael answered groggily, "Yeah, but don't worry about it. I needed to get up anyway. What's happening? Everything okay in Rome?"

"Well, I wouldn't know—I'm here in Chicago, at your hotel, in fact. I came in last night. I was going to surprise Hana, take her out on the town, show her Chicago. But after the last twenty-four hours, I think I'm going to surprise you even more than her. You are not going to believe what happened. I don't want to talk about it on the phone. I'll tell you why when I see you. Can you meet me for breakfast in the restaurant downstairs in about twenty minutes?"

"Yeah, sure. I'll take a quick shower and be right down."

"Great. I'll grab us a quiet table in the back."

When Michael got downstairs to the restaurant, he

found Aaron sitting with both Karl and Lukas at a booth in the back.

"We got you a coffee, Mikey," Aaron said, smiling. "I was tempted to get you something stronger, but I'm told you have trial again this morning. By the way, you are not going to believe what happened to me yesterday."

"Yeah, well, I bet I can top it, whatever it is." Michael said, looking at Lukas.

"Okay, well, here goes. One of my students, a guy named Viggo, works as a *scrittore* in the DDF. In the course of his normal duties he was picking up documents for shredding in the dicastery's offices—Bishop Sharma's, in particular—*after* Sharma left for Chicago. Anyway, Viggo had been watching the trial and knew what was happening, and when he looked at one of the documents in the shred box, he recognized it as a draft of the injunction, a marked-up copy of changes somebody wanted made to it before it was finished." Aaron paused, "Hey, how come you don't look surprised?"

"Because I'm not. I found out last night that the injunction was a fake."

"*What?!* How?"

"I'm afraid I can't go into it. I can't tell anybody."

Karl and Lukas exchanged a glance.

"Okay, but how about this one: the other document was a letter, a confession from Sharma—addressed to his boss, I think, although not by name—that says the whole plot was concocted by Sharma to embarrass and discredit you and the pope, and that his boss didn't know anything about it."

"But wait," Karl interrupted him. "You said it showed up in Sharma's shredding box *after* he'd already left for Chicago, so he couldn't have written it. Somebody else must have put it there, right? So if Sharma got in trouble, they would search his office and find evidence of the fake injunction and a confession that exonerates his superiors. How convenient."

"Aaron, where are those letters now?" Michael asked. "Did you bring them with you?"

"Well, I tried to. I got as far as O'Hare Airport with them, but someone grabbed my messenger bag while I was getting on an elevator to catch the train. I found the bag later, but the letters were gone."

"Hmm. Do you think that was random? After all that has gone on with this trial, I'm tempted to suspect it wasn't," Michael posited thoughtfully.

"I don't know. Only Viggo and I knew I was coming over with them. I doubt Viggo said anything about them. I didn't get a good look at the guy who grabbed the bag. I'm pretty sure he was male, dark hair, medium build. He was wearing a hoodie over his head, but I can't be more specific than that."

"You tried, and I appreciate that. I guess it's just the way this damned trial is going. I can't seem to catch a break."

"Well, that wasn't the weirdest part. This morning, just before I called you, I got a call from some guy named Jones. He said he was a friend of Karl's. He also said he had come into possession of the letters that were stolen from me at the airport. He refused to discuss how he'd acquired them, or how he knew that they were mine, or even how he got my number. It was quite strange and not a little disturbing."

Michael looked at Karl. "Yes, I do know him," the young guard said, "but I wouldn't call him a friend by any stretch. We met on the trip to Dallas. He called me this morning, too, and asked me to vouch for him with Aaron. So I called Aaron, who had just gotten off the phone with Jones. Aaron said he was going to call you, so we decided to all come down and talk together."

"Wait... This is all getting a little confusing. Did this

Jones guy say what he was going to do with the documents? It would be great to have them for the trial this morning. And I'd love to send a copy back to the Vatican so they can deal with that side of it."

"Actually, Jones said that he was discussing the letters with other interested parties and he would get back to me later today. He didn't know when that might be. But he said he couldn't send a copy of them till some decisions had been made."

Hana walked up to the table, a surprised look on her face when she saw Aaron.

"Hey, what are you doing here?! When did you get in?" she asked, giving him a quick hug and kiss.

"That's a long story," Michael interjected. "He can tell you in a minute. But since you're here, let me fill you both in on what happened last night." He gave them a rundown of the events of the previous evening: the meeting under the bridge, Kat and Ian coming in with the local Roma chieftain on a boat, the attack on Kat, the ride downriver and the return of the exhibits with Gunari. He omitted only the parts that were given to him confidentially.

Hana's eyes were wide with surprise. "Wow. Maybe I'm not so disappointed I wasn't there. I was really worried about you guys. Is everyone okay? Where are Kat and Ian?"

"Kat was a little shook up, but she's okay. She and Ian went to a different hotel with her uncle Gunari and her cousins. They are all going back home today," Michael said. "Well, you folks finish your breakfast. I need to go upstairs and explain all this to His Holiness before the trial starts."

Michael spoke to Nick Bannon at length before he was put through to the pope. Bannon was someone who got things done, and it would be easier for him if he knew all the details directly. When Pope Ignatius heard the wild tale Michael told him, right up to the latest revelations from Aaron, Karl, and Mr. Jones, he was both concerned and compassionate, as a father should be—even one who was the spiritual figurehead of a billion souls worldwide.

"Michael, I'm so sorry you've had to endure this. This is not so much about you as it is about me. The *papabile* are especially fractious already. It is the state of the world right now, with people letting themselves become entrenched in ideologies. It is dividing countries and cultures and will threaten to divide the Church.

"I am very concerned with what will happen when I am gone. This is just the first foray. But as we know, the Lord moves in mysterious ways. You have given me warning. I will not be caught unawares.

"But you might be interested to know that Cardinal Caputo has quietly called a press conference for a few hours from now. So be wary. Perhaps Bishop Sharma has something planned that Caputo is expecting to talk about. We will be watching, and we will be ready."

After Michael hung up, the pope called his secretary into the room.

"Nick, please call Colonel Scarpa and have him here in ten minutes."

FORTY-FOUR

om Anderson was getting settled in the courtroom when Michael entered with Hana, Karl, Lukas and Aaron. Bishop Sharma had yet to arrive.

"Hey, Tom," Michael asked, "is there a private place where we can all talk for a few minutes? A lot has happened since last night, and I need to bring everyone up to speed."

"Sure, Father. We can use one of the classrooms down the hall."

Tom led all five of them to an empty classroom, unlocking the door with his staff key. When they were inside, Michael locked the door and came to join them in seats around a small conference table.

He walked Tom through the events of the last twelve hours, starting with the meeting under the bridge, the attack on Kat, the identity of the thieves, the return of the exhibits, the discovery and loss of the draft injunction and Sharma's presumably fake confession, as well as the mysterious Mr. Jones.

"Also," Michael concluded, "I have a firm belief that the jury has been tampered with."

"By whom?!" Tom was stunned.

"I'm afraid I can't say."

"Why not?"

"The information was provided under confidential circumstances which I cannot violate."

"But you do have the exhibits back now?"

"Yes, everything except for the telescope and the fake injunction Sharma removed before the thefts."

"We should call the police!" Tom huffed adamantly.

"I simply can't call the police on the thieves. They are the ones who got the exhibits back for me, or at least they were involved in the return of them. And in any case, they're on their way out of the country. There would be no point. And while I know who hired them, I cannot do anything about that either because it would reveal how I know about it, and that would betray the confidence as well."

"Then what *are* we going to do?"

"I've given that some thought," the priest said, his brow furrowed. "Hana and Karl are going to take seats right behind Bishop Sharma's table. Lukas will be right behind ours. They will keep a sharp watch out for any physical threats. One of Sharma's men will not be returning today, so he only has the other one, Bram. You and I will have to do our best to try to get the people behind this mess to reveal themselves. I expect whatever Sharma has planned will occur this morning because his boss has a news conference scheduled for a few hours from now. I think he expects to have something to talk about."

"You're sure we can't get those documents from that Jones fellow?"

"Maybe, but you would know better than I whether

they would even be admissible or not. The chain of custody is complicated and may be impeachable. They were taken from a secure shredding box in Bishop Sharma's office by a person in Rome, who took them to a professor at his university. The professor attempted to bring them to me, during which time they were stolen, and subsequently returned by a person we don't really know. We also don't know who actually wrote them or how they got in Bishop Sharma's shredding box while he was here. I could imagine that Sharma doesn't even know they exist."

"Well, that's just grand. You're right. They probably are fake, and just being planted to set Sharma up if things go sideways here. Someone is covering his tracks."

"Okay, so we're together on this, Tom?"

"You bet. Let's do it."

THE GROUP FILED BACK into the courtroom, past the jurors waiting in the hall. The doors were closed, and the participants took their seats. Bishop Sharma was at his counsel table with Bram, whose mood had not improved since yesterday. He glared at the group as they came in. Sharma did not appear to be in any better mood.

The judge came in and addressed them all. "Any other matters to come before the Court before we invite the jurors in and get this thing wrapped up? I'd love to give this to the jury before lunch."

Sharma stood up. "Your Honor, as a result of information I received last night, I am asking the Court's permission to conduct a formal preliminary inquisition on Father Michael Dominic. This will take no additional time from this exercise." He walked over to the defense table and handed a set of documents to Michael. "This is a preliminary investigation for the recommendation of charges within the Holy Catholic Church. The charges are delimited within the documents I have just served on Father Dominic. They relate to incompetence, malfeasance, dishonesty and nepotism. I wish to deputize three members of the jury: the bishop, the monsignor, and the chaplain on behalf of the Church. I am authorized to convene a tribunal of clergy to hear the presentation of evidence, which in this matter will consist of Father Dominic's testimony under oath during this trial, and any discrepancies with the testimony he previously gave under oath, which I recorded and had transcribed." He patted a large stack of papers on the corner of the counsel table. "These men will be my tribunal and will recommend that charges be filed or not. I will be bound by their decision. If charges are recommended, Father Dominic will return with me, in my custody, to face more formal inquisition procedures at the Dicastery for the Doctrine of the Faith. I consider him a flight risk, and we are in a foreign country which creates exigent circumstances. This inquisition will be done concurrently with the testimony for this trial today so, as I explained, it will take no additional time on the part of the Court. The tribunal may render their verdict after the exercise is concluded.

"And, of course, Father Dominic is entitled to representation," Sharma proclaimed. "I hereby appoint Thomas Anderson to represent him. It is not required that his representative be a lawyer, nor a member of the clergy, just certified as an expert in canon law, a certification which Mr. Anderson possesses. But Mr. Anderson does have the distinction of having been, at least for a short time, a member of the clergy."

"Mr. Anderson, do you concur?" the judge asked. "Is Bishop Sharma correct in his assessment? Is he authorized to conduct this type of preliminary inquisition under these circumstances?"

"Your Honor, may we have a moment? This was highly unexpected. I need to speak with Father Dominic."

"Yes, of course. Take what time you need."

"Thank you, Your Honor." Tom took Michael to the very back of the courtroom, and they spoke in hushed tones.

"I'm sorry, Michael, but according to my understanding of canon law, his invoking exigent circumstances does authorize him to convene an ad hoc tribunal of clergy. As long as there is one bishop on the tribunal, the other two need only be clergy. And he can recommend charges, and if they concur, you would be taken to the DDF for formal procedures. I guess we now know what Cardinal Caputo is expecting to talk about later."

"What did Sharma mean about you being clergy once?"

Tom hesitated, slightly embarrassed. "Well, a long time ago, I fell in love with a woman named Leslie. It was right out of undergrad. We were thinking about marriage, but I wanted to go into seminary. We parted but stayed in touch during my formation. When I was ordained, we were reunited by circumstances. We were both assigned to the same city. She was a traveling nurse and I was a young new priest. We started seeing each other, just as friends at first, but then romantically. Not long after, we ran off to Las Vegas and got married. I had an apartment to myself, off-campus from my parish. We tried to keep it a secret. I liked being a priest. I couldn't bear to turn myself in and quit. But then, one of the other priests at the church just happened to stop by one morning, looking to borrow a book. He discovered Leslie in the apartment, dressed in her pajamas. I couldn't hide it any longer.

"Bishop Sharma was newly assigned at the DDF. He was sent out to investigate. He did the same thing: convened a tribunal. They recommended I be discharged. I went back to Rome with Sharma and he had me defrocked.

And that's why I asked those extra questions yesterday. I'm hoping that maybe this pope will be the one to allow married clergy. If the Church were willing to admit it was wrong about science and the literal interpretation of the Bible, then maybe they can admit they are wrong about celibacy. Think of how many more priests there might be if they could be married?"

"Believe me, I've talked to him about it. He's trying to lay the groundwork, but at present there is too much tradition and resistance. I don't think it will happen on his watch, though he did imply he has something planned, but, who knows?"

"Okay, so now you know my secret. I'm still married to her, by the way. So what do you want to do?"

"I think we have to go forward. If I don't, then that becomes the story. If I do, and they recommend charges, then that's the story. The only way we win is if we can convince them not to recommend charges, or if we can expose this whole fiasco without having to violate any confidences."

"You sure you can't break a confidence? The stakes are pretty high. This could mean losing your job and maybe even the pope's."

"No, sorry. Some promises can't be broken. And as much as there might be a few people who doubt it, I take my vows seriously."

"Well, then, God's will be done."

"Amen."

They walked back to the counsel table. "Your Honor, we accede to the bishop's authority. Let's bring in the tribunal and swear them in, then invite the rest of the jury in. We are ready to proceed."

Bram was dispatched to the hall to bring in the three clerics. They were briefed and sworn in. Michael noticed that the bishop did not seem surprised, while the other two registered shock on their faces. The rest of the jury and spectators were brought in and the judge called the assembly to order.

"Bishop Sharma?"

"Your Honor, the prosecution calls Father Dominic to the stand."

Michael took a deep breath, walked to the witness stand, and waited.

"Father Dominic, do you understand that you remain under oath?"

"Yes, Your Honor."

"Very well, please be seated. Bishop Sharma, your witness."

CHAPTER
FORTY-FIVE

With a script of several pages in his hand, Bishop Sharma slowly paced across the courtroom to stand just a few feet between the witness box and the jury. He paused, staring directly into Michael's eyes. *A fearful opponent is easy to direct,* Sharma reasoned. *You show them their fear, and then show them the less painful alternative. Like a scared animal, they will take the less painful alternative every time, just to make the fear stop.*

But seeing no sign of fear in the priest's placid brown eyes, he decided to change tactics.

"Father Dominic, can we agree that you don't really want to be a priest?"

That was not at all what Michael was expecting. He was anticipating something more along the lines of the questions he had endured yesterday. This was a completely different tack. *Well, honesty is the best policy. If you always tell the truth, you don't have to remember any falsehoods you'd said before.*

"I confess there are times I do still wonder about my

vocation, and whether I made the right choice. But there are other times when I believe I am on the ideal path for me. I wish I were one of those people who never has a doubt, but I guess I'm just human in that regard."

Sharma knew the jury would like that response. He also knew everybody had weaknesses. It was just a matter of finding them. Which he intended to do.

"You seem to spend an inordinate amount of your time in places other than at the Vatican, where you belong. Do you know how many countries you have visited recently?"

"No, not off the top of my head. Several, I'm sure."

"Let me help you with that. Several trips to France and Switzerland, a couple of trips to Israel and the Middle East, Scotland, Malta, and now the United States."

"Yes, now that you list them off like that, it does seem like quite a few."

"And in most of your trips, you stay in five-star hotels, dining at Michelin-starred restaurants, traveling by private jet...all due to the generosity of your journalist friend, Ms. Sinclair."

Michael's face reddened and his fists tightened.

"She has done nothing wrong. And much of that was at the behest of her grandfather, a member of the Holy Father's Consulta and a patron of the Apostolic Archive."

There it was, Sharma noted. *His fear. He is very protective of his friends. They are dear to him. He will sacrifice himself for their sake. How Christ-like. Very well. That shall be the vehicle of your undoing.*

"I didn't say she had done anything wrong, per se," Sharma smirked, looking back at Hana in the audience. "I'm sure she didn't mean to be a temptress, but you have to admit, you have been tempted. There is even a picture proving it." Sharma took the newspaper photograph and showed it to the jury, and then to Michael. "You cannot deny that you have kissed."

"As I have explained before, that was an obvious accident. Hana was just going to whisper in my ear, and I unintentionally turned into it. It's just the camera angle that makes it look that way."

"Still, it shows an inappropriate level of familiarity with a priest that she would feel comfortable whispering in your ear." Michael felt his face flushing again. He knew Sharma was baiting him. He had to stay in control.

"Tell me, Father Dominic, even if you say this wasn't a kiss, for all that it looks like one, you have kissed her before, haven't you?"

Michael mumbled out his truthful answer, embarrassed. "Yes."

"Well, goodness me. How many times, then? Two? Three? Or is this something you make a regular habit of?" Sharma did not really care what the answer was. Anything was damaging enough.

"Twice, I think."

"You think? A beautiful woman kisses you, a celibate priest, and you don't remember it?"

"I've known Ms. Sinclair a very long time."

"Oh, so this has been an ongoing problem for you?"

"No, it's not like that."

"Oh, I'm sure it's not. Whatever you say. But it's not just you, is it? You allow your employees to carry on this way as well, don't you?"

Here it comes, Michael thought. *How to answer this one. He really is good at asking questions with no right answer.*

"It is not something I condone. But they are adults, responsible for themselves."

"Oh, please, Father. Both Ekaterina Lakatos and Ian Duffy look up to you as a mentor. You knew those two had been sneaking off to see each other. You must have suspected how serious it had gotten between them. And you are Ms. Lakatos' ward. You are supposed to be looking after her to help keep her out of trouble. It was because she was in trouble that she came to your employ, was it not? Some sort of forgery issue?"

"Yes."

"So, do you really think it is a good idea to have someone with a history of forgery working in an environment with such valuable documentary artifacts?"

"I trust her."

"Yes, apparently you do. And look where that got you. You assigned the people to the teams watching the exhibits overnight before they were to be brought to this conference. You had two Swiss Guards available, yet you did not assign either of them to the first shift. You put Mr. Duffy and Ms. Lakatos together, on a shift that ran overnight. And let your Swiss Guard buddies have a night on the town. If you anticipated what happened, you are a facilitator. And if you didn't, then you are a fool. Which is it?"

"Objection! Argumentative."

"Sustained. Bishop Sharma, please watch your tone."

"Well, so you have been running around the world, living a lavish lifestyle, ignoring the moral depravity occurring under your roof, cavorting with criminals."

"What criminals?" Michael interjected, then immediately regretted it.

"What criminals? Well, aside from your little forger, there is the ultra-violent ex-commando who accompanied Ms. Sinclair. A Major Marco Picard, my notes tell me? How many people has he killed on your little escapades? I've checked. For some reason, wherever you two went, there were mysterious deaths in your wake. Coincidence?"

"I don't know. But on several occasions we were attacked, and Marco was simply defending us."

"Yes, you've been attacked. Taken hostage. Both Ms. Sinclair and her grandfather have been kidnapped, all so you could chase the occult and the arcane. And people have died. Meanwhile, fifty-three linear miles of manuscripts in the Vatican Archive remain largely uncatalogued. What do you think your job is, actually?"

"My job is to look after the Apostolic Archive, including acquiring artifacts and antiquities that belong there, and discrediting fakes and forgeries that do not."

"Yes, well, you don't seem to be doing a very good job of it, when some of the most priceless artifacts in your possession were stolen from under your nose while your employees were making out or falling asleep on the job, so you could get a pizza and kiss the girl. But the Apostolic Archive is the personal property of the pope, your father, which is how you got that job in the first place, isn't it?"

"I believe he recommended me for the position when he was a cardinal."

"I'm sure he did. In fact, he has recommended you during your entire ecclesiastical career, has he not?"

"That's something you should ask him. I wouldn't know."

Sharma walked over to the witness stand and got right up into Michael's face. "Well, let me ask you this. Did you not find it odd that your mother was his housekeeper, that you lived in his rectory, and that he acted the father figure for you, yet you never put two and two together? But he wasn't just a father figure, he was your father, and was never married to your mother. That makes you illegitimate. An ambivalent bastard priest hanging onto his daddy's coattails and enjoying his girlfriend's money."

"Objection!" Tom shouted angrily.

"Sustained. You do not have to answer that, Father Dominic," the judge proclaimed.

"Never mind," Sharma said, turning his back on Michael and walking back to the counsel table, "he doesn't have an answer for that anyway. No further questions."

FORTY-SIX

When Bishop Sharma rested his case, Cardinal Caputo turned off the live feed of the trial. He was uninterested in the outcome for Galileo. He was only concerned with the outcome for Michael Dominic and his father, the pope. And ultimately, for himself as one of the leading candidates to replace Pope Ignatius on his death or resignation, whichever Caputo could nudge into occurring first.

Cardinal Caputo was unfamiliar with American jurisprudence. He was not aware that Thomas Anderson would have an opportunity for cross-examination. No, instead, the cardinal spent the next hour making sure he had his remarks settled in his mind, and that he was as presentable as he could be for the cameras.

He intended to go out in his official red cardinal's cassock for his press conference and announce the initiation of an investigation into the position of the Prefect of the Apostolic Archive after the very public debacle in the United States. The tribunal would most certainly recommend charges and Bishop Sharma would be bringing Father Dominic back to Rome in figurative chains.

His gambit was almost complete. With charges of incompetence and nepotism, the pope would be directly implicated; and at his age, likely unable to properly defend himself. He would be pressured by the College of Cardinals and the Curia to resign to avoid a scandal. Or, it just might just kill him.

~

THOMAS ANDERSON STOOD UP. He did not have a clue what he was going to do. He looked at Michael, who looked back at him, pleading in his eyes. He looked at the jury, focusing on the three clergy amongst them. Then his attention was drawn to a man coming into the courtroom, one he had not seen leaving. Aaron Pearce came up the aisle, holding a few pages of paper in his hand. He leaned over the bar and handed them to Tom.

"Mr. Jones sends his regards."

Tom glanced over Aaron's shoulder, and saw an olive-skinned, dark-haired young woman next to a skinny, red-headed Irishman, huddled down in the courtroom gallery, trying to avoid being seen by Bishop Sharma.

He cocked his head, catching her eye, then silently mouthed a question to her: *Kat?*

She nodded subtly.

And now he knew what he needed to do. He turned confidently to Michael.

"Father Dominic, do you know a young novitiate named Viggo Pisano?" he asked.

"Objection," Sharma rebutted. "Relevance."

"Mr. Anderson, where is this going?"

"All I ask is a little latitude, Your Honor, given that the

circumstances have been expanded by the prosecution's request this morning."

"Very well, overruled. Proceed, Mr. Anderson, but get there quickly."

"Yes, I know him," Michael answered.

"How do you know him?"

"He is a *scrittore* for the Dicastery for the Doctrine of the Faith."

"That is a similar position to the one you had in the Vatican archives until your promotion—a records keeper, is it not? So he would have access to the records of the DDF?"

"Yes, in fact he was the one who brought the dicastery's exhibits for the trial to me to be transported along with the ones from the Apostolic Archive."

"So he would know if the injunction was among the records of the dicastery that were sent along with yours, and were entered into the shipping manifest? Did he sign the manifest when he handed the documents over to you?"

"Yes."

"I have in my hand that manifest, and a second document that was just handed to me. Can you look at those two documents and see if the signatures are the same?"

"Objection!" Sharma shouted. "Father Dominic does not have the qualifications to compare signatures."

Michael smiled, speaking confidently now. "On the contrary, Excellency, I have extensive formal training and experience in comparing documents to determine authenticity, including the handwriting and signatures."

The judge was satisfied. "Overruled. Proceed, Mr. Anderson."

"Now, Father Dominic, can you compare those two documents and tell me if they were signed by the same person?"

"Yes, they appear to have been. I'm quite sure. In fact,

the second document has also been notarized. It's a notarized affidavit, signed by Mr. Pisano."

"Will you read the affidavit into the record?"

"Objection!" Sharma was apoplectic. "There is no relevance, no foundation. I haven't even seen this document myself!"

"Let me see the affidavit, Mr. Anderson," the judge instructed.

Tom walked the document to the bench to let the judge review it. Bishop Sharma walked up to the bench and waited. The judge handed the affidavit to Sharma, who read it while turning an angry shade of red.

"Bishop Sharma, hand the document back to Mr. Anderson. I find that foundation has been established. Mr. Pisano is an unavailable witness, but as he is an employee of yours, you had ample time to elicit testimony from him had you thought you needed it. Proceed, Mr. Anderson."

"Father Dominic," Tom asked, "can you please read the affidavit into the record?"

"Yes, of course." Michael began reading.

"I, Viggo Pisano, swear under penalty of perjury that the following facts are true, and would testify under oath to the same.

1) I am a scrittore in the Dicastery for the Doctrine of the Faith;

2) I prepared the travel manifest of the Galileo exhibits at the direction of Bishop Sharma;

3) Bishop Sharma ordered me to include an injunction not previously in the holdings of the Dicastery;

4) I discovered a draft of this injunction in his shredding box after he left for the United States, even though I had already emptied the box after he left;

5) At the same time, I found a letter alleged to have been written by him that amounts to a confession; and

6) I gave the draft injunction and the letter to my professor, Aaron Pearce.

Signed, Viggo Pisano."

"Thank you, Father Dominic. You may be seated. I now call Aaron Pearce to the stand."

"Objection," Sharma said. "He is not on the witness list."

"Neither was Father Dominic, and I am calling him in rebuttal."

"Overruled. You may proceed, Mr. Anderson."

After Aaron was sworn in, the judge said, "You may take the witness stand, Mr. Pearce." Aaron sat in the witness box.

"Professor Pearce, you are a teacher at the John Felice Rome Center, and Viggo Pisano is one of your students. Is that correct?" Tom asked.

"Yes."

"And did he give you two documents that he told you he liberated from Bishop Sharma's shredding box?"

"Objection! Hearsay!"

"It is not offered for the truth of the matter, Your Honor, but to identify the documents, and this fact was already testified to via affidavit."

"Overruled. Proceed, Mr. Anderson."

"I want you to read these documents to yourself, Professor Pearce. Please take a moment to do so." Tom waited as he watched Aaron read the letter and the draft injunction.

"Professor Pearce, are these the documents you were given by Mr. Pisano?"

"Yes, they are."

"No further questions for Mr. Pearce."

"Bishop Sharma, do you have any questions for Mr. Pearce?"

"Your Honor, again, I have not seen these documents. How would I know what to ask?"

"Your Honor, Bishop Sharma is not entitled to see the documents until I attempt to introduce them into evidence or have them read in open court. At this point, I have only given them to the witness to read, to establish their foundation. Bishop Sharma's objection is premature."

"Overruled. Bishop Sharma, questions?"

"No, Your Honor."

"Then I recall Father Dominic to the stand."

Michael looked confused, but went back to the witness stand and sat down.

"You remain under oath, Father Dominic. Your witness, Mr. Anderson."

"Father Dominic, I would like you to read this letter."

Michael read the letter, his face growing pale, then flushing red.

"Now, Father Dominic, based on this letter, do you feel that the trial in this matter has been fair?"

"*No, absolutely not!*"

"Did the information in this letter surprise you?"

"No. I was already aware of most of it." Michael thought back to the night before. Kat could not look at him as she related her story. She revealed to Michael that she had gone to confession about her intimate relationship with Ian. As luck would have it, Bishop Sharma had been her confessor, as all members of the Curia were required to provide the sacrament on a monthly basis, a program Pope Ignatius had instituted to remind them of God's grace and forgiveness. To avoid her improper behavior being exposed to her uncle and Michael and losing her job, she was forced by Bishop Sharma to create the forged injunction. Under such duress, she complied. Michael had absolved her, both religiously and personally, but Kat could not forgive herself. She would have to figure out how to make amends.

"But you didn't say anything."

"I obtained my information in confidence, which I could not divulge. Although apparently Bishop Sharma does not feel similarly obligated."

"Objection! I want to see this letter!"

Tom took the letter from Michael and handed it to Bishop Sharma. Standing at counsel table, he read it. He turned bright red with rage and began shaking. Spittle flew from his mouth as he yelled, "This is outrageous! I did *not* write this letter. I've never even seen it before. It is not signed by me. Somebody is trying to frame me! There is no proof that the injunction is fake!"

The jury gasped on hearing the possibility that the injunction was fraudulent.

"Yes, there is!" a voice claimed from the gallery. Kat stood up and continued, "Because you blackmailed me into forging it for you!"

Chaos erupted in the courtroom.

"You're supposed to be dead!" Sharma exclaimed, shocked to see her, then put a hand over his mouth when he realized what he had just said.

The judge banged her gavel on the bench, repeatedly to try to restore order. Bram slipped through the swinging gate separating the courtroom from the gallery and made a beeline for Kat, a murderous look on his face.

Michael saw Bram moving toward Kat. Everyone else seemed to be distracted by Sharma's exclamations and the banging of the gavel. Michael leapt from the witness stand and moved to intercept Bram. As Bram approached Kat, he pulled the yawara stick from his pocket and swung it at her temple, a lethal blow if it had landed.

Thinking fast, Michael broke into a run, jumped onto one of the chairs in the gallery and launched himself at Bram's back. Lukas, just a row in front of them but facing forward, turned and made a grab for Bram as well, but couldn't get there in time. Michael fell onto Bram's legs, causing him to stumble just as he was about to land his blow on Kat. He fell short and hit Kat on the collarbone, snapping it but missing her head.

Lukas climbed over the chairs and leapt onto Bram's back, trying to take control of his weapon arm. Karl quickly charged in after Lukas, also trying to subdue Bram.

The judge continued banging her gavel on the bench, shouting, *"Order! Order!"*

Finally, Karl and Lukas got control of Bram. He was a trained fighter and gave them a few bruises, but Lukas and Karl's Swiss Special Forces training and mutual cooperation were tactically superior.

A law school security officer called by the dean from the bench came in and slapped handcuffs onto the struggling Bram, who, seeing that he was now effectively overpowered, stopped resisting.

The judge rapped the gavel again as her courtroom was clearly in chaos. Michael groaned and carefully got up, having been shifted to the bottom of the pile of bodies in the melee. He was going to have quite a collection of bruises tomorrow.

"What the heck was *that?*" the judge addressed the room at large. "And where is Bishop Sharma?"

In the chaos, it seems, Sharma had slipped out of the courtroom.

FORTY-SEVEN

C olonel Scarpa was on his way to meet with the Holy Father when his phone rang. He looked at the number, then ducked into a side hallway.

"Scarpa," he answered.

"Hello, Colonel. Nice to hear your voice again so soon. Do me a favor, right now, please, and take Viggo Pisano into protective custody. He could be in danger, and I have some news for His Holiness."

CARDINAL CAPUTO WAS WALKING from his office to the media relations department to give his press conference, with his new security attaché, Dieter Koehl, just a step behind. Finally, after years of suffering under this progressive pope, he would take a substantial step toward putting the Church back on the right track by initiating an investigation into the pope's son, which could not help but directly implicate the pope himself. It would be a scandal, but the Church had been through scandals before and come out the better for it.

And it would elevate his own brand, as it were. People would see him fighting for the Church, the true Church. The people, and more importantly, the College of Cardinals, would see him as a leader righting the ship, and placing him one step closer to being named captain of that ship. His deputy, Bishop Sharma, had done his job in America well, creating the crisis that he would capitalize on.

His cell phone rang. He pulled it from his pocket and looked at the number. He stepped into an alcove and tapped the green button.

"This had better be important. I'm on my way to a press conference."

"I know, that's why I'm calling. Did you watch the rest of the morning session, or did you turn it off after your little puppet did his show?"

"I don't know what you are talking about, Jones. I'm about to announce an investigation into Father Dominic's activities, so unless you want to be less cryptic, I have to go."

"That would be a mistake. Bishop Sharma was revealed to be a cheat and a fraud. It's clear he had that Galileo injunction forged to embarrass Father Dominic, and the indications are that you knew all about it. It might have even been your idea. But your little gambit didn't work. I appreciate your offer that if you were made pope we could use some of your facilities around the world, but we need someone we can trust. We are withdrawing our support for your cause."

"Wait! You can't do that! We are too close now. We had a deal. We've been working together too long."

"Do you hear boots approaching, Cardinal Caputo? I can hear them from here. So goodbye and may God forgive you."

The line went dead. Dieter waited just outside the alcove listening to a transmission on his earpiece.

To Caputo's surprise, he actually did hear boots approaching. He stepped out of the alcove.

"Cardinal Caputo!"

He froze. Colonel Scarpa was rapidly approaching with a contingent of six Swiss Guards. Caputo started to turn, but Dieter stood in his way. The guards quickly had him surrounded.

"Cardinal Caputo, you are under arrest for conspiracy to commit fraud and conspiracy to commit forgery." Scarpa leaned in, speaking more softly. "I know what you did, and I know why you did it. You aren't the only person who knows Mr. Jones. You are lucky it is we who have you and not him. But you might want to start saying your prayers. Come along now."

~

WHEN IT WAS DISCOVERED that Bishop Sharma had fled, calls were made back to Mr. Jones and Colonel Scarpa. An All-Points Bulletin was issued to Chicago police and the Transportation Safety Administration, but it was discovered that Bishop Sharma had gone straight to the airport and boarded a flight to Mumbai, India, before the APB was actionable. Indian authorities were contacted but could not find him on the plane when it landed. A review of the security footage showed Sharma having his ticket scanned at the gate at O'Hare, but then stepping out of the boarding line and back onto the concourse. As it happened, he'd bought a new set of clothes at an airport shop, changed in a restroom, and left the airport.

Then he vanished.

THE NEXT MORNING, Tom Anderson stood at the bottom of the airstairs to Baron Armand de Saint-Clair's jet. Around him stood Michael, Hana, Aaron, Karl, Lukas, Ian and Ekaterina, all waiting to board, their luggage having been transferred from Tom's minivan into the cargo hold. Ekaterina had her arm in a sling and her shoulder was wrapped in surgical tape.

Tom brought out a cooler from the trunk of his car and opened it. It was full of foil-wrapped Chicago hot dogs in their buns, still steaming hot, along with packets of condiments, a baggie of chopped onions, another of sliced peppers, and some individual bags of potato chips.

Tom spoke to the group. "I heard you were looking forward to having some of these, but the trip didn't actually work out like any of us planned. I couldn't have you miss one of the best things about this city. I hope you enjoy them on the flight home."

Michael reached out and shook his hand. "Thank you, Tom, this really means a lot."

"Good to be going home?" Tom asked Michael.

"Yes, especially with the exhibits and everyone intact. These two were already supposed to be home," he said, gently nudging Ian into Kat.

"We couldn't leave you to face that man by yourself," Kat said. "It was my fault. All of this. And still you were going to protect me. I don't know how to thank you. And I don't know what I'm going to do next."

"We'll talk about that when we get home. Personally, I would like to keep you on, but I think the reality of that is going to be something different. We'll have to see. Something will work out. I know your uncle would love to have you closer to home."

"What's going to happen to Bishop Loveridge?"

"He's being recalled to Rome. The pope has named a new interim Prefect for the Dicastery for the Doctrine of the Faith. Cardinal Caputo apparently planned all this with Bishop Sharma, who did the legwork. Caputo was trying to keep his hands clean, while at the same time trying to use me to get the pope to resign, from embarrassment or illness. Now Caputo is in custody waiting for an inquest into this affair. I daresay it will be fairer than what he had planned for me. And now that the trial is over, maybe the pope can get a little rest. I hated putting him through all this. He's been kind of under the weather recently, although I spoke to him last night and he said he was feeling a little better."

"It was nice of Dean Hastings to poll the jurors anyway, after the case effectively ended in a mistrial," Tom added. "Loveridge had already left, but the rest of the jury was unanimous in exonerating Galileo."

"Hey, did you hear that the Chicago police found Somchai Nguyen duct-taped to a chair, tied to a piling in the Chicago River near the cement factory?" Hana asked with a smile.

"Yeah, that's pretty funny." Michael said. "I hope Detective Mancini gets a laugh out of it. He's concerned about how this all ended. I mean, he's happy we got the exhibits back, but he seemed pretty upset that I couldn't tell him how we got them back and who took them. I had to explain that my information came from an inviolate confidential communication. As a faithful Catholic, he figured out what that meant."

"And you two didn't get to have your night on the town," Tom said to Hana and Aaron, who were standing together, shoulders touching.

"That's okay," Aaron said. "It was going to be a quick

trip anyway. I have to get back to school, and Hana has a couple of stories to write."

"Boy, do I. But then maybe Aaron and I can see a little more of Rome, or wherever our next adventure takes us."

"Thank you, Tom," Michael said warmly. "I don't know how all this would have turned out without you."

"Give my regards to your father, and to Galileo at the newsstand." They all laughed.

EPILOGUE

A week after the trial, Remi Shapiro relaxed on the poolside deck of Pastor Darwin's mansion overlooking the lake. The sun had set, and Darwin was looking through a telescope at Jupiter.

"I can see them, the moons. This is remarkable. A couple of little dots in a line around the bright dot. And to think this instrument is what started it all. That gives me an idea. I know just how we are going to display this. How did you get it?"

"Let's just say a friend of a friend in Chicago, an international antiquities dealer, let me know it was available. It was changing hands pretty quickly, because of how hot it was. I don't think I'd put it on display for a while. People are still gonna be looking for it."

"Nonsense. Finders keepers. I'll just pay whatever it takes to keep it. But possession is nine-tenths of the law, ya know…and being rich is the other one," Darwin smirked.

"Whatever you say, Boss. You always know best."

TWO WEEKS LATER, Michael was just coming back from visiting with his father. The scandals regarding the plot against them had eclipsed the flap engineered by Caputo with that photo. Though both Michael and the pope would be under continued scrutiny by some, others had come to accept—at least in private—that the priesthood was only human after all. The better news was that the pope's health had rallied and a new nutritional and prescriptive regime was giving him back some energy. All in all, Michael was relieved as he headed for his office when he got a call to come down to the shipping and receiving dock to pick up a large package.

"Hey, Ian. Grab a cart and give me a hand, will you? We've got some big package at the dock."

The two of them arrived at Receiving to find a wooden shipping crate, two meters long by thirty centimeters square. The shipping clerk gave them a hand cutting the nylon bands securing it, and used a small crowbar to pry open the case.

Michael was stunned to see what was inside. Encased in bubble wrap from one end to the other was the original Galileo telescope that had been given to the pope some four hundred years earlier. Someone had shipped it back from the United States. He and Ian pulled it out and unwrapped it.

Michael had given up on ever seeing it again, as he had been told the Roma had sold it before they knew where it had come from. There was no return address or shipping manifest. Michael rooted around in the remaining packaging, finding only a Polaroid photograph of a museum exhibit showing the telescope installed on a tripod against a starry backdrop, with Jupiter and its four Galilean moons. A headline banner at the top read, *"The Biblical Hall Museum Presents: The Telescope that Changed the Church."*

Peering into the now empty box, there was one more thing Michael found in a dark corner.

A red silk rose petal.

FICTION, FACT OR FUSION?

Many readers have asked me to distinguish fact from fiction in my books. Generally, I like to take factual events and historical figures and build on them in creative ways—but much of what I do write is historically accurate. In this book, we'll review some of the chapters where questions may arise, with hopes it may help those wondering where reality meets creative writing.

GENERAL

Edicola is a news kiosk. *Edicola Sacra* is located on Rome's Piazza del Risorgimento near the Vatican.

PROLOGUE

While the conversational elements are obviously contrived, Galileo's recitation of his experience is essentially accurate. We used the following references to guide the narrative:

Galileo's Mistake: A New Look at the Epic Confrontation Between Galileo and the Church, Wade Roland, Arcade Publishing, New York, 2012.

Behind the Scenes at Galileo's Trial, Richard Blackwell, University of Notre Dame Press, Notre Dame, 2006.

The Galileo Affair: A Documentary History, Maurice A. Finocchairo, University of California Press, Berkeley, 1989.

Retrying Galileo 1633 – 1992, Maurice A. Finocchairo, University of California Press, Berkeley, 2005.

The Trial of Galileo: Essential Documents, Maurice A. Finocchario, Hacket Publishing, Indianapolis, 2014.

In addition, we consulted online resources extensively.

CHAPTER 2

Historically, we couldn't find any record of Galileo giving Pope Urban VIII a telescope. But it seemed reasonable that he could have.

CHAPTER 3

The document archives of the Dicastery for the Doctrine of the Faith were invented for the book. They may or may not actually have their own records archives.

CHAPTER 6

This story takes place largely in Chicago. While some of the business names have been changed, the places where they are located actually exist. Ron spends about three weeks a year in Chicago, and described many of the locations from memory, with a little help from Google Earth.

• • •

CHAPTER 14

You can triangulate a cell phone's location from the cell towers it pings and the signal strength. As far as we have read, the cellular companies keep this information for some period of time.

CHAPTER 15

The bug detection routine is rudimentary, but reasonably accurate, at least as far as we were able to do with internet research. I'm sure there are more sophisticated devices both for listening and for detection.

CHAPTER 21

Just a quick note about the courtroom procedures. The "Retrial" is an educational exercise and not bound by any formal or official rules other than as agreed to by the parties and the host organization, so it gave us a lot of freedom in crafting the courtroom scenes. Astute legal observers may notice inconsistencies between the procedures invented for this exercise and the real procedures for any particular jurisdiction. That said, they aren't that far off either. We let the dean exercise her assumed authority as a judge might, and the parties accepted it as would be expected in such an educational exercise.

CHAPTER 23

The important part of this exchange was:
"Matthew 25:21" (*Well Done, Good and Faithful servant*).
A few moments later, a reply came back.
"Exodus 22:18." (*Suffer not a witch to live*).

The man texted back. "Matthew 6:10." (*Your will be done*).

(This is Cardinal Caputo and Bishop Sharma deciding to have Kat taken out.)

CHAPTER 33

Both the yawara stick and the coin purse sap exist. Yawara is used in a variety of Jujitsu styles and other martial arts.

CHAPTER 35

While the Injunction of 1616, if it existed, is probably lost to history, the Confession of Galileo in 1633 still exists and is accurately represented (in the part that was included) in the text. The complete confession is available online.

AUTHOR'S NOTES

Dealing with issues of theology, religious beliefs, and the fictional treatment of historical biblical events can be a daunting affair.

I would ask all readers to view this story for what it is—a work of pure fiction, adapted from the seeds of many oral traditions and the historical record, at least as we know it today.

Apart from telling an engaging story, I have no agenda here, and respect those of all beliefs, from Agnosticism to Zoroastrianism and everything in between.

~

Thank you for reading *The Galileo Gambit*. I hope you enjoyed it and, if you haven't already, suggest you pick up the story in the earlier books of The Magdalene Chronicles series—*The Magdalene Deception, The Magdalene Reliquary,* and *The Magdalene Veil*—and look forward to forthcoming books featuring the same characters and a few new ones in the continuing *Vatican Secret Archive Thrillers* series, so far comprised of *The Vivaldi Cipher*, *The Opus Dictum*, *The Petrus Prophecy*, *The Avignon Affair*, *The Jerusalem Scrolls*, and now this one, *The Galileo Gambit*.

When you have a moment, **may I ask that you leave a review on Amazon**, Goodreads, Facebook and perhaps elsewhere you find convenient? Reviews are crucial to a book's success, and I hope for The Magdalene Chronicles and the Vatican Secret Archive Thrillers series to have a long and entertaining life.

You can easily leave your review by going to my Amazon book page at https://garymcavoy.link/KkxTe, or just search Amazon for *The Galileo Gambit*. And thank you!

If you would like to reach out for any reason, you can email me at gary@garymcavoy.com. If you'd like to learn more about me and my other books, visit my website at www.garymcavoy.com, where you can also sign up for my private mailing list.

With kind regards,

Gary McAvoy

Made in the USA
Middletown, DE
26 September 2023